"It's no sh... It's n... all the ... after similar experiences."

William obviously had no experience with women who weren't trained from birth to rely on a manly pillar of strength. "I'm not most women," Mary said.

"So you seem determined to prove. May I suggest that even strong women need to sit and rest after an ordeal?"

Mary simply nodded, overwhelmed with exhaustion and shock. William started to walk off, and unexpected panic overruled her need to appear in control. "Wait, I... Don't go. Not yet."

William looked startled. Then his eyes softened and he sat down beside her. "You'll feel better after a little rest."

The fire's warmth seeped in and added to her exhaustion. Her head began to nod, and William pulled her near and supported her in the crook of his arm. It felt too right to protest. But although he might have saved her life and offered her comfort, he was a pastor. He would have done the same for anyone. She shouldn't make the mistake of reading too much into a man just doing his job.

DEBBIE KAUFMAN

never heeded her mother's advice to get her nose out of a book—except for when it was time to have adventures outside the written pages. Adventures like running a rural airport, working as a small-town journalist, teaching school and traveling to China to establish an adoption program, just to name a few. Of course, all these things were still accomplished with a good book in one hand.

Time and technology have marched on since her first visit to the bookmobile, but Debbie still likes her library to be portable. So these days you may find her with her nose in an e-reader that goes wherever she does. But mostly now, you'll find her perched in front of a computer creating her own award-winning stories. Debbie currently lives in Georgia and enjoys spending time with her husband and their four children, three grandchildren and two dogs.

DEBBIE KAUFMAN

The Doctor's Mission

Love Inspired

Recycling programs for this product may not exist in your area.

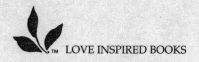

TM LOVE INSPIRED BOOKS

ISBN-13: 978-0-373-82894-4

THE DOCTOR'S MISSION

Copyright © 2011 by Debbie Kaufman

www.LoveInspiredBooks.com

Printed in U.S.A.

And we know that all things work together for good
to them that love God, to them who are the called
according to His purpose.
—*Romans* 8:28

To my husband, Bill, for always believing in me.

To my children,
for all the times I said, "After I finish the book."

To my children Emily, Dan and Dave,
for all the times I said, "After I finish the book."

And to my friends Sandy, Mae and Dianna,
for their faithful support.

Chapter One

~❧~

Liberia, Africa, 1918

William Mayweather placed his worn leather Bible on the table beside him and stepped out on the deep, shaded porch of the Newaka Mission Station. His evening devotions would have to wait if what he was hearing was any indication of what was to come. The smooth, hand-hewn rail transmitted the day's heat through his hand while he listened for confirmation of his hopes from the dense Liberian jungle.

There it was. His ears hadn't deceived him. The escalating cries of monkeys in the treetops telegraphed a clear message over and above the noise of the busy mission compound. Someone was coming. Finally.

The two-week delay here at the base mission station had seemed like forever despite the hospitality of his hosts, Hannah and Karl Jansen. William chafed to get back to the Kru people and begin his work anew. He didn't even mind the amount of physical labor that would be needed to restore his former mission at Nynabo after a year of unfettered jungle reclamation.

He looked past the rectangular compound lined with

tin-roofed wooden buildings to the welcoming arch at the entrance of the mission. No one yet.

The Newaka mission had long ago brought in tin from the beach to roof their home, the school and the dormitories. The other outbuildings were thatched just like his in the interior at Nynabo were—if they still stood. He squinted, as though his vision could possibly penetrate the dense jungle vegetation that lay a few feet past the mission entrance. Perhaps it was only a supply run, but given the dangers of travel in the bush, the regular caravan would have welcomed additional support and waited for the two new volunteers promised him by the Mission Board.

His pulse elevated with anticipation. Reviving the compound at Nynabo was back within his reach. Doubts it would ever come to pass had fled at hearing of the unexpected providence of God. God who had supplied not one, but two men now en route to join him in spreading the Gospel, and one a doctor no less. It spoke volumes about the character and dedication of these new volunteers that they dared see past the mission's deadly history and heed the call to evangelize the unreached peoples of the remote jungle interior. Now if they would just get here.

With his free hand he warded off the glare of the low-hanging sun. Behind him, the door opened and he turned to see a flour-dusted Hannah stepping onto the porch.

"Has the first runner come yet, William?"

"Not yet, Hannah. But the monkeys are in full chorus, so he should arrive any minute."

"Good. I don't want to miss greeting our new brothers." Hannah glanced down at the porch floor, a tight crease popped up between her brows and her Dutch cleanliness came out in full force. "Oh, dear. Company arriving and I haven't swept out here since morning."

William's chuckle escaped despite his efforts to suppress his amusement. Hannah's fight against common household dirt was legendary in the African bush. She would be scandalized if a guest caught her unawares. "The porch is fine. The only thing you might want to do is brush the flour off yourself."

Hannah's hands went straight to her apron to remedy the problem. "Fine for you maybe, but one of our guests is a doctor. He's bound to have high standards. We don't want to run off the first doctor the Board has ever sent us."

She removed her apron and gave her voluminous blue skirts a good shake. Her hands nervously smoothed her graying hair in anticipation of company.

"You look fine, Hannah. I'm sure once they get a whiff of your fresh-baked bread and realize they're in time for dinner, it will be a distraction from all else." William pointed to the birds rising and calling out in frightened flight.

"Dinner is only a simple affair. I didn't think they'd arrive so soon or I'd have done more."

"They are going to be glad to be out of the never-ending jungle. And I know your idea of a simple meal. You're going to spoil them, Hannah. Unless one of these men can cook, we're not going to be eating to your standards once we get to Nynabo."

"All the more reason for a good meal or two before you set off. I worry about you out there with no wife to take care of you."

Grief broke through his protective walls at the unexpected reminder of his loss. He schooled his face carefully into smooth lines to hide the effect of her casual words. "I think God already spoke on that subject."

"God doesn't expect you to grieve forever. It's been a year since malaria took your Alice."

"I am trying, Hannah. But grief or no grief, I could

never in good conscience take another wife into the interior. This is not a life for women. You, my dear, are the exception to the rule."

"Nonsense. How many women pioneered missions in this area before you were even born?"

Hannah's direct gaze left him at a loss for words. Grief had no logic at hand to argue with her.

His lack of an answer hung between them, dangling unsupported, until movement in the compound distracted her. She turned to her husband as he emerged from the schoolhouse across the way, his straight posture commanding attention and belying his advancing years.

Obviously aware of the jungle's message too, Karl Jansen nodded at the two of them and turned to greet the approaching caravan. Three shiny black torsos covered in little more than sweat and grass cloth entered the compound through the open arch. As the three unburdened themselves of the canvas-wrapped packs secured on their heads, the first of the hammock-chair bearers came into view. A single pole atop the circular corn-husk pad balanced on the porter's head, his counterpart in united step behind. Between them, a hammock swayed with the weight of the occupant they carried.

Karl moved to greet the new arrival, whose face was blocked from William's sight by the bearer standing at attention while his passenger disembarked. Karl turned and flashed a quick, unreadable look to William before giving his attention back to the occupant of the hammock chair.

As William approached to greet the travelers, Karl's liver-spotted hand reached out to help their guest alight. William's stomach registered the first knot of impending doom when a stout, stocking-clad leg came out of the chair. It was attached to a smiling, barrel-shaped matron in a newfangled split skirt and white shirtwaist. Her pith helmet was removed to reveal a neat, brown bun secured in the back.

A shock ran clear down William's spine. The Mission Board sent him a woman? A sturdy-looking woman of about forty years, but a woman nonetheless. What were they thinking? Had his last venture into the interior not proven Nynabo unsafe for the fairer sex? And matronly or not, a woman alone with two men deep in the bush would be compromised. Before his hopes of a quick return to Nynabo sank slowly into a bog of despair, a spark of hope and understanding hit.

They've sent me a married couple. Of course! The Board would never send a single, unchaperoned woman to serve with a man.

He shook off the worry and quickened his stride as the second set of bearers rounded the corner. He reached the hammock chair just as a slim, trousered leg complete with protective panniers and an impossibly small boot emerged. Fiery red hair peeked out from under the pith helmet and topped a porcelain complexion reddened by the heat. Intense and very feminine green eyes stared up at him. Karl nudged him and William's manners took over. He automatically offered his hand and let go of the breath he held.

Obviously these were no missionaries. Not two white women alone in the interior. Whatever sort of tourist trek these ladies were on, they must be hopelessly confused to have ended up here. He'd heard of the new travel fad of wealthy women, women who ran from the natural state of marriage to travel to exotic locales. But wasn't it confined to Arabia? Liberia didn't boast the excitement of ancient, lost civilizations that drew these types of sensation seekers. Yet here they were.

Disappointment at what would be a longer wait pulsed through him and he struggled to mask his irritation at receiving two adventuresses instead of two mission workers. Yet the hand he held, delicate in form, put him mind of his Alice. He'd not held a woman's hand since hers as she lay dying. He was saved from grief's hold by a hand that responded with a surprisingly sturdy grip.

"Thank you." Her voice was melodic. "I was beginning to think I would never get out of that contraption."

Despite his misgivings, William stood transfixed by the petite beauty as she emerged from the chair. The top of her head barely reached his shoulder. It was not until her eyes crinkled in a puzzled look that he realized he was staring. He felt a gentle tug and released the hand he'd held a little longer than was polite.

"Forgive me, ma'am. Pastor William Mayweather at your service."

"Excellent. Just the man I was looking for."

"Me? I do not understand."

"I'm Dr. O'Hara. I was told you would be expecting me."

Dr. Mary O'Hara lifted her chin and stared up past a broad chest covered in a white cotton shirt minus the traditional attached collar to find rich, mahogany eyes. Eyes that made her forget that every known muscle in her body ached, plus a few muscles she'd forgotten existed. Three days on the trail had taken their toll. Yet somehow the sight of this tall, rugged man took her mind off her mundane pains.

This was the pastor she was supposed to meet? If she hadn't heard his name from his own lips, she wouldn't have believed it. When she pictured herself working at a bush station with a missionary, she'd imagined a wizened, older man, glasses perched on the end of his nose and maybe even slightly stoop-shouldered from bending over his Bible. Nothing prepared her for this magnificent, broad-shouldered, six-foot man without a stooped shoulder in sight. She certainly wasn't expecting the warmth that radiated from his hand or the spark of awareness igniting. She tugged her hand back just to recover her ability to think straight.

Piercing eyes stared at her in frank amazement, probably doubting she could handle living in the jungle. Quite understandable. Men often looked at her like that when they first heard she was a doctor, underestimating her. The inevitable banter would follow while they tried to get her to admit she was joking. Last would be a final look of disgust or horror when they realized a member of the fairer sex had overstepped the bounds of propriety and actually studied human anatomy in detail.

She'd thought she'd hardened herself to the inevitable path that first encounter took. But for the first time in a long while, she regretted the disappointment she would soon see. Might as well get on with it.

She squared her shoulders and tilted her chin higher than her five foot four inches normally allowed her to see. "The Mission Board sent letters. Weren't you informed of the impending arrival of Mrs. Smith and myself?"

His eyes flashed disbelief and despite his polite tone, she could see the resolve of his answer in the set of his jaw. "I was indeed informed of the arrival of two new mission workers, Miss O'Hara, one a physician. I just did not expect the Board to send women, because of the deadly history of the jungle interior. I'm afraid you've been sent to the wrong place. I simply cannot take someone so delicate and unsuitable for the dangers to the compound at Nynabo."

Unsuitable? She wanted to laugh at the irony of being found lacking after having just left a frontline mobile field hospital for this man's *dangerous* jungle. She took a deep breath to steady her voice. It wouldn't do to sound shrill and create a negative opinion of herself. She needed this position; was, in fact, desperate for it.

"Obviously, Pastor Mayweather, we are both surprised to find someone whom we did not expect. But I assure you that while your opinion is no different than most other men in society, ones who do not carry Bibles at their ready, it is entirely unwarranted."

Mary could only imagine what her dear mother would say if she could hear her now. She'd managed to keep a polite tone but still broken her mother's cardinal rule— don't challenge a man in charge. Her own loving mother had never found herself able to hold an opinion that wasn't first that of her husband, Mary's father.

Pastor Mayweather's eyebrows raised and his mouth opened, drawing in breath for the next volley. Before he could launch it, a matronly older woman put her hand on his arm and pushed herself forward. Mary couldn't help but catch the disapproving frown the woman gave him before smiling at her visitors.

"Welcome to Newaka." Thick arms enveloped Mary in a hug and squeezed the breath right out of her. "I am Hannah Jansen. My husband Karl and I serve here at this station."

Hannah Jansen was as plump and well-rounded as her husband was spare. Mary resisted the urge to check her ribs when the apple-cheeked matron stepped back. "I'm Dr. O'Hara. But you may call me Mary." She telegraphed the stuffy Pastor Mayweather a look over Hannah's shoulder that she hoped said, "And *you* may not."

"Hannah, this is my friend and travel companion, Mrs. Clara Smith."

Clara stepped toward them and smiled. "We introduced

ourselves while you were meeting Pastor Mayweather, Dr. Mary."

"Yes," Hannah said. "Dr. Mary, this is my husband, Karl." She pointed to the tall gentleman who had helped Clara from her hammock chair.

Karl stepped up and took one of her hands between his bony pair and pressed gently. His eyes twinkled with good humor that carried in his voice. "We are so pleased to have you, Dr. Mary. I can't tell you how happy we are to finally be assigned a physician in our area."

"Why thank you, Pastor Jansen. It's very polite of you to say so." Mary avoided looking at William. "Most men are less accepting of a female doctor."

"We just didn't expect such a beautiful young woman." Karl chuckled and offered Mary his arm. "Let me show you and Mrs. Smith to our home. Someone will bring your bags in a moment."

"Dr. O'Hara?"

Mary swung around and forced a civil smile in spite of William Mayweather's serious countenance. "Yes?"

"Please don't unpack more than the essentials. I plan on sending you back when the porters are ready to return. Or, if the Jansens don't mind, you can wait here for a more suitable posting at one of the safer coastal stations. While I'm sure your skills are more than adequate, regrettably I cannot take you and your companion into the interior with me."

Shock at his highhanded assumption froze Mary's tongue into silence. Silence he must have taken for acceptance as he turned and walked away. The nerve of the man. Drop his little piece of emotional ordnance and walk off before the explosion hit. Good thing she didn't intend to answer to him in this decision.

* * *

Disappointment laid itself heavily on his heart as William walked away from the two workers who should have been his entry back to Nynabo. With his back to the sun's glare, despair managed to cloud his vision. He'd prayed about the workers God would have assigned to Nynabo. But where was God in this obvious mistake? What reason could He have to delay William's return to Nynabo? Was this some sort of test or temptation? He wouldn't have believed it, but Dr. O'Hara, with her long, red locks and smattering of freckles across the bridge of her nose, was even more beautiful than his beloved Alice.

William stopped short at the base of the porch steps. Where did those traitorous observations come from? He ran a hand through his unruly black mane and rebuked himself. Widowed only a year and reacting to a pretty face. It wouldn't do.

He took the porch steps two at a time and entered the relative cool of the mission house. If he was so easily noticing this woman's beauty, he would have to flee temptation's possibilities. If it wasn't inhumane to the porters, he would've ordered them to simply turn around and start back. Even if he could have done so, Hannah and Karl would have none of it. Basic hospitality dictated that the women be fed and rested along with their carriers.

He understood Hannah welcoming another woman with open arms, but he'd been shocked when Karl reacted kindly, as if not seeing the obvious problems. The fatherly man had heard William's heart many times on the subject since he'd returned from his stateside leave. Well, he would have a man-to-man talk with Karl later, and then William would make sure that both women went on their way back the moment the porters were rested.

A lilting laugh flowed through the open windows. The

petite doctor no doubt. The sound stirred the buried pain of the lost laughter of another precious woman, one he'd buried at Nynabo. He had no intentions of burying another woman there. The jungle's interior was just not the place for a delicate female.

Oh, Mary O'Hara had pluck. He'd give her that. But she also had no true understanding of the dangers of practicing medicine among hostile natives, most of whom had never seen a white person of either gender before. This time he'd make sure a member of the fairer sex didn't die on his watch. The sooner she was sent packing toward the safer coastal regions the better. Even if she stayed here at Newaka, it would be substantially safer than Nynabo.

William made a quick decision. He would spend as little time as possible in her company. It would alleviate some of the guilt he would inevitably feel at crushing her dreams of working in the interior. With that thought in mind, he headed through the kitchen, out the back door and around to the boys' dormitory. There would be enough work there to legitimately occupy him until the women were settled in for the night.

Later, he could talk to Karl and make arrangements. The Mission Board's policy on malaria would force him to stay longer here at Newaka until replacements could come or William contracted his first bout of the inevitable disease. There was enough work here and he enjoyed the Jansens' company. Surely this was all in God's ultimate plan.

He rounded the corner to the boys' cottage at the same time the door flew open, disgorging seven chattering little brown bodies in their khaki drawstring pants, minus the white shirts they'd worn in class. As if all one confused sculpture, they froze silently in place when they saw him. Seven sets of eyes flitted their gazes between him and each other, finally coming to rest on the tallest boy, Sabo. The designated speaker of the pack swallowed hard, took a deep breath, and straightened his bony spine before asking, "Nana Pastor?" Sabo managed the honorific title and paused before blurting his question. "Is it true more white mammies have come and one is a medicine woman?"

All eyes turned to him for an answer. William bit back a growl and mentally chided himself for not realizing this would of course be big news for the children. He'd come to escape the frying pan and walked straight into the proverbial fire. He chose his next words carefully, well aware that the boys were from a world that saw women as property. None of these children had ever seen a white woman before Hannah Jansen, a married woman in the company of her husband.

"Yes, it is true that we have two new guests and one is a doctor."

Seven voices clamored with questions. He put up his hand and waited to be heard. As they quieted down, the smallest one braved a question. "Are her conjures strong?"

It was William's turn to freeze like a statue. It was so easy to forget that even though the boys had been baptized, they still struggled between beliefs from two vastly different spiritual worlds. Their education wasn't such yet that they would see what Dr. O'Hara did as science and not magic. A male doctor wouldn't have been such an event for the boys. Medicine could have been explained rationally. *Her presence was already causing trouble.*

Trouble he had to straighten out now.

"Boys, let's go back inside and talk."

In unison, seven little faces frowned their distress, realizing they were losing their chance to go see the new arrivals. Before any could protest, William put his body between them and their intended route of escape and waited till they turned and shuffled barefoot back into the cottage. He closed the door behind him and prayed that God would give him the words to explain the difference between their medicine men's fetish bags of charms and a female doctor who practiced science. But more important, how faith in God was stronger than what their medicine men offered.

Mary pushed her chair away from the dinner table. "Oh my, Hannah. I haven't eaten this well since before I left home two years ago. Fresh fruit is such a luxury."

Clara nodded vigorously, sending her double chin to jiggling though she was still chewing a mouthful of bread.

Hannah responded. "Most of the fruit grows naturally here without planting. You'll find it the same where you're headed."

Karl's thick brows knit together. "Two years. I knew the Kaiser disrupted ocean travel, but who'd have thought it would take that long to make all the connections to cross. It's a good thing the Allies finally put him in his place."

Clara spoke up. "Well, it was the Kaiser, but not the way you think."

Mary chided nicely, "Hannah and Karl don't need to hear our war stories."

Karl smiled. "We don't get much news about the rest of the world here. So we'd love to hear any stories from the outside."

Before Mary could think of another way to change the subject, Clara launched into her tale. Normally she was such a quiet woman. Why did she have to become loquacious on the one subject Mary preferred to avoid? Even though the armistice was signed, the Great War was still a big topic. She just preferred not to talk about her part in it, though avoiding the topic hadn't stopped the unmerciful memories.

"Dr. Mary and I met at Argonne. We both worked for the Red Cross at the field hospital."

Hannah's hand froze over the plate she was about to pick up. "You were at the battle they called the Big Show?" Her fingers fluttered over her heart. "Even here we've heard about that battle. How horrible for you."

Mary put on a professional mask as best she could while Clara nodded and said, "It was truly. If Hades exists anywhere on earth, it would have to have been there at Argonne Forest. So many young boys lost tragically, brutally." Tears brimmed in Clara's eyes. "Why Dr. Mary here…."

The chair legs screeched against the floor when Mary abruptly stood. "Clara. I don't think we need to burden the Jansens with those horrors. I'm sure their imagination will suffice." The last thing she wanted dredged up was the death of her brother. That wound was too raw to touch. Even now pain stabbed through her chest as she tried to shut out her memories—that final glimpse of him alive, bloody and barely breathing. Would she ever be free of that horrible image?

She caught the questioning look on Karl's face. Those eyes saw too much. Before he could ask any questions, she turned to Hannah and asked, "May I lend you a hand with the dishes? I'm not used to being idle while others are working."

"You'll both be busy soon enough once you get to Nynabo. Tonight you're our guests. Next time you come, I'll put you right to work."

"If Pastor Mayweather has his way, there won't be any Nynabo in our futures. And certainly not a next time here."

Hannah laughed as she continued her tasks. "Karl will set him straight on that. Won't you, dear?"

Karl stood and pushed his chair under the table. "I'll try, but it would be better if he realized the severity of the situation for himself, Hannah."

Mary seized on what sounded like a life preserver. "The severity of what, Pastor?"

"Well, if he refuses to work with you ladies, he won't be able to reestablish Nynabo for quite some time. When you consider how possessive the jungle is, any more significant delays risk the station not being restorable. He might have to start from scratch once the white ants get finished with an unoccupied compound."

Clara asked, "The white ants?"

"African termites, dear. The natives call them bugabugs," Hannah answered.

Mary's curiosity overruled her good manners. "What's stopping him from going on without us?"

"The malaria policy." Hannah tossed the answer back over her shoulder on her way to the kitchen.

"Pastor Mayweather hasn't had malaria yet?" Mary asked.

Karl shook his head side to side.

Clara's confusion threaded through her voice. "What policy? Isn't it a good thing that Pastor Mayweather hasn't been sick?"

Mary heard the back door open as Karl explained. "Until missionaries have come down with the White Man's Death the first time, and lived through it, the Mission Board will not allow them to staff any mission post on their own. Without you, William must remain here until a replacement can arrive. That could take precious months that he doesn't have to spare."

Mary watched as William stepped out of the shadows

by the back door and into the room. Anguish churned across his face and his hands were clenched into fists tight to his sides. "I would rather give up my call than be responsible for the deaths of these two women."

Mary's arms and hands trembled as the tiring day and disappointing reception from Pastor Mayweather finally caught up with her. Anger coursed through her veins. "Responsible for our deaths? Why, you…"

Everyone but Clara froze. She moved quickly to Mary's side and placed her arm around Mary's shoulders, attempting to herd her out of the room. "Dr. Mary, please. We're all tired and it's been a long day. Do not say anything you will regret. He means no slight."

Mary pulled away from what was meant to be a calming embrace. She deliberately lowered her voice to avoid its strident tones. "Clara, dear, I am not going to be stopped from speaking my mind any longer."

Mary lifted her eyes and looked toward William, addressing him with her most formal of tones. "I am sorry to learn that you are one of those men who cling to antiquated ideas of women's roles and set themselves up as Lord and Protector." A bit of the exasperation she felt crept out. "It's the twentieth century, for goodness' sake."

Mary glanced to Hannah for her reaction. The plate in the older woman's hand looked dangerously close to slipping to the floor, so rapt was her attention. Karl looked down, but was that a smile he was trying to hide? William readied himself to answer her, but Mary raised her hand to stop him.

"Please, let me finish, sir. You, Pastor Mayweather, aren't responsible for me. I am responsible for myself, my own actions and my own consequences. If I were afraid of dying, I would have never signed my agreement with the Mission Board after they spelled out the possible dangers."

William wedged in a quick answer. "With all due respect, Miss O'Hara…"

"If you wish to accord me respect, then please address me as *Doctor* O'Hara."

"Doctor O'Hara, then. I don't see how you can possibly understand what you might be getting yourself into." William relaxed his fists and stretched out his hands in an apparent plea. "The interior is fraught with dangers, and even if you manage to live through your first bout of malaria, there are still wild animals and hostile cannibals to face."

A blanket of emotional exhaustion wrapped itself around Mary. The man meant well. It was tempting to just walk away. But where would she go from here?

Returning home to her parents was out of the question. Her father's reply to her last letter clearly stated his anger and grief over what she'd done. Better to stay here where she could hope to do some good, to atone for her brother's loss.

Resolved, Mary straightened her spine. "I thank you for your concern, Pastor Mayweather, but I had malaria as a child back in Virginia. The animals and cannibals I'll deal with when the time comes. I have orders to establish an infirmary at Nynabo, and Clara is to run the school. While I would prefer to have a man of your experience along, I will do so with or without your help."

William sat on the front porch rocker after the women retired for the evening and wished the inky darkness would simply swallow him whole. What was he to do with this impossible woman? Nothing he said dissuaded her. And to make matters worse, she was right. Her orders gave her all the permission she needed to proceed without him. It would be a total disaster and she would undoubtedly get both herself and her companion killed. Or worse. The only mission posts run by women tended to be on the coast where help was more readily available. Even government troops hesitated to travel the interior, a fact he'd ignored when he'd taken Alice to the bush.

His sweet Alice. She'd wanted nothing more than to please him when he'd told her he felt the call to salvage the mission where his uncle and aunt had been martyred. She'd trusted him. He'd let both her and God down. The year of compassionate leave helped, but what he really needed was to put his hand back to the proverbial plow once again. But not while responsible for not one but two women this time.

Panic at the very thought brought William to his knees, using the railing as if it was a makeshift altar.

Father, why have you sent me this woman? Have I incurred your displeasure that my task would be made so impossible? Please, God. Turn her heart. Show her the error of this decision or show me what I must do to end this foolishness.

"Am I interrupting?" Karl's voice jolted William from his silent pleas. Karl stood in front of him with a kerosene lamp.

"No. I was just finished."

"This is one of my favorite places to pray." Karl settled himself in one of rockers he'd made with his own hands as a gift last year to his wife. "I can see you are struggling with the direction things have taken, William. It is good that you are taking this to the Father."

"I don't know what else to do, Karl. There is simply no dissuading her. Even in this short time I realize she has to be the most stubborn female I have ever met." William returned to the rocker next to Karl's. The lamp Karl set on the floor cast the older pastor in an eerie light.

"She reminds me of a stubborn young missionary I know."

Was that a trick of the shadows or did Karl have a twinkle in his eye? He wasn't seeing the seriousness of this situation. "Is it merely stubbornness on her part? How many funerals of fellow missionaries have you presided over, Karl? It is one thing for a man to choose the risk on his own, but a woman in the interior?"

"My Hannah would tell you that God calls us all alike, Jew and Greek, male and female."

"God also expects us to learn from our mistakes. I understand now what my uncle must have known before he and Aunt Ruth were killed."

"I'm sure that he and your aunt knew the peace of God over all else, my son."

"But next to God, he loved my Aunt Ruth more than life itself. Surely he knew in those last moments that taking her to tribes that cannibalize their enemies was a mistake. He must have regretted being responsible for her horrible death."

"You mean like you feel responsible for Alice's?"

"Exactly. I should have learned from my uncle's failure, but I didn't. And my ignorance cost Alice her life."

"Malaria cost Alice her life, William, and your aunt and uncle were in God's hands." Karl stood and picked up his lantern. "You're letting your grief blind you to God's bigger plan. You need to trust that He is in control, that He is sovereign in all things."

"I trust God. It is this place I do not trust. You can't tell me it is the Divine plan for the women we are charged to protect to be put in such needless danger when we can avoid it."

"No, I can't tell you. It's up to God to show you His

plan." Karl moved to the front door. "I'll pray earnestly for you, William, that God will reveal His plan in due time."

"Thank you, Karl. I covet your prayers."

The illumination receded with Karl as William sat alone in the darkness. A thousand lights burned their autumn patterns in the sky above him, but it was the light of an idea beginning to burn in his mind that captured his attention. He *would* go to Nynabo, no matter what. He could see to it that neither woman was exposed to the dangers of the interior any more than necessary. Especially not the cannibalistic tribes of the Pahn.

And he would die trying if that's what God's plan required.

William rose and headed into the house to find stationery. He might not be able to stop them from going to Nynabo, but a letter to the Mission Board would shorten their stay there. Once he explained his dissatisfaction with Dr. O'Hara and her unsuitability for the post, the Board would have to act and both women would be sent packing for safer quarters. God's work would continue and he'd avoid ventures into the more dangerous territories until her replacement arrived.

He couldn't give his Alice the long life she'd deserved, but he'd do everything in his power to see the women temporarily in his care didn't meet the same end. Dr. O'Hara would live to use her talents for God some place safer. Some place far more suitable.

Chapter Two

Mary slapped at the millionth mosquito trying to make her a meal. Futile, but instinctive. Ten hours into the journey to Nynabo should have taught her that swatting was a waste of energy. Clara was smarter. She had stayed in the hammock chair and draped netting to keep the pests away. Mary, on the other hand, just had to prove she was capable of walking on her own.

The waning light through the heavy jungle canopy told her evening was near. Night's fall brought a sudden inky blackness that only campfires relieved. So surely William would call camp sometime soon. No, not William, she corrected herself. Pastor Mayweather. It wouldn't do to think of him in anything but the most formal of terms. The man acted as if she were his own personal trial.

Mary's foot hit a root and the jungle floor came rushing toward her. She threw out her hands to break her fall just as strong arms grabbed her from behind and righted her. Mary turned and found herself face to chest with the object of her ruminations. How had he moved up so far in the single-file line of the caravan without her knowing? She'd thought he was still at the back trying to encourage some of the stragglers.

"Careful. Are you all right, Doctor?"

"I'm tired and I stumbled, that's all. Thank you for coming to my aid."

"Are you sure you don't want to get back in the hammock chair?"

Mary bristled like a cat stroked the wrong way. "Most assuredly. My poor porters are obviously exhausted from the day's trek and I'm perfectly capable of walking."

"It was never my plan to carry two women into the bush. The two days of preparation after your arrival was not enough time to engage additional bearers if we were going to get to Nynabo and complete repairs before the rainy season begins."

Now she'd gone and offended him. She turned and walked forward down the trail, as much to avoid unintentional conflict as not to halt the progress of the porters behind them.

"We'll be stopping at the next clearing."

"For the night, Pastor Mayweather, or is it another rest break?"

"For the night."

Silence fell, and Mary decided that even if she had been inclined to speak further, the trail itself was a barrier to companionable conversation. She'd wondered on the trek to Newaka why the trail wasn't widened to make travel easier. Watching the men with machetes where the jungle encroached had answered that question. The amount of time needed to deal with even small patches of overgrowth was astounding. The arduous trail from coastal Garraway to Newaka was an after-dinner stroll in the garden compared to this route from Newaka to Nynabo.

When she rounded the next bend, the path appeared to broaden. Thank goodness. At least she could walk beside Clara's hammock chair and pass the time amiably.

But no. They were stopping. The porters ahead of her were already disgorging their packs and scurrying around to make camp. Pastor Mayweather moved past her, and Mary turned and waited for Clara's hammock-chair carriers to catch up.

Mary gave Clara a hand alighting. Clara glanced around and wondered aloud, "Where are we supposed to sleep? This space isn't enough for all of our tents."

"It does appear small. Still, I am ready to stop. This trek reminds me too much of those eighteen-hour shifts in the field hospital with no end in sight."

Pastor Mayweather's voice thundered an interruption in the small clearing. "Hannabo." The porter in charge jerked up his head in response and stepped closer to the pastor.

The two huddled in conversation and then Hannabo barked out directions Mary couldn't understand. Order began to fight its way out of chaos. Porters arranged packs around the outside ring of the camp as large stones were placed in the middle of the clearing, edging a small stack of firewood. A three-legged iron pot found its home on the stones and Mary's stomach began to rumble.

Food! Oh, thank goodness. The afternoon's repast of fresh bread and fruit Hannah had packed for them was long since a distant memory in their travel day.

A porter brought her the night's bedding and then repeated the gesture for Clara. Clara stopped the retreating figure and asked, "Where is our tent?"

A simple shoulder shrug was the answer.

"Mary, are we expected to sleep out in the open with all these men?"

"It is beginning to look that way. Wait here. I'll have a word with Pastor Mayweather and get this situation remedied."

Mary laid her bedding on top of her pack and headed

across the clearing. Pastor Mayweather had come to a sudden reversal about their assignment to Nynabo. Too sudden. Was depriving them of a normal amount of privacy part of a campaign to get rid of them or just an oversight? She intended to find out.

Nothing Pastor Mayweather could dream up could compare to the ingenuity of a professor in medical school unhappy with the enrollment of a female student. If the good pastor thought he could embarrass her and force her to leave, he was in for a rude awakening.

William saw his mistake. The clearing was too small to support their tents, but the sun was almost down and there was no time to move on. He'd called another porter, Jabo, and ordered only the bedding to be unpacked. Objections were swift. No sooner had the porters stacked the ladies' bedding than Mary crossed the camp with an obvious target in mind.

His ear.

"Pastor Mayweather. Doing without a tent is wholly unacceptable." The good doctor stood with her hands on her hips a mere two feet from him.

Rivulets of sweat ran down her neck, their origins hidden in her pith helmet. Sparse, dampened red tendrils flirted with his vision, their origins also secreted in the headgear. Little warnings went off in his brain. He should not be focusing on her physical attributes, but her annoyance factor. Instead, his mouth followed its own plan and upturned in a smile.

"Do you find discomfiting us amusing, Pastor Mayweather?"

"What? No, of course not. I'm sorry. My mind was elsewhere occupied."

His excuse sounded weak even to him. To her credit,

the woman did not roll her eyes. "Then tell me please, why are we not to have a basic measure of privacy tonight?"

"It is only a matter of space. I cannot in good conscience ask the porters to sleep off the trail to give us more room. Not when they could become dinner for a roaming leopard."

Mary's hands left her hips and crossed her chest. This time she did roll her eyes. "Leopards? Am I supposed to believe that? Perhaps I should quake in fear and beg to be returned to Newaka?"

A loud report resounded in the near distance. Hannabo must have gone hunting nearby to add to the supper pot. A quick glance around confirmed he was not present. When William looked back at Mary to answer, he found all the blood had drained from her face and her freckles were the only color that remained.

He grasped her upper arms, concerned she would faint on the spot. "Are you unwell, Dr. O'Hara?"

The delicate doctor's eyes blinked twice and then seemed to regain focus. "Please unhand me," she insisted, pulling to free herself. "I'm fine."

William's touch fell away as if he had held glowing embers. What was it with this woman and his reaction to her? "Your appearance gave me reason to believe you were about to swoon."

Sudden shards of crimson heat stained her cheeks. "I assure you, I'm not given to swooning like some ninny in a corset. But back to this leopard you claim will endanger us."

"Listen to me, please, Dr. O'Hara." He tried for a rational approach. "Leopards are only one of many dangers out here. I will not erect tents in this small space and force these men to sleep unprotected away from the fire and the watchmen." .

"You are serious?"

"The threat is very real. I would advise you not to wander outside the camp tonight. Now, if there is nothing else?"

"What about our..." She searched for an appropriate term. "Necessities?"

It was William's turn to blush, and he felt the heat rising up from his collar. "I will make arrangements for a separate privy area. Just do not go without an armed escort."

"Thank you." Mary headed back to her friend.

Lord, if I had to be saddled with members of the fairer sex, why couldn't they both be sturdy, easygoing women like Clara?

That woman was a salt-of-the-earth type who didn't stir feelings that he'd thought were buried with Alice. He wasn't sure which was the bigger danger on the trail right now. A hungry leopard on the prowl or the small-boned little redhead in men's trousers marching away from him.

William turned his thoughts back to camp chores and making sure all was secure. Hannabo had returned with his catch dangling over his shoulder.

"I see you have had good hunting."

Hannabo grinned. "Yes, Nana Pastor, I got a fine monkey. We eat soon."

"Good. If you need me for anything, just call out. I'll prepare the evening devotions while the light is still good."

Hannabo nodded his agreement and headed off to skin and prepare the main addition to the meal.

William was deep in the Word when Hannabo appeared again at his side. From the sun's position, he'd studied for almost an hour. A blessed hour of no interruptions from anyone, especially the women.

"Nana Pastor, the meal is ready. Would you and the mammies like to eat now?"

"Thank you, Hannabo. I will gather the ladies so we can bless the meal."

William pulled his tin bowl and spoon out of his pack and headed toward the women. "Ladies, the evening meal is ready."

"Thank the Lord," Clara intoned. "I am starving."

Mary nodded agreement and rummaged through her pack for utensils.

When all were gathered round the three-legged cook pot, William gave the signal to Hannabo and bowed his head to pray. "Dear Heavenly Father," William paused at short intervals for Hannabo's translation. "We thank you for this safe day's journey…and the food we are about to consume. Be with us tonight as we sleep…and may we, through Your Divine Providence, arrive safely in Nynabo."

Once Hannabo finished translating, William held out his hand to indicate the ladies should be served first. William followed next and sat on the ground a slight distance from Mary and Clara after he was served.

He wondered how long it would take before the realities of meals outside of Newaka became apparent and the complaints began. If his experience with his wife Alice was any indication, it would be soon.

It was Clara who broke the silence first. "What is this meat in the rice? It tastes like pork."

Mary's first bite was halfway to her mouth when Hannabo answered. "You like? It's monkey. I shot special for you and Mammy Doctor."

William dropped his chin to hide the smile when the doctor's eyes went wide and she asked, "Monkey? Monkey like the ones overhead in the trees? Those monkeys?"

Hannabo's head bobbed in delight with her understanding. Clara paled and set her bowl down. William held his breath. He should have warned her. He could not afford to lose his best guide and translator over a finicky woman. It was childish to want Mary's surprise and revulsion to prove a point about her being unsuited for this trip. He let his breath out slowly, muscles tensed for her reply.

Mary looked straight at Hannabo and finished the fork's circuit to her mouth, chewing thoughtfully. When she swallowed she said, "It is the best monkey I've ever eaten. Thank you for your trouble, Hannabo."

William stared in shock. The doctor was full of surprises. Alice had gagged and refused to eat more the first time she was served monkey. There was more to the doctor than he thought.

The rest of the meal passed in silence. Clara resumed eating, but seemed to be picking through the rice mixture. Mary finished hers and said, "If you will excuse me, today's exercise has me ready for sleep. I'll be heading for bed now."

Clara rose. "I think I'll join you."

"Ladies, we will leave at first light. Please be ready."

"Of course, Pastor Mayweather. Clara and I will be ready promptly."

William waited to turn in until he saw that they were settled for the night. Rifle at the ready, he climbed into his own bedding. Despite his exhaustion, sleep was elusive. Even the presence of the women could no longer dampen his excitement at the nearness of his goal. His longing to be at Nynabo surprised him with its strength. Following God's call on his life was joy enough, but to step into the broad footsteps of the uncle who had raised him as his own made it all the more meaningful. Despite the losses he'd suffered, achieving this goal was like a Christmas present in a shiny bow demanding to be opened.

Karl's private conversation with him three nights ago had provided some comfort about taking the women. The doctor would have gone on without him anyway, taking her companion with her. No doubt about that.

His prayerful agony the night before he announced he had changed his mind didn't leave him with complete peace; more like a restless armistice with his fears. In the end, he concluded he must go or leave two inexperienced women to fend for themselves. At least he could keep them from the worst of danger until they were replaced.

And replaced they would be as soon as the letter he'd left with Karl made its way to the Mission Board with his request for male workers. He prayed the wait wouldn't be lengthy.

In the meantime, he would maintain a professional relationship, nothing more. Dr. O'Hara had managed the difficult trail with minimal complaint, handled the unique foodstuffs without giving offense and held her composure at the realization roaming leopards were a danger. He had to admire a woman like that. He also had to be sure admiration never crossed a line into something more. Not with Dr. O'Hara, not with any woman, while he served in one of the more dangerous parts of the world. Besides, she and Clara would soon find themselves on a caravan back out of the jungle.

He felt a pang of guilt for the letter he had sent, but brushed it off like the beetle scurrying across his blankets. It was for her own good. Dr. O'Hara didn't understand the danger, so he had made the decision to ask for a reassignment for her.

He thought of how well she'd handled Hannabo's feelings despite her obvious discomfort, and it caused his conscience a slight twinge. Examined rationally, there was no real reason to feel guilty over his actions. Wrestling with irrational guilt turned out to be as futile as getting comfortable where he lay. The hard jungle floor made its every bump felt through William's bedding. He was on a first-name basis with most of them before sleep finally claimed him. His last thoughts were of how to most effectively protect the two women until the day they were recalled. Especially when the village of the warlike and lecherous Nana Bolo lay between them and Nynabo.

Chapter Three

Mary's new boots had rubbed an angry blister on her right foot. The second day on the trail and her old boots were a fond memory whose faults she'd forgotten. She should've taken care to break the new ones in better before this trek. If the caravan didn't stop for a midday break soon, she would be forced to ask for one. The risk of infection from an untreated blister in this humidity was high. Memories of field amputations flooded her brain, and she shuddered.

"Are you getting sick?" William asked, right at her back.

Mary almost jumped out of her own skin to stand beside herself. How did he do that? She could have sworn he was several places back. She would never get used to the noise of the jungle animals, the way it covered the most mundane sounds.

"I'm as healthy as the proverbial horse. Why do you ask?"

"You were shivering. While you may have had malaria as a child, you must know it frequently recurs. Often with no real warning."

He, the pastor, was lecturing her, the physician, on malaria? "While I may not remember much from my personal experience, I'm perfectly aware of the disease and its on-going nature. Medical school, even for females, was not a social experience."

The short laugh from behind her was edged with bit-terness. "You don't know malaria until you have actually seen its devastation in this land."

The intensity of his answer held her unruly tongue for her. Who had he lost to bring such pain to his voice? He probably wouldn't appreciate her asking.

William edged past her while she answered. "Rest as-sured, I am not experiencing any symptoms of the dis-ease."

His back to her, he lengthened his strides to move ahead. "Speaking of rest, we will be stopping for a thirty-minute period shortly. Be prepared to march again after we've eaten."

"Thank goodness," she murmured. She didn't want to start limping and be subject to more of a lecture. Both their tempers had been edging toward a real fandango.

It was bad enough the gunshot last night had affected her. The constant barrages at Argonne initially hardened her. But since her brother Jeremy's death, she heard every shot in a new way. She would have been useless for front-line hospitals if the Armistice hadn't come. She'd covered up her reaction last night, but she didn't need to give this reluctant missionary guide another chance to look down on her and see weakness.

A long half-hour later, the caravan halted. Lunch was a quick and quiet repast of cold rice, absent monkey meat. No William in sight either, giving her time to tend her blister.

Sitting on a fallen tree at the edge of the path with Clara, Mary unfastened her panniers, the leg coverings she still wore for protection from mosquito bites, and unlaced her left boot, carefully removing her sock. An angry red swelling on the outside of her small toe brought a hissed intake from Clara.

"That's not good."

Mary forced a smile in Clara's direction. "I know. Do you think you can get me my small pack?"

Clara returned, pack in hand. "It doesn't look infected."

Mary agreed. She used gauze and canteen water to clean the blister and applied a small plaster for protection. Mindful of the imminent call to move, she reached for her discarded sock.

"Uh, Mary?" Clara tipped her head to indicate Pastor Mayweather's approach.

She tried to stuff her foot in the sock, but didn't succeed before the pastor got an eyeful of her exposed bandage.

"Is there a problem?" His deep rumble easily crossed the short distance between them.

"No, no problem at all." Mary pulled the sock snug and reached for her boot.

In one swift movement, William snatched the boot from her hand and squatted in front of her, concern across his face. "Take off the sock."

"No. I have a small blister and I've taken care of it. I'm not going to waste my plasters to satisfy your curiosity." She stretched her hand out for her boot.

"Blisters in the jungle are serious. Any open wound is."

If only she could get to her feet. He obviously meant well, but she still had an urge to knock him off his know-it-all hobby horse. "Medical school managed to cover both malaria and minor scrapes in my training."

"Too bad your training didn't extend to proper foot-wear. Those shiny new boots will probably rub both of your feet raw before we reach Nynabo." William stood, forcing her to crane her neck to look up. He held out her boot. "You need to take the hammock chair. Let your foot heal."

Mary laced her boot and Clara handed over her pannier, looking amused over the whole exchange. Mary joined the hooks and stood. She was so close that she could easily breathe in his earthy scent. "I'm perfectly capable of walking." Even to her, the irritation in her voice sounded petulant.

The corner of his mouth turned up and he inclined his head. "Obviously. Otherwise you wouldn't have a blister."

He made no move to step back and put a more polite distance between them, causing her an awareness of his nearness she hadn't expected. She stared up into eyes that turned serious.

"Please, Dr. O'Hara. I would appreciate it if you would take my advice on this matter. Even if I do know more of the Bible than medicine." He stepped aside and motioned to her hammock-chair bearers.

Mary's first thought was to refuse. His eyebrows knitted in concern as he waited for her decision. His plea seemed genuine without any hint of an order behind it. She took a couple of steps and decided the hammock chair it would be.

The smile that lit the faces of her bearers surprised her. "Carry Mammy Doctor? Yes. Yes."

Their enthusiasm was such that it occurred to her she might have offended them by refusing their services before. Only the depth of her ignorance of the pidgin they spoke kept her from inquiring further.

When the call came to move on, two eager men bore the poles on their heads, and Mary climbed into the canvas conveyance. She was soon fast asleep from the rhythmic sway and the sound of drums in the distance, tattooing out a deep bass beat.

A sudden stop broke her rest and Mary woke, embarrassed at having slept while others labored to carry her.

"Pastor, Pastor." Cries from the front of the caravan, all of which had come to a screeching halt, reached Mary's ears. She sat up and glanced around. Through an opening in the canopy, she could see the tropical sun hanging low in the sky. She must have slept for hours.

A few feet behind her, Clara was standing near her chair, taking advantage of the opportunity to stretch. Mary did the same. William pushed his way back from several spots forward. When he came level with her, she asked, "What's going on?"

He ignored her and gave instructions to her bearers in a staccato native dialect. The narrowing of his eyes, the tightness around his mouth, both coupled with the insistent tone to her bearers, needed no translation. Her stomach tightened.

He started to walk off once he finished talking, but Mary grabbed his arm. "I asked you what is wrong?"

"Nothing you need concern yourself about. Just wait here and follow any instructions your bearers give you." He pulled his arm from her grasp and moved away.

"I am not a child to be either coddled or ignored, Pastor Mayweather."

"No," he tossed back with barely a glance. "But you are under my care and I'm telling you to wait here."

Mary stood in the interminable heat, sweat pouring down her back. Nearby porters failed to rest in their usual sprawl. Her bearers flanked her closely. Mary yearned for the vocabulary to explain the social decorum of space in her culture.

She was keen to walk forward and see what was happening. Trouble was she didn't know what she'd be walking into.

Clara moved up and joined Mary. "Do you think there are hostile natives up there?"

"If there are hostiles, I fail to see how they could possibly win out over our acerbic pastor."

Clara's barking laugh echoed off the canopy above and set birds to scattering.

With nothing left but waiting, Mary turned her attention to the porters nearest her, all of whom shifted nervously. Those who carried rifles with their packs now had them slung through the crook of their arms, pointing down. Words in dialect tumbled back from the front of the caravan and the overall agitation level around her rose. She felt her mouth go dry as the porter in front of her slid the bolt on his rifle to chamber a round.

"Did you see that?" Mary asked Clara.

Clara inclined her head. "The one with the rifle?"

"He's getting ready for something. Whatever message just passed through the ranks has them all on edge."

Clara said, "I'm not sure whether to wish I understood the language or not at this point."

"After the last year, I think we both understand enough of men with their guns to translate anyway."

"More than enough. What do we do if shooting starts?"

If shooting started, could Mary trust herself not to panic like she did when Hannabo unexpectedly shot dinner? It was only one rifle shot that affected her last time. How would she fare if they ended up embattled with guns firing all around? "I assume the men guarding us so closely will know what to do if the time comes. It's Pastor Mayweather that worries me. He's up in the thick of whatever is going on."

"Do the natives in the bush even use guns? Some of our men carry spears."

"I don't really know. Our indoctrination session back in France said the missionaries before Pastor Mayweather were the first of any whites that far into the jungle interior. How would they have even gotten rifles?" Curiosity was replaced by a shiver of apprehension running down her spine. Rifles or spears, either were deadly in an enemy's hands.

An eternity passed in silence while they waited. Mary's nerves frayed. Maybe William was right. She didn't belong here. Not if she turned into one of those vapid women she despised every time a rifle was used.

Then she thought of his pinched lips and creased brow when he had lectured her before they left Newaka. She'd had a hard time taking him seriously when the wind kept blowing his unruly brown hair into his eyes.

Mary's thoughts exploded with the crack of a single rifle shot. Porters grabbed Clara's arms, hauling her off into the bush for cover. Mary resisted the ones who tried to grab her and stood rooted to the spot. Who was shot? Was William injured?

Her bearers reached again for her arms and pulled. "Is someone shot? Please, I'm a doctor, I must help."

The younger man shook his head vigorously saying, "No savvy. Nana Pastor say Mammy Doctor must be protected." His pressure on her arm increased.

Part of her longed to give in and seek cover in the surrounding jungle. The tree sheltering Clara looked so appealing. Her oath as a doctor won out.

She pulled her arm free and took advantage of her small stature to duck around him, striding quickly. The excited chattering and his at-heel position confirmed he hadn't given up his quest to stop her. Fortunately she kept her immediate supplies in the pack she carried. She doubted she could have convinced any of these men to get it for her.

Ignoring the dread weighing down her stomach, Mary forged ahead. If William was injured, or even another man, she had to help, not cower in fear.

Sheer shock at her charge forward paralyzed the remaining porters still on the trail. A heavy sigh behind her told her that her shadow was still attached. She passed several more armed men, some with spears, before the jungle fell back and opened. She scented the wood smoke before she saw the tendrils reaching upward. Smoke escaped at random intervals throughout the yellow undulations of dried grass roofs.

They had arrived at a village. If the rifle shot was any indication, an unfriendly one.

Looking down the hill to the spot where the path widened at the village edge, Mary saw William. Hannabo was on one side and another porter, Jabo maybe, stood on the other. She stopped where she was to take in the scene. No one lay on the ground or clutched a wound. Who or what had been shot?

All of her dramatic worries and it was just a serious discussion with a group of natives. No one was at war here.

All of them were deferring to the one native in a worn black bowler hat and bright red loincloth standing with his arms folded across his chest, a chest hung with some type of decorative necklace. Must be the chief.

Whoever he was, she knew the moment he became aware of her. He put out a bony finger and pointed. *Was he pointing at her?* All conversation ceased.

William turned to see what Bowler Hat was pointing to, and if there had been any doubt in her mind she was the object of attention, the glare from William removed it.

Bowler Hat began to speak. Mary wasn't close enough

to hear anything. By the frequency of gestures, there was a debate or perhaps a trade. She knew that trading was one way a missionary made inroads into a tribe's favor.

The conversation ended abruptly. Bowler Hat's arms were back in place across his chest. William and Hannabo turned and headed toward the caravan. Hannabo looked on stolidly, but William's face morphed from blank and emotionless to raw fury.

When he drew near, his voice came out as a low hiss. "I told you to stay put. Turn around and follow behind me."

"I beg your pardon. I…"

"If you don't want to be that old man's newest wife, you'll do as I say and you'll do it right *now*."

Chapter Four

William tried to ignore the sputtering sound behind him. Amazing what it took to make that woman speechless. Now if he could figure out how to get her to follow his instructions.

She didn't stay speechless for long. "What do you mean I could end up as that old man's wife? I assure you…"

The villagers out of sight, he wheeled around to give Dr. O'Hara the dressing down she deserved. Except he misjudged how closely she was following and ended up with her walking right into him, knocking her pith helmet off her head and sending her backward. He caught her before she tilted to the ground.

A hundred and ten pounds of warm femininity snapped back into his arms. Soft skin and womanly curves seared his bare arms. He loosed his grip and stepped back.

"Thank you, Pastor Mayweather. I'm not normally so clumsy. My apologies." Mary bent over to retrieve her helmet.

"If by following me too closely you mean you didn't stay put where you were told to, then you certainly do owe me an apology. Me and this entire company."

"What?"

"Can you not follow simple instructions? I distinctly told you to wait where I left you." His temple pulsed and throbbed. This healer would be the death of him yet.

"I heard a shot. What in the world did I do that was so wrong? I came to see if someone was injured."

"No one was injured. Negotiations for passing through the village got a little difficult. Jabo overreacted when directly challenged by one of the warriors. He fired into the air."

"I had no way of knowing that. Someone might have been injured. I only came to see if my skills were needed."

She meant well, but William couldn't find it in him to absolve her actions. Not considering. "Well, while you were busy seeing, you were *seen* before we'd negotiated simple pass through the village. It would have saved us hours on the trail. Now we're expected to stay the night. By Nana Bolo no less."

"Nana Bolo? Is that the older man in the bowler hat? The one you said wanted me to be his wife?"

"That would be the one."

"Well, tell him I said no. Politely, of course."

William blew out an impatient breath. "For an intelligent woman, you don't know much about the way things work here."

"A quick indoctrination in France before you climb on a freighter hardly covers everything. And excuse me if I don't know the customs of the Liberian bush. I've been a little busy lately. France. The Great War. Maybe you've heard of it?"

"The war affected us all. It took me months to get passage back here from leave in the States with transport at such risk."

"Right. Try actually serving in the war instead of staying home in some cushy church job. Then we'll compare notes."

"Cushy church job...." He snorted at the idea a compassionate leave qualified as cushy. Then the rest of what she said hit him. "Wait... You served in the war in France? How? The Army didn't recruit women."

"I already went over this with the Jansens at dinner, something you would know if you'd had the manners to join us. The Red Cross did the recruiting and the Army used us despite their public objections to enlisting female physicians."

William felt the proverbial rug go flying out from under his feet. All of his assumptions...could he be wrong about her? The image of his delicate Alice on her deathbed tamped that idea down without hesitation. "Nevertheless, your knowledge and experience don't extend into this battlefield. And make no mistake, it is a battlefield. A battlefield for men's souls."

"I am aware, Pastor Mayweather. But I intend to deal with men's and women's bodies much more than their souls. I'll leave the cure for eternal damnation to you."

Vehemence blew through Mary's words, and William was hard put to understand. But they'd gone too far off track and he needed to deal with the situation at hand. "A good mission station is one where everyone works together toward the salvation of the heathen. However, we have to first get through the night alive in this village."

Considering his plans for her quick removal from the mission, he wasn't sure why he bothered with the lecture on teamwork. The only thing of real importance now was surviving the situation she'd created.

William crossed his arms and gave Mary his most serious look. "So you, Doctor O'Hara, must do exactly as I tell you tonight so you do not find yourself married or get us all killed. Nana Bolo will not accept your refusal. He thinks of women as property, and property does not make its own choices."

Mary's brow knit into a frown and her mouth opened in a small "oh." The look didn't last. What looked like fumes of outrage bubbled to the surface. "Well, you can set him straight on that right now. I am no man's property."

She punctuated her words with an adorable little foot stamp. William would have chuckled if the situation they were in was not so dire. "Tonight while we are in this village, you are. It's the only concept he understands. Since you and Clara are under my care, I explained to him I was not willing to trade you despite his several generous offers." William leaned down closer to her eye level and said, "And believe me when I say the bullocks, goats and chickens he offered are looking pretty good about now."

Each step down the path to the village might as well have been on hot coals instead of rough dirt for the effect on Mary's temper. Once her jaw began to hurt as they got to the village perimeter, she realized she was grinding her teeth. The nerve of the man. She'd made a mistake, but an understandable one. One he completely discounted.

Quick orders were exchanged between the tribesmen, Hannabo and William. As the carriers and porters were separated from them, a frisson of unease snaked down Mary's spine. Leaving those familiar faces behind, familiar faces with weapons, unnerved her. William and Hannabo were armed, but what could two men do against a village? The iron-tipped spears in the warriors' hands carried a sure promise of death.

Or better yet, what *would* two men do? Did missionaries have a code against defending themselves? Not to kill, or something? Her sense of vulnerability projected itself in stomach knots. It was like a residency all over again. Classroom training couldn't compare to actual experience.

The booming artillery at Argonne had been unnerving, but shells rarely reached the mobile field hospitals and both sides strictly left the Red Cross personnel alone, keeping in mind they themselves might end up in need of their services. Captured enemies were treated alongside soldiers. The only fact she could remember about the Liberian interior was that many missionaries had died in the attempt to break evangelistic ground here. She knew the fatality rate of malaria. How many died at the hands of the natives?

"Dr. Mary, look." Clara gave a slight nod of her head. They followed a hut-lined path through the village, stepping around the roaming chickens and one stray piglet. A break in the huts revealed a small work area, complete with a low cook fire and large iron cook pot with steam rising.

Mary glanced over and saw a group of about ten young children, including one nursing baby, all sans clothing. The older ones were eminently curious. Three of the youngest fled behind their mother's legs to peer out from safety as soon as they had seen them. The oldest of the bunch, not more than seven, stood stock-still and tried to look fierce, not quite pulling it off. Of the five women present, presumably their mothers, although there was little doubt about the one who was nursing, expressions ranged from wary to curious to downright hostile on one thin woman with blue cloth covering her modestly while she stirred the pot.

Without exception, the rest of the women wore nothing more than a cloth skirt fastened about their waists and a small fetish bag she'd come to expect hung around their necks. Mary found herself gawking and forced herself to take her eyes off the uninhibited display of uncovered skin. Even as a physician, the unabashed nudity discomfited her. Why did some cover more than others? Was it a status indication?

As much for herself as Clara, Mary said, "They might not have ever seen a white person, Clara. Try not to stare. I think we're scaring the little ones."

"Then we're on equal footing. Some of those warriors scared me. All those tattoos on their faces. I've never seen anything like it."

"Me neither. Maybe it's something just this tribe does. None of our porters bear those kind of markings. Although Hannabo's patterned scarring on his face resembles them a little."

"Well, the children are adorable. I can't wait until we're in Nynabo and I can start the school."

"Let's hope it won't be much longer. The excitement of jungle travel wore off soon after we left the beach at Garraway and headed to Newaka. I'm ready to be settled."

Clara laughed. "I know what you mean. The first few miles when we left Garraway city behind, the trail seemed so exciting. So different."

Mary adjusted the medical satchel she carried. "I agree. The endless dirt track, tree roots waiting in ambush and all the insects lost their novelty for me."

Clara glanced around. "Well, we should be careful what we wish for, because there's a lot of novelty here."

Novelty aside, they passed in a tired, companionable silence through the rest of the village, the tableau of cooking they'd seen repeating once more. The village, large and well laid out in several divisions from the perspective of the hilltop trail, was different when you actually walked through it. Now an endless maze of mud huts, topped with the low-hanging dried brush used for thatching, surrounded them. Mary feared she would get lost in the sameness if she tried to navigate alone.

A wooden palisade wall came into view and the tribesman leading them halted before a hut outside the entrance to the private compound. He gestured to the hut and to the women, and Mary assumed it to be their quarters for the night.

Before she could enter the hut, William put his hand up and conferred with Hannabo, all the while with his back still to them.

Arrogant. That was the word that normally came to mind when she thought of Pastor William Mayweather. Then he took off his pith helmet and ran his hands through that wavy brown hair and the word changed. Striking. And worried.

William crossed his arms when Hannabo conveyed something to the tribesman and the tribesman shook his head and repeated his gesture indicating the hut. What was the problem? Was he holding out for a better hut? They all looked the same to her.

The weariness settling over her as the sun dropped halfway below the horizon overrode her resentful obedience and she stepped forward. "What's the problem? Is there something wrong with this hut? Because it looks fine to me."

William turned to her with narrowed eyes, glaring. She flinched. If those rich, brown eyes had been spears, she would have been impaled on the spot.

She'd done it again. Whatever *it* was.

William's deep rumble came out deceptively low. "I'm sure the hut is quite fine." He came closer, crossed his arms over his chest and leaned down and in until he was only inches from her face. "If, that is, you don't mind being separated from Hannabo and myself. Alone with only your sharp tongue for protection. Of course, we could always share the hut."

William pulled back, the discomfort of being close enough to Mary to see her smallest freckles befuddling his thoughts. He had tried counting to ten, reciting Proverbs to himself about the futility of arguing with the foolish—none of it worked. No sooner did he get things back under control than this obstinate woman tried to insert herself right back into the thick of things. At least Alice let him be in charge, hung back and allowed him to do the man's work. This woman wanted to literally and figuratively wear the trousers. At least…

William derailed his mental train of thought on the memory of Alice and traveled back to the reality of an impatient redhead in front of him with her eyes bugging out at his sarcastic statement about sharing a hut.

Oh, so her suffragette sympathies didn't extend to sharing a hut with him. The shocked look on her face proclaimed outrage. Good to know. At least her morals stood firm, not loose like her definition of a woman's place in life. What had the Mission Board been thinking to send him this female physician?

Mary took a deep breath in and out and straightened her spine, all under his careful observation. Indignation rolled off of her. "That is quite unacceptable. No tents on the trail were one thing, but sharing a private hut is another."

William's smile wasn't one his Aunt Ruth would have approved of if she had been there. "My point exactly. Now maybe you'll let me continue making my point with this tribesman so neither of us ends up indulging in scandalous behavior."

"Can't we be in separate huts but next to each other?"

"Not possible. Let me finish here and I'll explain."

The slight tic in her right eye gave away the fact Mary had more to say. Much more she suppressed with a great deal of effort. He turned his back to her and planted himself between her and their appointed village guide's line of vision. He nodded to Hannabo and continued his negotiation.

He walked a fine line to accept the hospitality and yet require his own special guard for the women without impugning his hosts. When it became clear he risked insult to village hospitality, he'd explained his concern for the crazy woman with red hair wandering away and getting into trouble. Certainly true. Just not the whole reason.

When his tribal host laughed, he knew he'd won the day. Troublesome women, the universally understood notion among men.

The best negotiating ploy too, although the good doctor would have a conniption if she could only translate the language. Why couldn't she understand he was in charge without constantly challenging him?

She thought western sensibilities would prevail in the situation with Nana Bolo. That sort of attitude would have her married and bearing the chief's children in no time.

Hopefully, the idea that she was troublesome and a little crazy would get back to Nana Bolo. That wily schemer caught the turn of the phrase where William avoided claiming her as his wife. By indicating she was under his care, a phrase the chief took to mean Mary was William's property, he left himself wide open to this. The chief would think he only held out for better terms.

Of course the only other option available to him would have been lying and saying that she was his wife. Not an acceptable course for his conscience or the mission of winning souls. Scripturally, lying about Sarah backfired on Abraham twice.

This way he could protect the women to the best of his ability. He would go to the palaver hut, an honor reserved for male guests only, but leave Hannabo to sleep at the threshold of the women's hut. He may not want women in the interior with him, but he couldn't leave them undefended this close to the chief's compound.

Even if they were more trouble than they were worth.

Dr. O'Hara did have a tendency to forget to stay put. Her reasons may have been admirable. How many women would have run toward a gunshot to help? But now more than before, he needed her out of the sight of the villagers. She would be easier to protect once he could get to Nynabo. He refused to think about her return trek out of the jungle when the time came. She would be someone else's responsibility then. He'd be sure they steered clear of Nana Bolo on her return trip.

He outlined his plan to Hannabo, who nodded. Taking a deep breath, he turned back to Clara and Mary. "Ladies, for your protection, our hosts agree Hannabo will stay with you, sleeping outside the threshold of your quarters. I would do the chief a grave insult if I don't sleep in the palaver hut allotted to honored guests. And, as women are not allowed in that hut, you will stay here outside the palisade walls."

Clara's hand fluttered to her chest.

"Not to worry, Mrs. Smith. We will keep you safe." With a sweeping hand gesture, he indicated the doorway of the hut. "If you need something, ask Hannabo. I will be just on the other side of the wall."

Mary's voice filled with concern. "Pastor Mayweather, our needs should not deprive Hannabo of his comfort for the night."

William laughed despite his desire to attract as little attention as possible. "I assure you your comfort levels will be quite equitable. At the most, you will sleep on planks to elevate you off the dirt. I promise you sleeping directly on the dirt is little more hardship."

Clara's face echoed Mary's surprise as the two exchanged looks. It was Clara who finally spoke. "But can we not retrieve our camp beds from the porters and set them up in the hut? I know the trail was too narrow for tents where we camped the first night, but surely this hut will easily hold them."

William understood her desire. The relative comfort of his folding cot would be a nice reprieve from the hard surface. "I'm afraid not, ladies. Don't insult our host by refusing his provision."

"That's too bad." Clara's voice held the same longing for her own bedding William ascribed to his. "I guess we'd better just make do."

Mary offered no argument. Surprising.

"I'm going to have to ask you ladies to stay inside the hut till morning. No matter what you hear. There will undoubtedly be a lot of revelry tonight." William hoped his plea wasn't words to the deaf.

He reached over and laid his hand on the physician's arm. "Dr. O'Hara, I am only one man. Our caravan is too small to intimidate the chief here. Please, don't put us in any more situations where I might not be able to talk our way out."

Conscious of Mary's eyes on the hand still resting on her arm, he pulled back and stuffed his hands in his pockets. "I'm begging you. Consider all our lives in this."

Chapter Five

Mary clutched the extra blankets Hannabo had surreptitiously secured for them from their gear and followed Clara, ducking into the low opening of the mud hut. Once inside she straightened. The conical roof gave more openness than she'd realized. The floor was smooth, packed dirt with faint round marks overlapping at regular intervals. The smooth clay walls lacked a window and the only real light came from the open doorway.

Squinting against the dimness, she made out two elevated wooden pallets to her right. They seemed high for a bed, sitting a few feet off the floor. She placed the blankets on the one closest to her.

She slid her pack off her shoulders and laid it at the foot of the pallet. Clara groaned in relief enough for both of them as her pack came off and said, "Right now almost anything looks comfortable. Even wood covered with a thin reed mat."

"Not exactly my idea of comfort. But I'm too exhausted from being such a troublemaker to care."

"You aren't a troublemaker, Dr. Mary." Clara's grin came through as Mary's eyes adjusted to the low light. "You're just used to being in charge."

"Exactly. If Pastor Mayweather would only talk to me instead of barking orders, maybe I wouldn't have caused him such problems."

"Rare is the man who can treat a woman like an equal. Even at the hospital they wanted to relegate you to anesthesia and not surgery."

The pain of loss stabbed Mary's chest. "They were right. The most important operation of my life and I botched it." Tears threatened to flow. Exhaustion was breaking down both her muscles and her emotions.

Clara stepped close and put her arm around Mary. "You didn't botch anything. Your brother was too far gone by the time he arrived at the hospital. Not even that braggart Dr. Hubbard could have saved him—no matter what he said."

Mary looked at Clara through unshed tears. "I wish my father saw it that way. Jeremy died on my operating table. Father's letter spelled out whom he held responsible for his only son's loss."

"Now, now. Grief did his speaking for him. Grief will pass and he'll think it through. He'll come around. Your father loves you. He supported your studies to become a physician in the first place."

Mary pulled away and picked up the blankets. "I don't know, Clara. He made his opinion pretty clear that nothing I did could ever atone for costing him his only son." Mary arranged the blankets over the planks as best she could. "I'm afraid I agree with him."

"Nonsense. A German soldier killed him. Men die in war, plain and simple."

Mary sat down on the pallet and unhooked her panniers one at a time. "Well, what's my excuse this time? If I hadn't reacted to that gunshot and just stayed put, we wouldn't be in any danger."

Clara's belly laugh startled Mary. She looked up from unlacing her boots. "Dr. Mary, we're in the middle of the Liberian jungle with heathen tribes known for their cannibalism. Of course we're in danger. You think the chief wouldn't see or hear about a pretty woman with red hair anyway?"

Mary turned up the corners of her mouth despite her fatalism. She reached and pulled the pins from her hair, letting down the long plait and wagging the tresses ruefully. "I suppose you're right. My hair has always been a beacon for trouble."

Clara's face turned serious. "God made you exactly right, my girl. From the color of your hair to the desire He gave you to be a doctor. We just have to trust that He will protect us in this eternal battlefield."

Mary slid off her right sock and removed the plaster from her small toe. No signs of infection, but she pretended to study the healing area awhile to take in what Clara said. It sounded like what William had said, only without the anger. They both envisioned God's plan so clearly. She just wanted to bury herself away, do some good with her training and not think so much about God's plan for her. Since Jeremy died, her faith had faltered to the point she wasn't sure she could even know God's plan in her life anymore.

Mary took the fresh plaster Clara offered her from her bag. Even if the God of her childhood was real, did He have a plan for their lives? Otherwise, why would Jeremy have died? Jeremy and so many boys like him. Where was God's protection, his plan in the Forest of Argonne?

Clara's soft voice interrupted her contemplations. "We all have doubts sometimes, Dr. Mary. Take them to Him. He's the only one with real answers for them."

Mary's tears hung back at the border of her lower lids

and she blinked to dispel them. Clara generously pretended not to notice while she explored the small hut. "No place for a fire. I thought there would be some sort of pit in the center."

"I don't know. This hut seems a lot smaller than the ones we passed. Maybe they have them. Or they do all their cooking in the open like the groups we passed with cook pots."

"True. Speaking of food, I wonder what we are to do about dinner."

Mary formed a reply, but Hannabo stuck his head in the doorway first. "Mammies, food is here."

"Oh, thank the Lord. I'm starved." Clara's enthusiasm was infectious and Mary's stomach rumbled in response.

Two of the village women entered single file. One, a young girl of about fifteen whom Mary hadn't seen on their walk through the village, smiled shyly. She wore twice the amount of necklaces Mary counted on the other women they'd passed and had a bright red skirt wrapped and tied around her hips and chest. Her well-fed appearance made sense when she bent to place a wooden bowl of steaming liquid in Clara's hands. Pregnant. And so young. Only four to five months, but pregnant nonetheless. Mary hoped her own expression didn't mirror the shock on Clara's when she seemed to come to the same conclusion.

This girl, still a child in many ways, at home would have been in school, giggling with girlfriends, maybe even mooning over a handsome boy. Here she was already someone's wife.

Mary stole her attention from the girl's pregnant belly and focused on the wooden bowl offered to her. Steaming soup. What kind she didn't know.

The woman in the faded blue skirt she'd seen earlier

stirring the cook pot stood in front of Clara. A lot less jewelry adorned her. Was this a sign of status? If so, this young girl outranked her older counterpart. This woman looked to be only in her late twenties, but a hard life displayed itself in the weariness, the long lines around the woman's mouth. Her life story was summed up in her face.

The same face also clearly advertised the woman's feelings. Was all that hatred directed at her? Why?

Mary wondered as she took the steaming bowl and the women stepped back. The two women gave no indication of leaving, and Mary questioned if there was a ritual to the meal. Getting no cues from the women, she lifted the bowl up and inhaled the aroma.

She took a glance at Clara who sat holding her bowl with one eyebrow raised as if to say, *you first*. Ha! Afraid of monkey again.

Mary smiled at the two women now standing to the side, watching intently. She infused her voice with a cheery note and said to Clara, "Probably chicken soup. Whatever you do, let's not offend them."

Mary lifted the bowl to her lips and took a small sip which she balanced on her tongue, mouth open to cool the heat. Heat which never cooled.

She swallowed. Real tears came to her eyes and her sinuses began to run. She managed to stutter, "A little spicy." Somehow she kept the smile plastered to her face. The younger woman giggled behind the hand now covering her mouth. The older one lifted her chin as if in challenge.

Mary managed to take another sip and smile. After all, once her tongue started singing soprano, what did more spice matter? The older woman's eyebrows went up ever so slightly. Respect? Mary couldn't be sure. But she never backed away from a challenge.

She finished the bowl completely and waited to grab for her canteen until the women backed out of the hut.

Clara's face flashed between pale and a little green. Sweat poured off her. "I don't know how you swallowed the soup, Dr. Mary. I'm not sure mine is going to stay down."

"Did you catch the expression on the older woman? She expected her food to be insulted."

"What was in that anyway?"

"Pepper of some kind. Let me ask Hannabo." Mary stuck her head out the door. William and Hannabo held their heads together in conversation. Surely she hadn't done something else she didn't understand.

Hannabo caught sight of her and said something to William. He turned around and walked over to her. "Is there a problem?"

"Not unless you consider having our tongues completely numbed from dinner." She tried for a smile so he'd know she spoke in humor.

The serious look on William's face dropped instantly and his eyes crinkled in merriment. "Red pepper. A country-wide favorite. Since you're an honored guest, I am sure the spicing was generous."

"You could have warned me. I'm not sure I'll ever be able to taste food again."

"You will. It was a little tough to swallow my first time, too. The wives looked pleased when they left, so you must have held your tongue, so to speak."

Mary marveled at this lighthearted side of William. She'd begun thinking he possessed only a serious side. "Why Pastor Mayweather, is that a pun? Humor becomes you."

And just as quickly as it was there, the smile vanished. "Is there anything else you need for the night, Doctor?"

Mary wasn't sure what to make of the sudden turn in demeanor. "No, we're fine. Did I say something wrong?"

"No, of course not. Not this time at least."

Of all the things to say. Couldn't he just be nice and let it go at that? She bit back a scathing retort as he said, "If there's nothing else then, may I remind you a lot of celebrating will go on in the village tonight. A lot of religious ceremonies are conducted after nightfall."

Mary shuddered despite the waning heat. "What kind of ceremonies?"

William's eyes narrowed and he tilted his head for emphasis. "None you need to be attending."

This time she did sputter. "I assure you, I hadn't planned to attend. I was merely curious."

"See that you keep your curiosity in check this time."

Of all the gall. He turned on his heel and returned to where Hannabo was waiting. Mary stood rooted and gape-mouthed at the man's insolence. After a few seconds, William walked off and Hannabo came to stand at the entrance to their hut.

"Where's Pastor Mayweather going, Hannabo?"

"Nana Pastor, he goes to speak to Chief. He hopes to show Nana Bolo the one true God and get him to put away his fetishes. He will not succeed."

"Why not?"

"Nana Karl has tried for years. Nana Bolo's devilmen are powerful. They have already given him what he wants. He will not listen to the stories of the white man's God."

"Devilmen? What do you mean?"

"They hold the magic. Their conjures are strong. The young girl who brought you dinner?"

"Yes, she is with child, I believe."

Hannabo's head nodded vigorous assent. "Because of

the Devilmen. Nana Bolo made his offering when she did not conceive for some time."

"Nonsense. Conception is not a sign of magic."

"Devilmen do many things, miracles sometimes, Mammy Doctor. I believe in the Jesus God, but I've seen devilmen work. They hold much power."

A shiver that belied the heat ran through her. Evil seemed so distant back at home in a Virginia church. Not so distant on the battlefield. Witchcraft prevailed in this darkness.

"Our worlds are very different this way, Hannabo."

He nodded in response.

"There is another difference I wanted to ask about. Why do some of the women cover their…uh, chests and some do not?" She felt silly being embarrassed, but it was one thing to examine someone and another to ask about modesty issues so specifically to a man.

Hannabo replied as if it was no issue at all. "Young girls who are not promised in marriage wear only the skirt. Once they are promised or married, they wear more to show their status."

So it was a question of status, just not the way she'd thought. She said good night and went back into the dark hut, feeling her way to her bed. Clara was stretched out, already snoring. Mary sat on the hard pallet and wondered what kind of witchcraft Hannabo had seen to make him think it held power. Exhaustion took a stronger hold than her questions, and she lay back to fall into a fitful sleep filled with the rhythm of drums, shouts and fervor.

When quiet finally reigned, she sunk into a deep inky blackness even dreams couldn't penetrate. Later, a rooster announced the dawn. More than once.

Foolish fowl. The sun wasn't up yet. She tried to shake off the hold sleep claimed but kept dozing off.

The only thing finally piercing the veil of slumber and startling her completely awake were the screams.

Chapter Six

William heard the women's wailing over a loss before Hannabo reached him. It was an unmistakable sound in the bush.

Someone had died.

Hannabo came running, out of breath, tension pouring out of his very skin. The smell of fear was strong. They all had to leave the village before accusations began.

Hannabo's words confirmed it. "It was one of the warriors in Nana Bolo's personal guard."

"I'll get the women. You get the rest of the caravan. We'll meet you on the trail just outside the village. Hopefully all eyes will be busy elsewhere with the mourning ritual and we can be long down the trail before someone points the finger."

Hannabo nodded and set off to roust the rest of the caravan. Most were probably packing up already. Some may have already headed into the bush, taking no chances with their lives.

He saw a familiar red head peek out of the hut door. Her long hair was loose and mussed. She was dressed, however, and looked like she'd slept in her clothes last night.

"Pastor Mayweather, what's all the wailing? What's happening?"

"One of the warriors has died in the night. Grab your things. We must leave immediately or risk death."

Mary paled and her eyes widened.

"It will be all right. But there is one chance to save ourselves and it is now. Grab your gear!"

She spun around and headed back into the hut. He headed back to the palaver hut to get his pack. The separate compound looked empty, probably in response to the wailing. Custom required the widow receive comfort from the entire village. Custom also required punishing the responsible party. The inevitable witch hunt wouldn't exclude guests.

He couldn't let another woman die because of him. The idea of his own death did not bother him; he had settled where he would spend eternity when he was but a boy of twelve. But what about Mary and Clara? The Mission Board had assigned them, but the assignment being given was no absolute guarantee. Do-gooders with no real salvation experience had slipped through the process and come to the mission field before.

Where did the women stand with the Lord? Hot shame lodged in his chest. He'd been so set on getting rid of them, he hadn't bothered to find out. Now he might not have the chance. Bad enough a man had died here last night without accepting the Gospel.

He rolled his bedding and attached it to his pack, then left the chief's compound and headed back to the women's hut. Rounding the corner he came face-to-face with both women, dressed and with their packs on their backs.

"We're ready." Mary's voice carried a faint tremor. He'd obviously scared the wits out of her. He'd apologize later. Provided they all lived.

Clara's face was pinched and drawn, her eyes reflecting her own wrestling match with fear. One she appeared close to losing.

"Dr. O'Hara. Clara. Keep your heads down and follow behind me as if it was a normal leave-taking. Don't make eye contact and don't stop for any reason."

Clara nodded and they both followed. Behind him Mary asked, "Pastor Mayweather, what is going on? Why does this warrior's death put us in danger?"

Maybe some explanation would help her to understand, but he was loath to slow them down. Mourning would turn to anger quickly and he wanted to be well down the trail before that happened. He condensed his answer. "Nothing is considered an accident here. They'll want someone to blame. We would be a good target right now."

Clara startled. "Someone murdered him?" She swayed on her feet and Mary took her arm.

"Not necessarily. But I have my suspicions. The timing is too coincidental. Here unexplained death is considered a result of witchcraft. And the witch must be found and punished."

Mary's keen sense of reason reflected in her answer. "And one of us could be the witch. We're outsiders."

"Exactly. So we must leave now."

"Will they follow us?" Surprisingly Mary's voice no longer held a tremor. His respect for her rose. No wonder she'd managed in France.

"They might. Swift travel is the order of the day. No stops unless we must."

Clara took in a deep breath and seemed to strengthen at Mary's calm. "We'll keep up. I'd rather this not be my final resting place."

"Good. Follow me. No obvious haste till we are outside the village." William turned to leave and just as quickly turned back. "And pray. We need His protection and deliverance here. Otherwise we are lost."

He turned again and set off. He trusted they would follow his instructions and didn't glance back. The village had begun stirring earlier than normal because of the wailing and grief. Most would already be at the hut of the dead man consoling the family.

Bouts of wailing punctuated the glory of the sunrise as they followed the footpath out of the village, scattering chickens in the wake of their progress. A few startled faces, sleep still creasing their cheeks, looked up from their doorways as they passed, but no one raised an alarm at their leaving. Now if only the same was true for the rest of the caravan.

By the time they left the village perimeter, his shoulders ached from the tension he couldn't let go of despite his nonstop prayers. His eyes searched for the first sight of Hannabo and the porters, wanting reassurance that they had made it out. They were a mile down the trail before he found them waiting. William blew out a breath he had not realized he had been holding. *Thank you, Lord.*

Maybe they would make it. But they weren't in the clear yet. Nana Bolo would soon realize they were gone. The question was if he would come after them or not.

Mary's legs burned in rebellion at the prolonged march. The sun had long passed the midday mark. She wasn't sure she could take one more step. Rest stops had come only twice and then for too short of a time for her muscles to recover.

Instead of stopping when Clara stumbled and twisted her ankle, William ordered the bearers to put her in the hammock chair and carry her as a precaution. Mary knew better than to complain or call a halt when it was their very lives in danger.

She reached for her canteen and realized it was less than half full. Well, she would hydrate while she could. Better to be well saturated now; later may not matter. Still, she wondered about a water supply. If they made it to safety, wherever that was, would there be a ready source she could purify?

Mary swallowed several mouthfuls of tepid water and continued on. She wished she could stop and tend to Clara's ankle, see if it was swelling. She'd given her a wrap from her bag and instructed her to wrap and elevate it. It didn't look bad at the outset, but she'd feel better if she could see for herself.

She wiped away sweat running freely down her face and mentally chided herself for worrying. She focused on water and Clara's ankle only to keep her mind off the obvious.

Would they all be dead by nightfall?

Glancing back, she caught no sight of William. He and Hannabo were in the rear of the single-file caravan. They would be the first line of defense if the tribe came after them. She shuddered at the thought of William Mayweather dying to protect her. Was she going to be responsible for another man's death?

True, she couldn't have predicted her little brother would enlist, trying to follow in her footsteps when she signed on with the Red Cross. But he followed her lead, if for no other reason than to escape their father's expectations for him. Michael O'Hara was a strict but loving father who'd always encouraged her dreams. It was Jeremy her father wanted to study law and take over his own practice one day. Jeremy, who would rather have been behind a plow, riding a horse or baling hay before he'd ever want to set foot in a courtroom. He'd been her shadow since he'd learned to walk.

Murmurs reached her ears and interrupted her memories. As the sound rippled forward she realized they were calling a halt. The line moved on until a clearing appeared ahead. The porters shed their packs in record speed and collapsed beside them. Mary waited till Clara's bearers caught up and helped her alight.

Clara stepped out gingerly and placed weight on her injured ankle. Her narrowed eyes spoke initial discomfort and then opened wider in relief.

After she took those few tentative steps, Clara recognized the slight limp in Mary's walk before Mary concealed her own discomfort. "You're hurting. Is the blister worsening?"

"The blister hardly compares to trying to keep the pace. You seem to be walking all right. How's the ankle?"

"There's no swelling, just a little soreness. I can walk on my own now. You should take the hammock chair."

"No. The men need a rest. I can't ask them to keep carrying my weight when I can manage on my own. I'm just going to rebandage my blister now before we get started again."

"I wonder how long we'll stop for. My stomach feels the lack of breakfast. Not that I won't wait versus ending up a meal for our friends back there."

"I'm with you. Although I didn't get the impression they were one of the cannibal tribes. I don't know how long we are stopping, but here come Pastor Mayweather and Hannabo. Let's ask."

Mary started in their direction, but Clara took her arm and stopped her. "I'll find out. You go sit and take care of your foot."

Mary complied. If the stop was short, she'd need every

minute to get ready to walk again. Clara returned before she'd gotten the fresh plaster on. "Oooh. That's looking awful red."

"Hand me the kit, would you. I'm going to put a little of the Vitogen antiseptic powder on before I cover it again."

Clara rummaged in the bag and brought out the blue vial. "Here you go. We've got about ten minutes before we move on. Pastor sent some of the men to gather fruit, so we should have something to eat as we march."

Mary capped the vial and returned it to Clara. "Fruit sounds heavenly. My navel is too well acquainted with my backbone as it is."

Clara laughed. "Mine, too! And you know how I love to eat." She patted her sturdy stomach for emphasis. "Funny how we still think of the ordinary when we could be some-one's main course."

"I guess it's like humor back in the operating wards. Seems out of place, but keeps us from going completely mad."

Clara nodded. "Do you want me to hand your pack over to one of the carriers? We left in such a hurry."

"No, I think I'd rather keep the medical pack on me. I'd hate to be separated from it if anything happened."

"Good point." Clara's head bobbed her agreement. "I guess you never know what might happen out here."

"I wonder what our chances are of being attacked."

"Pastor Mayweather and Hannabo were talking about making the river. If we make the river, we're likely to be safe."

Jabo headed in their direction, bananas in hand. An-other porter held a basket and went around the camp passing out the fruit. No sooner did Jabo hand them the much-welcomed fruit but the call to leave went up.

Clara shook her head when the hammock chair carriers came to her. Mary did the same. Hammock travel was slow and she didn't want to cost them precious time.

The rest of the day's trek passed in extremes, boredom overlaid with exhaustion and fear, as adrenaline waned and surged in waves.

Everyone was jumpy. A swift green lizard scurried across her path and Mary almost jumped out of her skin. All eyes turned at jungle sounds the whole party had ignored till now.

What was that new sound? Water? Definitely moving water. Not a falls, but movement. They must be running parallel to a river or stream. Maybe the river Clara had heard about. Could they be near safety?

In answer, the jungle pulled back and gave a clear view of a wide, lazy-looking river.

Clara came up behind her. "This must be the river they were talking about. Now what?"

"I don't know. I don't see any boats or a ferry. I assume we're supposed to cross, but how?"

"Using a rope line," William said, walking up behind them. "Think of it as the only opportunity to wash off some of the trail grime before we get to Nynabo."

Attempting levity, a sweat-soaked William, his shirt clinging and rivulets of sweat running down his neck into his collar, grinned. She glanced down and realized she didn't look much better. Clara was her mirrored image. The pace hadn't been kind. But wait… "Do you mean we are actually going wading in the river?"

"Yes, this one isn't crocodile infested, so it's reasonably safe. We'll string a rope across for you to hold in case you lose your footing in the current."

Clara turned the color of thin parchment. "Crocodiles? Are you sure there aren't any?" Clara asked.

"I've crossed this river before. There are no crocodiles,"

he assured her. "Mostly the problem is the current. I know it doesn't look treacherous, since it's the dry season. But even at its lowest point, it does have a temper."

Mary studied the lazy river. "It looks pretty tame to me."

"Don't let that deceive you. The last time I crossed this river, one of my men died."

Chapter Seven

William saw shock on both women's faces. "Don't worry. That was the rainy season. I will do everything I can to secure your safety. Just don't underestimate the potential for danger."

"Do we have to cross if it's so dangerous?"

"If we camp here or follow the river to a better spot, we risk Nana Bolo's men catching up with us."

"Can't they just cross over too?" Clara looked puzzled.

"Yes, but with us on the other side, it becomes more dangerous for them. We watch and pick them off with our rifles while they are fighting the current mid-stream." William glanced at Mary. Her face was a study in seriousness. She was staring at the river as if it was to be her grave.

He tried for reassurance. "If they start losing warriors, the price of the sasswood trial becomes too high."

Mary seemed to focus back in on his words. "A sasswood trial?"

Another thing she didn't know. If only she had known how ill-suited she was for this place. "A sasswood trial is the African form of a witch hunt. The witch must be found and punished for the safety of the tribe. That's where the sasswood comes in."

Mary's head tilted in thought. "So is sasswood a poison?"

"Exactly. You drink the poison and, if you live, you are innocent. If you die, the witch has been punished."

"It sounds like a lot of the punishments in early America. A so-called witch had no real chance," Clara intoned.

"Well, what exactly is this poison? What does it come from?" Mary's medical curiosity seemed to bring her attention back from her fear of the river.

"And is there an antidote?" Clara asked.

"The poison comes from the tree bark of the sasswood tree. And no, there is no antidote I have ever heard of being used."

William looked past the women to make sure Hannabo had all the preparations underway. He saw the rope was already secured to a sturdy, nearby tree and Jabo stepped up to have it tied around him.

"If this is common, then I'll need to know more about this poison. Maybe I can come up with a treatment. What I don't understand is why Nana Bolo would want to blame us." Mary wiped her brow with a kerchief from her pocket. "I thought the tribesmen liked to create trade relationships with the missionaries. That trade, schools and medical care drew them in to hear about God."

William debated deflecting her comments. No, it was too important for her to understand how things worked in the jungle to shield her from the truth. "Trade is important and we have something he wants. You. He wanted you from the minute he saw you and, since I refused to sell you to him, he wants me out of the way."

"So he would blame you? Kill you?" Her eyes grew huge and she looked about to faint. He and Clara both reached for an arm and led her to a log to sit down. William looked to Clara and asked, "Does she have smelling salts in her pack?"

Clara nodded. "I'll go get them just in case."

Why did this revelation throw her? She'd been such an oasis of calm and strength to this point. Just when he thought she possessed the strength to make it out here, she brought him back to the reality. A woman's frailty.

Mary looked up from the log where she was sitting. "He would kill you over me." It was a flat statement. A trail of tears slid down Mary's cheeks.

William sat beside her and took one of her hands in his. He wanted to impress upon her the seriousness, not devastate her. Now he only wanted to take away the pain he saw in her eyes. "In all fairness, I probably could not have kept your presence known from him for long. He is notorious for adding to or replacing his wives as the notion strikes him. You met two of them at the village. They served your dinner."

Mary's tremulous voice gave way to indignation. "You mean that young, pregnant girl we saw was his wife? She is a child."

"Out here once a woman is able to bear children, she is marriageable."

"That's horrible. But you said wives. He has more than one?"

"Yes, the older woman you met is his chief wife. At least for now. If the girl gives him a son, her status will rise." William glanced up, looking for Clara's return.

"Oh. It was jealousy."

"What was jealousy?"

"The older wife. I kept thinking she hated me, but it didn't make sense. She must have thought her husband was going to trade for me and she would lose her status."

Mary used the back of her hand to wipe away the vestiges of her tears. "Poor woman. To always wonder if you could be replaced."

William formed his reply, but a shout stopped him. "Nana Pastor, come quick."

William hurried to the river's edge and joined Hannabo. He could see Jabo's head bobbing in the current. He was about three-fourths of the way across and a few yards downstream. He asked Hannabo, "What happened?"

"He is stuck on something. The line snagged."

"Have you tried pulling the line back in from this end?"

"Yes, Nana Pastor. But he does not move. I am afraid to pull any harder lest we break the line and he be swept down the river."

Mary and Clara caught up to him. Mary asked, "What is he trying to do out there?"

Hannabo answered her. "He was to tie the rope on the other side so we can cross over holding it."

Mary asked, "What do we do now?"

"There is only one thing to do now." William turned to Hannabo. "Start a new line, have the men secure it. I'm going out to get him."

Mary felt helpless. All this was her fault. If they hadn't had to escape in the first place, they could have found a safer crossing spot. Now William and Jabo both faced danger.

She no longer needed the stimulation of the smelling salts Clara brought. They both stepped closer and watched in morbid fascination as Hannabo secured the rope around William's waist and he stepped into the water. He controlled a shiver as the water quickly reached his waist, but goose bumps rose on his arms. Surprising. Despite the overall heat, the water temperature must be cold.

Halfway across and water reached William's mid-back. He moved slowly, as if at war with the invisible hand of water insistently pushing him downstream. Hannabo and two other men held the rope like a tether and let it out slowly when William's raised hand signaled. For every foot across, it seemed he went downstream two. Would he overshoot Jabo's position and have to start again?

"We should pray."

Clara's suggestion embarrassed Mary. Heading to a mission field and prayer came in dead last in her thoughts. "The last time I asked God to save someone, it didn't work out so well."

"God's Word doesn't say things will always work out the way you want them to. It says they will all work to the good."

It was too much. She tore her eyes away from William's progress. "Whose good? Jeremy's? Mine? Pastor Mayweather's?"

Clara's voice gentled even more. "Maybe if you stopped blaming yourself and God so much, He would be able to show you."

Cheers rose from the men on the bank. William had reached Jabo and together they were both moving toward the other side. When they climbed up the other bank, both men secured their lines to adjacent trees and signaled Hannabo.

Hannabo turned from the small celebration and walked over to Mary and Clara. "Please Mammies, put everything in your packs for carrying by the men. They will keep it dry on top of their heads. Then come. I will tie the new rope to you so you can cross."

The knots in Mary's stomach multiplied. The cold sweat breaking out heralded the fear coursing through her body. Clara didn't look much better, but her lips were pressed together in grim determination. It was amazing what you were willing to do to survive.

She and Clara laid their packs at the bank and waited while Hannabo untied the same rope William had used from its tether on this side. The thick coarse hemp tightened around Mary's waist and she barely found the breath to gasp. "I still need to breath, Hannabo."

"Sorry, Mammy Doctor. But it is worse if the rope loosens and you…." He broke off, unwilling to state the obvious danger of drowning. Suddenly the rope felt just right.

"What do I do? While I'm crossing."

"Step in slowly. Hold the other rope to stay steady. Slow steps till you get to the other side." Hannabo grinned as if it was an easy, everyday thing. "You are not a tall Mammy, so in some places the water will be here." Hannabo indicated a place about six inches over her head. "When your feet do not find bottom, pull on the ropes with your hands to move forward until your feet touch bottom again."

Mary glanced back at Clara. "What about my friend? Once I cross, there is no rope to tie her."

"Mammy Clara will come after you. The rope will be untied and pulled back."

Clara chewed her lower lip. "So we all go one at a time?"

"No. No. Just the mammies use the rope. We men will hold the guide rope only. No problem for men."

For once being thought the weaker sex paid off. She wanted every bit of security the rope offered. She hugged Clara and infused her voice with confidence she didn't feel for her friend's sake. "It will be all right. Watch me and see how easy it is."

Two porters stepped into the water in front of her, one hand holding the rope, the other securing the packs on their heads. Her turn. She grabbed the rope, and with

Hannabo steadying her from behind, she stepped into the water.

Even though expected, the cold took what little breath the rope around her waist had left her. Still below her knees, water surged through the lace holes and into her boots. She took a couple more tentative steps. The river bed was uneven. She tried to get the feel of it before she put all her weight down. She should have gone barefoot like the natives. Her boots would take forever to dry. She didn't want to think about how hard they would be to swim in if she lost hold of the ropes.

The rough hemp lines bit into her tender skin as her hands grasped and pulled to maintain her balance. Harder than it looked, but doable.

Further in, the current flow gave a vicious push. This living, throbbing pulse of water demanded she go with it. She resisted and held tight.

The porters neared the other bank. She tried to pick up the pace so the rest could move forward. Any delay left the men on the riverbank behind her vulnerable to Nana Bolo and his men.

Halfway across, the water reached just below her shoulders. With each new level of skin contact her shivering intensified. Note to self—never complain about the jungle heat.

Her foot reached out for the next step, but found no purchase on the riverbed floor. Too deep.

Gripping the rope harder, she began to pull herself forward, grateful for the hand and arm strength she'd built as a surgeon. Her boots acted a little like an anchor and her feet half floated, half dragged behind her. The current kept pushing her sideways while her boots pulled her down.

The arm strain was starting to get to her. Her chin trembled with the effort and the numbing cold. Could you get hypothermia in the jungle? The other side beckoned its warmth. She looked up to see how close she was. The two porters in front of her had already exited the water and were out of sight.

William stood at the edge of the bank, shifting his weight from foot to foot impatiently. Didn't the man know she was going as fast as she could? Or was he worried? She reached forward for the next hold. A lot of his problems would be swept down the river with her if she didn't make it.

Mary's left boot scraped bottom and relief flooded through her. Finally, she could touch bottom again. She put all her weight down, then waited for her foothold to steady before she relaxed her cramping hands.

Big mistake. Strong fingers of current wrapped around her legs and shoved. Her feet swept out from under her and her mouth filled with river water.

Don't breathe. She held her breath as best she could and clawed for the guide rope. Her fingers grazed it, but it only taunted her with its closeness and waved goodbye. She fought against the weight of her boots and surfaced. A half gasp was the best she could do before she went back under.

The rope around her waist gave a strong jerk. They were trying to pull her to shore. Would she drown before they succeeded? Panic coursed through her veins. She couldn't find the surface. She wasn't going to make it. She would drown before they could get to her and no one but Clara behind her knew what to do to revive her.

Another strong jerk of the rope heaved her backward. The river rushed by her as she folded in half from the tether's pull and came right into a strong grasp that lifted her into blessed air.

Heaving air into her demanding lungs, she saw the grim

face of William in between the locks of hair plastered to her face. He had saved her! His grip around her waist held her tight to him and hauled her back toward the shore. Teeth chattering from the cold and the fear, she tried to stand up in the lesser depths.

"I have you. Relax and let me get you to shore."

For the first time in a long time, she gave in to offered comfort. She leaned into his grip. It had been so long since she'd allowed anyone to comfort her, but right now she needed his quiet strength. He held her tightly against a hard-muscled chest that belied all her notions of a minister who only lifted a Bible. Warmth radiated from him and seeped into her. Her jaw stopped its staccato motions. An unfamiliar feeling teased her. Safe. She felt safe, protected.

At the bank's edge, Jabo and another bearer reached down and grabbed her under her arms, hauling her away from the comfort of William's grasp. Another grabbed William's hand and pulled him out of the muddy flow. Water ran off them in sheets.

With solid footing under her squishy boots, Mary looked to see if Clara fared any better. A white-faced Clara stood within a few feet of the shore, flanked by two men. Apparently they had learned from Mary's little fiasco.

The other caravan members moved in single file behind the trio. Only one man still remained on the other bank. Pursuit, if it indeed existed, was nowhere in sight. Had the fear been for naught?

After an arduous crossing, Clara came dripping up the riverbank looking acutely uncomfortable. Mary stepped toward her only to have a hand on her elbow hold her fast. William stood right beside her with a blanket in his other hand.

"Clara is fine. Jabo is getting her a dry blanket. You, on

the other hand, need to sit down and rest." Without waiting for a response, William draped the blanket from her shoulders and lifted her straight off her feet, carrying her away from the shore.

Really, the presumption of the man. It was one thing to haul her to safety, but quite another to manhandle her at will. "What do…"

"Sssh. I will put you down in a minute. You looked about to collapse."

True, but she couldn't afford to have him see her as weak. Not if she wanted to work here. "I was not. Please put me down."

And he did. She was instantly sorry and quickly ashamed that she wished herself back in his arms. Arms now folded across his chest in companionship to the scowl on his face. She wondered if he read minds when he asked, "It's no shame to admit your weakness. It's not necessary to be strong all the time. Most women collapse after similar experiences."

Ah, there it was. The weaker sex. He obviously had no experience with women who weren't trained from birth to rely on a manly pillar of strength. "I'm not most women."

"So you seem determined to prove. The men are starting a fire and setting up camp. I'll make your tent and camp bed available tonight. In the meantime, may I suggest that even strong women need to sit and rest after an ordeal?"

He turned and barked an order. One of the men scurried to comply. Pointing to a log near the fire, William suggested, "Stay wrapped up in the blanket and get warm. Your dry clothes will be available soon."

Mary simply nodded, overwhelmed with exhaustion and shock. William started to walk off and unexpected panic overruled her need to appear in control. "Wait, I.... Don't go. Not yet."

William looked startled. Then his eyes softened and he sat down beside her. "You'll feel better after a little rest."

Out of the corner of her eye, she saw Clara approach from the bank wet but blanketed. Clara looked over but oddly did not join them. She was too tired to even call out to her friend.

The fire's warmth seeped in and added to the exhaustion. Her head began to nod. After the second jerk of her head to her chin, William pulled her near and supported her in the crook of his arm. It felt too right to protest. When had she relaxed her policy and allowed a tradition-bound man to get close to her? The answer teased her consciousness, the one fighting sleep. When you started falling for him, that's when. No, oh, no, this man didn't even like her. He might have saved her life and offered her comfort, but he was a pastor. He would have done the same for anyone. She shouldn't make the mistake of reading too much into a man just doing his job.

Chapter Eight

William stood at the riverbank peering across to the other shore. The dry clothes he had changed into were a welcome relief against his skin. The full moon lent enough light for him to be sure no contingent from Nana Bolo stood on the other bank. Maybe he had jumped to conclusions.

Hannabo appeared by his side, surprising him with his stealth. William always felt loud and clumsy in the jungle compared to Hannabo, a man who bridged both worlds with his missionary education and his native origins.

"Nana Pastor, I posted guards. They will keep watch at the river. The mammies are sleeping in their tents. You rest."

"Do you think they will come still?"

"I cannot say, Nana Pastor. Nana Bolo wanted this woman, but he is smart enough to realize the trouble he would be in with the government if he took a white woman captive. Even the government soldiers would be forced to brave the jungles then."

"You're probably right. Not much else would get them here though."

Hannabo laughed. A harsh break in the midst of the

night noises. "This is truth. They leave the missionaries to civilize us, hoping all the tribes will lay down their spears. When it is safe, they will come and make their roads."

"Let us hope Nana Bolo considered this."

"Nana Bolo has outlived three devilmen and many wives. He will not put his foot in the trap so easily."

"Still, some poor soul will pay for that death."

"Nana Bolo will use this to rid himself of an enemy. It is how he has survived long. If he doesn't come after you to drink the sasswood so he can have Mammy Doctor." Hannabo shrugged as if to say this was just the way of it.

"All right. I am going to my tent, but wake me and I will take a turn on guard."

Hannabo nodded and William headed for his tent.

Sleep did not come. The camp bed should have invited his dreams after the last nights without it. He tried to blame his upcoming watch at the shore in two short hours.

Instead, thoughts of Mary going under the water and the panic that gripped him over losing her rolled through his head. The relief when he reached her and she took a breath of air. And the feelings she stirred when she was in his arms and later when he drew her to his side at the campfire and she fell asleep, those feelings challenged his memories of Alice. Memories he'd set aside as too painful.

God help him. He needed to remember his calling. He'd vowed to take up the Gospel in his uncle's place at Nynabo. He'd vowed to never endanger another woman to fulfill that commitment. That same vow now mocked the feelings Mary O'Hara stirred from deep within him.

How could he fulfill his calling to the Kru people and keep a wife safe at the same time? He felt like Jacob wrestling with God till he had an answer. Not possible. Yet here he stood.

Father, why have you put this woman in my care? To fix her misguided plan to serve in this dangerous place? What do I need to help her see?

The answers proved more elusive than sleep. And sleep didn't last as once again the night was shattered with screams.

Mary's dreams were plagued by muddy water and elusive ropes. Exhaustion's depths sucked her into sleep as effectively as the currents moved her down the river. Shaking. Shaking. Not from cold. Someone was calling her name and shaking her.

She swam to the surface of consciousness and found Clara standing over her. She blinked to be sure she wasn't in her dreams.

No, Clara still stood there, oil lamp in hand, concern plastered all over her face.

She sat straight up. Nana Bolo. Had he caught up with them? Her pulse started to pound and her mouth went dry as she tried to get the words out to ask. "What?" That was all she could croak out.

"Come quickly, Dr. Mary. She's dying." Clara's voice urgently conveyed the appeal, but it didn't make sense.

Mary swung her legs over the edge of the cot. She was dressed in dry clothes. She had a vague memory of changing with Clara's help before she fell back to sleep in the cot. She had a stronger memory of falling asleep in William's arms.

Clara grabbed her arm and started to drag her from the bed. "Please, you've got to come now. She's dying."

The last vestiges of sleep fled at her friend's distress. "Who? Who is dying?"

"Grab your bag. I'll explain. She's out here."

Mary looked for the black leather doctor's bag, a gift

from her father upon graduation. It sat next to her small pack between her cot and Clara's. She ignored the pang of grief at remembering his proud presentation of the bag, grabbed it and followed the hastening Clara outside the tent.

Several of the men huddled around a form lying on a blanket near the fire. Undoubtedly the "her" Clara kept referring to a minute ago. William stood looking grim and Hannabo was near her head.

Hannabo was wet. Had he been swimming?

The men parted at Clara's insistence. Mary knelt on the blanket and started assessing her patient. The woman from the village. The older of Nana Bolo's wives. Her wet blue skirt peeked out in confirmation from under a blanket that covered her from the neck down. Hannabo knelt at her head.

"Someone tell me what's happened here." Mary asked.

"Sasswood." Hannabo said nothing further, just stood dripping, slightly out of breath.

Mary reached under the blanket and took the woman's arm. She looked around. "Her pulse is high. Someone tell me more about sasswood. I can't treat her if I don't know."

William knelt down beside her, placing his arm on her shoulder. "No known treatment exists. Sasswood is too powerful a poison."

Anger flared. "Maybe you're willing to just give up, but I can't stand by and do nothing while a woman dies."

Mary lifted the woman's eyelids and met with slight resistance. Not in a coma, but not quite conscious. Her pupils still reacted to the change in light from the fire. She reached in her bag and pulled out her stethoscope, confirming the rapid pulse she'd felt. The heart was working too hard, so it could be an alkaloid-based poison. Purging might help.

A subdued Hannabo interjected, "Sometimes they live. The only protection is the fetish bag worn to keep the poison from being harmful." His head dropped in sorrow. "Hers is gone. They must have removed her protection before they made her drink."

"Hannabo!" William rebuked. "You know those things have no power."

Mary threw up her hands. "Your theology can wait. She can't. How long since she drank the sasswood?"

"Hannabo saw her on the bank not quite an hour ago. We watched, helpless, while the devilmen caught up to her and forced the sasswood down her. Once she passed out they left."

Mary nodded. "And Hannabo went to get her, right? He's wet."

William seemed to apologize. "We couldn't leave her there. There's always a small chance she may survive." Hannabo nodded his assent.

She rummaged through her bag for an emetic. "How long since they forced her to drink? I can try and purge the poison." Where was it? There. Ipecac. "Clara, get the charcoal from my other pack. And I'll need a bowl and water to mix the charcoal."

William knelt beside her and placed a hand on her shoulder. "It's futile, Doctor. The kindest thing is to make her comfortable. Not put her through more agony."

Hannabo's eyes lit up. "You can save her?"

William shook his head. "There is no cure for sasswood poisoning."

"Well, I can't just do nothing. Clara, you mix the charcoal while I get the emetic down her."

Clara hesitated. "The poison has been in her for a while now. Do you think it will do any good?"

"We lose nothing by trying. She loses her life if we don't."

Clara and Hannabo left to get the necessary items. William sent the rest of the men back to their posts.

Once they were alone with her, William asked, "What do you possibly hope to accomplish by giving them false hope? You will destroy their trust when you lose this woman to the poison."

The nerve of the man. "What do you possibly think to accomplish by giving them no hope? If the situation is so futile, why aren't you praying? If there's nothing my medicine can do, then where's your miracle? Aren't they your business? Miracles?"

In answer to her railing, he stood and stepped back, looking as if she'd slapped him. The only thing missing was an actual hand mark. The man of God finally seemed stunned speechless.

He should. Death was something to be fought, not accepted. A flash of something else in his eyes. Bleakness? Despair? The unidentified emotion flitted through the depths of his deep-brown irises. His head dropped and his shoulders slumped.

"You're absolutely right. I have forgotten myself at this woman's expense." Eyes closed, he prayed over her. Which, in her estimation, still did no good unless she got the medicine in the victim.

Mary opened the ipecac. "Someone help me lift her."

Hannabo returned with a bowl and placed it at her side. He sat on the ground and held the woman's head up in his lap, cradling her like a baby. William asked, "What else can I do?"

"Pray for me this time, for this to work."

Mary instructed Hannabo. "Turn her more to her side

as soon as I get the medicine in her so she won't choke on her own vomit."

A breathless Clara brought the charcoal, setting it to the side for later.

Mary hoped the woman wouldn't choke. That she wasn't too far gone to swallow. She stopped for a moment and thought. Looking at Hannabo, she asked, "Does anyone know her name?"

Hannabo answered, "Anaya. She came from my village before her marriage."

"Then talk to her. Call her by name and tell her this is a good medicine. She has to swallow so it can help."

Hannabo nodded and spoke to Anaya. There was a flutter of her eyelids, but no acknowledgement.

Mary poured the brown, viscous liquid into Anaya's mouth and closed her jaw. Anaya began to turn her head side to side and moaned.

"Hold her mouth shut. She needs to swallow." William and Clara complied. Hannabo continued speaking in soothing tones until finally Mary saw the bob in her throat indicating she'd swallowed.

"Hannabo, turn her to her side now. She's going to throw up whatever is left in her stomach in the next few minutes."

Clara moved out of the way. She knew what to expect. Mary watched Anaya for any signs of the imminent vomiting.

Prodigious heaving ensued from Anaya's slight frame. Eventually they were down to dry heaves.

Hannabo looked at Mary. "Will this fix her?"

"Keep talking to her. The will to live is important." Mary dodged the real answer, one full of doubt, and turned to Clara. "Is the charcoal ready? I think the vomiting is passed."

A subdued William stepped in, "Is there anything else I can do?"

Mary looked him in the eye, a much humbler eye at that. "Keep praying."

After the administered charcoal stayed down, hopefully binding up the dangerous leftover poison, Mary stumbled back to her tent to catch a little more sleep when Hannabo promised to keep watch.

She'd done all she knew to do. Now if Anaya's kidneys wouldn't shut down, her liver wouldn't fail, her... Mary stopped the recital of potential problems in her head. She was doing the same thing she'd accused William of earlier.

She was a hypocrite. Accusing a man of God of doubting and not doing his job while fear and doubt had brought her here in the first place. Fear that defeating death was beyond her reach. Doubt that hindered her ability to fully function as a doctor. If this woman had required surgery, would she have been able to act? She hadn't held a scalpel since her brother's death.

Oh, the irony of coming to a place where life, both eternal and temporal, hinged on shoving all doubt aside. Would Anaya live after her treatment? Her brother hadn't. Where was God in that? Or her training, for that matter?

All of her training rendered useless at the damage German ordnance had done. How could she ever operate after watching Jeremy's life slip away in her hands? His death was her fault. *Where were you then, God? Will it be the same with this woman?* Above the crickets and the cries of the jungle night she couldn't identify came an insistent voice.

Pray.

The compulsion was so strong, she shifted off her bed onto her knees and began to pray. Maybe her imagination had conjured it, but she wasn't about to disobey that voice.

It had been a long time since she felt God had answered one of her prayers, but maybe he'd do this for Hannabo, who seemed greatly upset and somewhat possessive of Anaya. What that was about she'd have to learn another day. Now she only wanted to sleep. When she awoke, she would see if Anaya still lived. If her prayers still received answers.

Chapter Nine

Another night of wrestling with his thoughts of Mary left William woolly-headed halfway through the morning's trek. She had been the last thing he wanted on this mission. Now he found himself looking for her first thing every morning. The sight of her stirred him with feelings he couldn't afford to have for any woman. He tried to focus on something besides the fact she was only twenty feet behind him staying near the hammock that carried the weak, but living, Anaya.

Soon they would make Nynabo. Alice waited for him there, buried under one of the large cottonwoods that shaded their former home. A sense of disloyalty to his delicate wife and her memory filled him and set off a sharp pain in his chest.

He'd wrestled this grief and regret so often the pain had become a familiar companion. Somehow he had to come to terms with the fact that he'd brought a new bride to a country with so many inherent dangers. She was with God now. He had made a solemn vow at the spot where he had buried her that he would never again endanger another woman to fulfill his calling.

Oh, he had made plans to have this unconventional

woman sent back as soon as possible. This whole journey with Dr. Mary O'Hara was only to keep her from harm since she'd insisted on going. If only he could have kept her at Newaka or returned her back to the Garraway mission on the coast before she had gotten any further in the jungle.

But no, he thought as he wiped the back of his neck with a handkerchief where the sweat ran freely. There was no stopping the good doctor once she made up her mind.

Until the night before last that had meant one disaster after another. But now a woman was alive despite a deadly ordeal and his faith had fallen short in the process.

He was the experienced missionary, but it was Mary who reminded him to pray for Anaya. A strong sense of shame burned its way through his gut. He should not have had to be reminded to pray. Mary was a distraction to his faith even as the threats of the jungle should have been sharpening it. The sooner she left this dangerous interior, the better. For her and for him.

"Nana Pastor." Hannabo's voice brought William out of the endless jungle of his thoughts. "We will be in the open soon. We should stop then and let the mammies rest, eat."

William was loath to halt the journey when the goal of reaching Nynabo coaxed him forward, but Hannabo was right. "Strike a cold camp once we are clear of the jungle. Distribute the smoked cassava from last night and any fruit on hand. We stop for one hour."

"Yes, Nana Pastor. It shall be done."

The thinning vegetation soon gave way to a familiar rolling plain.

"Pastor Mayweather, what are all those small hills? They resemble a valley of stalagmites without a cave."

Clara had made her way to his side while their temporary camp was taking shape.

William pointed in the distance to one of many such structures. "Those are the homes of the white ants. Their hills are strong enough to support a man's weight if he climbs on them."

"White ants? The ones Hannah mentioned might have damaged your mission? Bugabugs, right?"

"Yes, you would know them better as termites. And out here they can easily devour a home or turn their attention to the contents of one of your trunks and eat every piece of apparel inside rather quickly."

"Oh dear. I had no idea."

"If you think they're something, how do you feel about elephants?"

"Truly, real elephants?"

"I don't want to get your hopes up, but this stretch of plain is sometimes a pathway the herds travel."

William glanced past Clara's astonished face and watched as a weary looking Mary emerged from the forest. Anaya's hammock followed next and Mary helped her alight on wobbly legs.

"Pastor? Isn't it time you put aside your animosity?" Clara suggested. "She's not the enemy, you know."

William glanced back at her and felt the heat of embarrassment flush his face. He'd been caught staring.

"No, she's not the enemy, but her actions put Anaya in jeopardy in the first place."

"Nonsense. It was Dr. Mary who saved Anaya when the rest of you would have given up."

William refocused on Clara and his irritation overcame his discretion. "Did you ever stop and ask yourself why Nana Bolo would have one of his own wives accused of witchcraft?"

Clara's brow knit together in puzzlement. "No. I don't claim to understand heathenish ways."

"It was to clear the way for Mary to be his bride. Nana Bolo had tired of Anaya, but he might not have taken any action with one new young wife to keep him happy." William pressed on, determined now to get the whole truth out. Maybe if the women understood, they would be more accepting when the time came for them to leave. "But he saw Mary, a complete novelty to him. Not wishing to support a third wife with her own hut, he decided to clear the way instead."

Clara's head shook disbelief. "But I thought you said you were the one he would try and kill to get to Dr. Mary."

"When he realized we'd left, he sought to remove Anaya first. Had we not gotten across the river when we did, I would have been next and both of you slated for slave-brides in his village."

A gasping sound caught his attention. Mary had approached while he was talking to Clara. Too late to soften his stance now. They had to get the seriousness of the danger in the bush. "Without Dr. O'Hara on this journey, none of this would have happened in the first place."

Mary felt the piercing blow of his words as he made a weapon out of her own secret fears. She'd caused this. She might as well have poured the poison down Anaya's throat herself. She'd almost been responsible for another person's death. Again. Not able to take his glaring accusation any longer, Mary turned on her heel and retreated to Anaya's side.

Hannabo patiently offered Anaya some of last night's meal and tried to tempt Mary with a plantain. Mary desperately needed a distraction from her thoughts, so she sat and took the food Hannabo offered her. She chewed out of sheer habit. Right now anything would taste like sawdust, and cassava, smoked and tasting like a cross between a potato and a pumpkin, wasn't as tasty when you ate it several nights in a row. At least it wasn't more rice.

Mary peeled the plantain and listened to the rhythm of the dialect Hannabo and Anaya shared. She didn't understand him, but the gentle tone was apparent. His upset and tenderness toward her hadn't made sense until he'd revealed they'd both grown up in Nynabo together.

But they weren't just long-lost friends. Hannabo appeared smitten. She thought about asking, but didn't when she saw Clara approaching. Mary rose and brushed off her trousers, trying to act like the conversation she'd just heard between William and Clara hadn't affected her.

Too bad Clara saw right through her. "Don't be blaming yourself for any of this, Dr. Mary." The heat of anger in Clara's voice surprised her. "I don't care what Pastor Mayweather says, none of this is your fault. How could you be expected to know some tribe chief would try to murder someone just because he wanted you?" Clara's hands went to her hips and she leaned in closer to Mary to emphasize her point. "I say he would have done the same thing soon enough anyway. Pastor Mayweather is looking for a scapegoat."

Mary took one of Clara's cocked arms by the elbow and pulled her away from Anaya and Hannabo. After a few steps she stopped and said, "I'm afraid he's right, Clara. I can't seem to stop endangering others. Anaya or even Pastor Mayweather might have died because of me."

"Nonsense. Just like I told him. If it hadn't been the sight of you, it would have been something else soon enough. And then she would be dead." Clara harrumphed. "If you hadn't come along when you did, there wouldn't have been anybody to save her when it finally did happen.

You think about that instead of sitting over here sulking and blaming yourself."

"Sulking? I am not a child, Clara."

Clara's eyes narrowed. "Then maybe you're grown up enough to realize that everything isn't your fault. God brought you to this faith-forsaken place for a reason. Maybe it's time you stopped blaming yourself long enough to see that."

Mary's hand flew to her mouth to cover the "oh" of surprise at hearing Clara, sweet, supportive Clara, speaking to her like this. It was beyond shocking.

It was a wake-up call as clear as the reveille they'd heard every morning in France and as jarring as the artillery shells that shook the makeshift buildings where they'd operated.

"Clara, I…."

"No, don't apologize. I'm the one who's sorry here."

"Whatever for? You've been nothing but supportive and tolerant of my headstrong insistence on burying myself in the jungle to nurse my grief."

"Exactly the problem. As a friend, I've coddled you too long. You've run through grief headlong into self-pity."

"You're right. I've only been thinking of myself lately. I was so wrapped up in my wallowing that I've barely given a thought to others until Anaya's crisis." Mary lifted her shoulders a little further and straightened her spine as a horrible thought popped up. "Why, I've given no thought to dragging you to this place with me."

Clara's quick laugh startled Mary. She blinked as if it would change the grin on Clara's face. "Why, Clara, whatever is funny?"

"The idea that you dragged me here. I heard the call to teach loud and clear." Clara's hands came off her hips and went to Mary's shoulders. "I knew this was where God meant for me to be. Teaching the children at Nynabo is what I am called to do. You could have not dragged me *away* from this adventure."

The warmth and certainty in Clara's face doused the horror she'd felt over bringing Clara with her to the Liberian jungle. "I only wish I could be so certain. I've always followed my impulses. Like deciding to serve in France."

Mary swayed as Clara gently shook her shoulders. "Impulses maybe. Or perhaps God's direction in your life."

"How can I be sure?" Mary put her hands on top of Clara's, drawing them down between them. "How can I know God's will from my impulses?"

"Ah, that I cannot tell you. God himself holds the answer to that question. You must pray for those answers." She felt the light squeeze of assurance from her friend. "But it's no accident or impulse you're here, Dr. Mary. The steps of a righteous man are ordered. God says so in Proverbs. The question is, what would He want you to do now that you are here in His service?"

Mary gave Clara a quick hug. "I will spend time listening for the answer when I pray." Mary nodded toward William across the way. "Although if Pastor Mayweather prevails, the answer will be nothing at all. How in the world will I ever win Pastor Mayweather over to the notion I could be a part of God's plan at Nynabo when I'm not even certain of it myself?"

Clara's face took on a mischievous grin and one eyebrow raised conspiratorially. "Leave that one to God. You cannot change the man's mind for him."

"Easy for you to say. You're not the one he actively despises."

Clara's eyes crinkled up with her smile. "Oh, he doesn't despise you. You're the first one he looks to protect when there's trouble."

The heat and stress had addled Clara's brain. Mary snorted. "More like trying to keep me from escalating things."

"I'm telling you, the good pastor has eyes for you."

"Watching me constantly for signs I'm about to cause more trouble is not exactly a sign of romantic interest from a man."

Clara smiled. "If you say so. He's looking at both of us right now. The caravan is moving on."

Mary turned and saw an impatient-looking pastor motioning for them to come. See? That's what she wanted to say to Clara's retreating back. William is only interested in one thing. Getting to Nynabo as quickly as possible.

Chapter Ten

Clara pulled off her pith helmet and wiped at her brow. "Even with the sun, what a relief to be out of the jungle."

Clara walked side by side with Mary in the open plain. More jungle beckoned in the distance. The caravan's members stretched out in front of her like a lazy game of connecting dots. "I can't agree more, Clara. Although I'm starting to feel a little well-baked."

"Well, from what I hear, we may wish for the sun once the rainy season begins."

"Pretty soon you will see my home, Dr. Mammy." Hannabo's eagerness touched Mary until she remembered she might never see her own again.

She forced a smile for Hannabo. He didn't deserve her sadness to intrude on his joy. "I look forward to it, Hannabo. Is your village close to the mission?"

"Very much. Nana Pastor's uncle bought the land from my chief four summers ago. The village is on the other side of the mission."

"His uncle? I thought this was Pastor Mayweather's mission."

Hannabo looked at her with surprise. "Yes, yes, but Nana Joseph and Mammy Ruth came first."

"Where are they now?" Even as she asked, the suspicion grew. Malaria killed more than half the missionaries sent here in their first few months. This place lived up to its name as a white man's grave.

Hannabo's head hung and the normally boisterous man whispered his answer. "They died."

"Was it the malaria, the shaking sickness?"

Hannabo met her gaze and shook his head. He pointed to a mountain in the distance. Its imposing peak jutted upward. "They died there. Nana Mala wanted their medicine."

"I don't understand, Hannabo. Were they doctors like me?"

"No, not like you. They brought healing through their words and hands. They prayed to Father God and put hands on a dying man. He was wasted away from leprosy."

Like all great storytellers, Hannabo's hands illustrated his talk. His voice rose with such intensity that Mary wondered if he'd witnessed this event.

"They told him about the white man's God, Jesus, and when he laughed and said even the devilmen couldn't make him better they told him the story of the Father God and his Son. Nana Joseph said their God was more powerful than the devilmen. When the dying man challenged them to prove it, Nana Joseph prayed and his hands grew hot."

Hannabo's chest swelled and his face shone beyond the glow of sweat that covered him. "After, the dying man grew stronger and better every day until he was in good health again. Word spread because this healed man told everyone far and wide what had happened to him."

Privately, Mary doubted this healing tale. She'd bet the story traveled and grew with each telling. Prayers of dying men had assaulted her ears at Argonne and no heavenly relief came. Her own were uttered in vain.

She concealed her thoughts so as not to destroy Hannabo's fervor. Instead she only asked for clarification. "How did this lead to their deaths? You say Nana Mala wanted their medicine? Who is Nana Mala?"

"Nana Mala is an evil man who does not know the true God. When he heard of the healing, he sent for Nana Pastor Joseph and Mammy Ruth. They went to preach, but Nana Mala just wanted the secret of their magic. When he did not like their answers, he killed them and took their magic for himself. This is my fault." Hannabo's eyes looked downward in shame.

Oh my. This explained a lot about Pastor Mayweather's calling. But Hannabo shouldn't carry the guilt for what another tribesman had done. She sought to reassure him. "This is not your fault, Hannabo. You are not to blame for the actions of others."

"But Mammy Doctor. It was my fault. I was that man."

"Which man are you talking about?

"The one Nana Joseph healed. I bragged to many people, especially Nana Mala."

"Oh, I see." Mary masked her surprise. Hannabo believed he'd experienced a miracle firsthand. She couldn't tear apart his faith, but she could set him straight on his guilt.

"Hannabo, it was fine to tell others. The Bible often tells of people who were healed and told many others. It's natural. What's strange is Nana Mala believing he could get magic from Pastor Mayweather's aunt and uncle."

"No, no. Not strange. Every bush man knows how to take magic."

"Okay, so how did he think he could take their magic?"

Hannabo cocked his head to one side and looked at her

like she was a simpleton. Even his tone seemed one of patient explanation to a lesser mind. "By eating them, of course."

Mary looked at the jungle looming ahead. She'd been assured this was the final leg of the journey. Nynabo was close. She'd had plenty of time to think about Hannabo's revelation, a stunning reality of this harsh and beautiful land. She'd rather busy herself with setting up her clinic than have more time to dwell on Pastor Mayweather's family's death by cannibals. A shuddering thought even for someone well acquainted with the various methods of destruction man offered in the name of war. She shuddered even though Hannabo had assured her that no one knew for sure that the missionaries were eaten, just that they died.

Clara startled her. "Never thought more jungle would look so good. You, my girl, haven't worn your hat nearly enough."

Mary touched her cheek. "I know. The sun has given my fair skin a bit more color than is comfortable." The caravan leads stepped into the taller grass that led into the jungle canopy.

"Well, here comes the shade. Two days in the canopy before Nynabo should let your skin heal. And then—" Clara wagged her finger "—you start keeping your hat on in the sun."

Mary laughed. "You're sounding like my mother again, Clara."

"Well, someone has to look out for you. You stay so busy looking out for everyone else."

"Speaking of which, does it seem like the number of physical complaints among the porters has risen?"

"Dramatically. Ever since our Anaya recovered, you've been the center of a lot of attention."

"Do you think that's what sparked it?"

"From what I understand, vomiting is the key to surviving the sasswood. But to hear Hannabo and Jabo talk, only those who throw up right away survive. They'd never seen someone live who'd had the poison in them that long."

They reached the taller grass and a barely trampled path forced them back to single file, straining their conversation. Pushing through the spiky grass stalks, Mary surveyed the towering vegetation ahead while she considered her answer. "After talking to Hannabo, I'm rather concerned most of them think what I do is magic and not science."

"Well, it's what they know, Dr. Mary. You can't expect them to go from believing in devilmen to understanding science just because Pastor Mayweather tells them it's different."

"True, a lifetime of beliefs is hard to change. I…" Mary drank in the sight before her. "Oh, Clara. I've never seen such beauty."

Clara stepped in behind her. "Oh, my. It's like something, something…holy."

A cathedral. It was like the aisle of a cathedral. Tall cottonwoods with massive roots able to hide a choir of angels in their folds lined the footpath through the jungle. Light filtered through in random streams that caught the color of orchids adorning the vines, vines winding their colorful blossoms up and around the smaller trees. Even the animals seemed to respect the solemnity, and little sound penetrated. For a time Mary walked in awe of the beauty, forgetting how much she'd wanted to be done with this trek.

Ahead, a massive, fallen tree sprawled across the trail

like an altar in the distance. Porters scrambled over its limbs and disappeared from view. Mary walked on, fascinated. Clara kept pace behind her.

The heavenly atmosphere held until she drew close enough to see William standing at the blockade in front of her, an impatient scowl planted firmly on his face. Jabo waited at his side, smiling in bright contrast.

"Wonder what I did now?"

"What are you...oh, I see that look. Pastor Mayweather does look a little more unhappy than usual."

Mary deliberately locked onto Jabo's smile and returned one of her own. William's demeanor wasn't going to mar the beauty of this place for her.

"Ladies," William said. She saw the problem, the tree extended deep into both sides of the trail, creating an impasse for less agile travelers. She had tripped on enough tree roots to qualify.

William explained the process. "These roots that spring from the side go on for a short distance. We'll have to walk on the tree trunk and roots to pass on."

Clara piped up. "I'm game for anything once."

A smile strained William's face. "Unfortunately, it will probably be more than once. No one here clears more of a trail than they personally have to use. Lightning fells the trees and we're left to deal with them."

Mary eyed the trunk, which was taller than the two men before it. "How are we going to do this?"

"Jabo, could you please show the ladies?"

"Yes, Nana Pastor. Mammies, watch me please." Finding invisible toe and handholds, Jabo scrambled up the side.

"I'm not sure Clara and I are quite as experienced as Jabo."

"That's why he will help you from the top, and I will

give you a leg up to the first hand and foot holds. Once you're there and reach up, Jabo will help you the rest of the way."

Clara eyed it warily, so Mary volunteered to be first. Did she have to be so close to the man to do this?

William stood with his right side to the tree trunk and bent over, lacing his fingers together for her foot. "Put your hands on my shoulders and then your right foot in my hands. I'll boost you up and you reach for a handhold. Then put your left foot in the space a little above my shoulder and pull yourself up. You should be able to reach Jabo's hand after that."

Mary moved closer. Stop being such a ninny. Think of him as just a ladder.

William's raised eyebrows asked what she was waiting on and she put her hands on his shoulders. No ladder she'd ever climbed had such handsome brown eyes, the rungs had never made her feet feel as small as they did between his powerful hands.

Mary nodded when he asked her if she was ready. Even though she really wanted to stay right where she was a while longer looking at that slight stubble and strong jaw.

Reflexively, her hands squeezed his shoulders as she lifted upward.

He gave her a moment to balance and asked, "Can you grab on with your hands?"

Reluctantly, her fingers went from clutching cotton to rough bark. She dug her fingers in as best she could and followed his directions to find her toeholds. She hung there feeling awkward but little danger from the small height. Once she straightened, she reached up and grabbed Jabo's hand and finished the process.

She moved to the side so Clara and the pastor could

follow, hunting even spots to put her feet down. It might not be that high, but no point in risking a broken limb.

Once the four of them were all up, William motioned her forward. When she went to pass him, he took her by the arm. "We're walking down a maze of roots. I don't want you to fall."

"I'm perfectly fine, Pastor Mayweather." She tried to extricate her arm.

He firmly held. "Considering I've had to catch you on more than one occasion when we were on the ground, I believe this way will save me the trouble."

Rude. Rude. Rude. The minute she thought he was trying to be nice, he had to go and ruin the illusion by pointing out she was trouble. She took two steps forward and immediately squelched her mental protests. This was hard. She drew on all her concentration to keep from falling. All those childhood years spent climbing trees should have better prepared her.

"It's your boots. You wore the wrong shoes for the jungle. Without rubber soles to grip you're going to slide. Place your feet carefully and I'll be here to stop any missteps."

Did ungracious speech just come naturally to the man? Ignore it. No point in her being fractious on top of a tree. She looked at Jabo leading Clara down one of the root paths. "I don't think my feet are tough enough to go without shoes like our porters. I own rubber rain boots, Army issue, but they're packed away."

William shook his head ruefully while he guided her to the next offshoot. "It didn't occur to me until we got to this part of the forest to ask if you had other footwear."

"Why Pastor Mayweather, is that an apology?"

The tension of his grip increased. If she wasn't so painfully aware of his nearness, she might have missed it.

"Merely a statement of regret. It would have made it easier for both of us if you had the right footwear."

A very unladylike snort was the only answer she gave.

"What? Did I manage to offend you somehow yet again, Dr. O'Hara?"

She kept her reply matter-of-fact. "For a man professing his love of God, a missionary no less, well, I've seen better manners in the field hospitals by overworked and overbearing male doctors. And believe me, they ruled the kingdom of rude."

Three more steps and he let go her arm and took an oversized step to the ground. Her legs didn't have the same reach. Should she jump?

He turned and reached up to her waist and lifted her off the last root and planted her firmly on the ground. And held her there, boring into her eyes with an intensity that bespoke a fervor of God.

"Maybe my manners aren't perfect for your drawing-room sensibilities, or even as good as those in the medical community, but politeness won't keep you alive and uninjured in the bush."

How to even answer? Galling, just galling that he was right.

Pastor Mayweather removed his hands and stepped back, staring at her. "Is the exertion of travel getting to you? I don't recall a time in my company you've ever held your tongue."

"I am tired, Pastor, but more from sparring words with you than the trip itself. A bad habit on my part. Perhaps we could simply declare a truce, our own version of an Armistice agreement?" Mary brushed errant hairs back from her face. "We can agree to dislike each other, and I'll concede you find me unsuitable in every way for the position in Nynabo."

"I do not dislike you, Dr. O'Hara. However, we do seem to bring out the worst in each other." A flush of shame crossed his face. "I concede your assessment of my manners is accurate. I'm sure after observing you with Anaya that your medical training is adequate, but the bush is still too dangerous for you and Mrs. Smith."

"So we remain at an impasse. To keep the peace, perhaps we should simply ignore each other and allow our areas of purview—mine of medicine and yours of saving souls."

"An equitable agreement, considering. I only have one question."

"Which is?"

"If your only mission is medicine, why trek to an isolated spot where the main focus is to spread the Gospel?"

William was surprised at Mary's reaction. He considered his question a reasonable one considering the world's need for doctors.

She looked at him like a trapped animal seeking a fast escape. When she finally spoke it was softly with great reserve. "My reasons for coming here are my own business, Pastor. I assure you they will not affect the quality of my medical care at Nynabo and the outlying villages."

At least she didn't try hiding the fact that she was dodging the question. Despite the truce, he couldn't let her go on to Nynabo with a false understanding. "I respect your privacy, but at the risk of stirring up more trouble, I must set you straight on your duties in Nynabo."

Seeing Jabo with Clara attempting to dismount from the tree, William took Dr. O'Hara by the elbow and moved her so the two could descend. She started to protest but caught sight of her companion's descent and moved.

A few steps away, she stopped and folded her arms

across her chest. "I'm pretty sure I know my medical duties. What could you possibly have to correct me on this time?"

"You seem to be under the misconception you'll be engaged in medical treatment outside of the Nynabo Mission Station."

One eyebrow rose and despite his expectation of her explosion, she stood quietly waiting for him to finish.

"I can't allow you to travel outside the compound. There's too much to go wrong, too many customs you don't understand. The eternal salvation of these people is in my hands and I can't allow you to endanger either yourself or that goal."

Even in the dim light, he registered the flush spreading across her cheeks. Might as well get it all out now. "Once at Nynabo, I expect you to stay within the compound and treat only the women and children who come to your clinic."

Exasperation laced her voice. "Only the women and children? I suppose I should be grateful you allow me to practice at all?"

"Despite any orders you carry, the Mission Board recognizes my authority in my own compound. I am responsible for you and Mrs. Smith and I can't have you endangering all our lives. Again."

He nodded to Jabo and Clara as they walked past. More porters scuttled from over and under the branches and roots and cast a wary glance at the two of them as they passed. "The women and children occupy a lower status among the tribes. If treatment is unsuccessful, there will be less chance of harm to the compound."

Dr. O'Hara looked at him a moment longer. Then she adjusted her backpack, turned and began to walk down the trail. Without a single word.

The surprise threw him off, but he caught up with her in a few strides. "I need to know you understand and will comply with this, Dr. O'Hara. Even if you disagree."

She spun on him like an out-of-control children's top. "Of course I disagree. You talk as if the women and children don't matter. As if you must protect patients from me. I'm not sure which is the more offensive."

"No. I did not mean to imply women and children aren't important. Not at all. They are a downtrodden part of tribal society. I can only hope an understanding of the Gospel's message will improve their lot."

"But you're not convinced I will."

"I thought we agreed to a truce of sorts."

"Perhaps we should be sure we've ironed out all the issues first. My competence seems to be one for you."

"On the contrary, I was very impressed with your care of Anaya. But we have to be extremely careful in the bush world, Doctor. One misstep and even a friendly tribe turns deadly out here." He searched for the words to settle the issue. "Can you guarantee a sick or injured man would not die under your care?"

The flush on her face immediately fled. "No, Pastor. No one can make that promise. Or at least no one should."

Finally she seemed to get the seriousness of the situation. "If a man of the tribe dies under your care, you and perhaps the whole compound could be accused of witchcraft. Or we could be simply killed outright. I can't impress upon you enough how unforgiving the family would be if you failed to save a male patient."

"I'm pretty sure I can understand exactly what you're saying. Forgiveness is out of reach when you lose a male family member in any society."

Pain, sorrow, or maybe regret? What was the emotion

that flashed across her face before she turned and started walking? "Doctor O'Hara?"

She answered without looking back. "Not to worry, Pastor Mayweather. I will confine myself to the women and children. You've made your point and now I would prefer to concentrate on the trail without distraction. The roots are especially well hidden under the accumulated rot of the jungle."

He knew dismissal when he heard it. Victory should make him feel relieved, happy even. Not uneasy that he'd tapped into something he didn't understand. Anger he could handle. Sorrow radiated from Dr. O'Hara and baffled him, leaving him feeling wholly inadequate. Give him a hostile tribesman any day.

Chapter Eleven

Mary stood at the top of the rise that held the mission compound, taking in the sight of her new home. "Looks like we got here just in time. The overgrowth makes the jungle appear to have hands, creeping vine hands reaching out to grab the main house."

Clara took a second to catch her breath from the upward climb before answering. "The growth is close enough to start climbing the buildings any time now."

Mary surveyed the forlorn compound. Vines crowded over a wooden fence, one that defined the perimeters but offered little in the way of protection, unlike the taller palisades she'd seen in Nana Bolo's compound. Didn't matter, since warriors wouldn't man the compound's fences. Two buildings lay in front of her. Central in the compound was a wooden home, with what appeared to be intact thatching on the roof. The house sat on a stone foundation of evenly spaced pillars about five feet off the ground. A deep veranda ran across the front with four wide steps flanked by handrails on each side. To the left was a similar building, same style, only smaller. From the front, the thatch looked a little spotty, but basically intact. To the right stood an open structure with wooden pillars at the four corners and a larger wood column in the middle. Little thatch remained. Maybe a meeting area or open-air chapel?

"Dr. Mary, look out over there." Clara indicated a dense fog that rolled into the distance almost as far as the eye could see. In the foreground, small hills rose like tiny atolls dotting a calm ocean. Farther on was a large mountain, possibly the same one she'd spotted from the plains, although she wasn't quite sure of her directions at this point. "Oh, my. What a view. I could stand here all day just enjoying the sight."

"I wonder how tall the mountain is. We're on a hilltop now."

"I don't know. I don't think this country is known for its mountains."

"Unlike France's peaks."

"Definitely not. Here comes Pastor Mayweather. He can tell us about the geography here."

He approached with a new bounce in his step. She'd noticed the change the last two days on the trail. He was excited to be back.

"Ladies, welcome to Nynabo. The building to your left was originally planned as a schoolroom and infirmary. It will be quarters for both of you and the clinic."

"Will we build a school for my students, Pastor Mayweather?"

"Yes, and eventually I'd like to build dormitories over there," he gestured to the right behind the open structure. "For now, students will be only local and they will walk the short distance to the village every day."

"Where is Hannabo's village from here?" Mary asked.

"If you stand just past the chapel, you can see the village once the mist burns off."

Mary's desire to get started overcame her curiosity about the village. "May we use the building now?"

His jovial look faded. "The building needs to be checked for damage. Once safety is assured, you may move in tonight. We can work on any minor repairs around you."

Anticipation mixed with wonder and awe. This was really happening. She had made it here and all their talk on those monotonous freighter-bound days to Liberia was a reality. A shiver of excitement ran down her back. And was quickly quenched.

"As to patients, it will probably be awhile before any venture here. Although I'm sure word will get out eventually."

Mary stared at the man's retreating back. Good thing he'd walked off, or her new resolution, to stay out of arguments, was going to flop again. She'd follow his orders not to treat the men, but surely there was a safe way to get the word out and start building trust in her new neighbors?

Anaya! Her first real patient was returning to her family home in the village, promising to come back as a cook in a few days. She could help Mary learn some of the language or at least some pidgin to communicate. She hoped Anaya's presence would help spread the word.

Mary turned to share her plan. "Clara, why don't we…" The sheen of perspiration on Clara's face stopped her. "Are you feeling ill?"

"I think I need to sit down. Unless I'm mistaken, the chills I'm feeling mean we've gotten here just in time."

Mary turned and yelled to the nearby Hannabo. "Hannabo, Mammy Clara is sick. Bring a camp bed and set it up in the infirmary. I need all my trunks." Hannabo took one look and hurried off. Mary called out to his retreating back. "And tell Pastor Mayweather."

Mary grabbed a shivering arm and led Clara to sit on

the steps of the medical building. "Don't worry. We'll have you a bed and medicines in a few minutes.

"I'm not worried. I don't want you to be either. You have to promise me something, Dr. Mary."

"A little early in the process for promises. You'll be fine, Clara."

Clara shook her head, giving her a wry smile. "Now that's not a promise you can make, dear girl. No, what I want from you is your word you won't blame yourself if I die."

William knew his duty as a pastor to pray for Clara, but fear for her life almost paralyzed him. Now, as he waited for Dr. O'Hara to allow him into the sickroom, his stomach churned. Clara was asking for him, and he couldn't let her down.

The walk from the main house to the infirmary had been like a prisoner's march to execution. Memories of Alice's last few days flooded his brain and left him drowning in a cold sweat.

Father, give me peace so I may minister your peace to Clara.

His own thoughts so occupied him, he startled when Mary exited the sick room.

She looked up. "I see Hannabo found… Are you all right? Are you sick?"

"No, doctor. I'm fine." How did you explain the lasting effect of something so personal as holding your dying wife in her last few hours as malaria racked her body? "I have a confession."

Mary double blinked. "A confession?"

"For a pastor, I have a very poor bedside manner with the infirm. I'm just not very good with sick people." This was enough of the truth to explain his appearance and skirt around his own personal issues.

Mary managed a small smile and placed a reassuring hand on his arm. Not the reaction he expected. "Pastor Mayweather, most people I've seen visiting the sick don't understand how to handle things either."

Then she cocked her head and looked at him with real understanding. "How do you do your job? I thought visiting the sick with prayers was a large part of it. At least for pastors back home."

William tried to laugh it off. "My impediment does cause me some difficulty, but I'm here. How is Mrs. Smith doing?"

"She's suffering, as you would expect. I'm hoping she acquired one of the less deadly forms. It will be a couple of days before I can say for sure and then a couple of weeks before she's able to get around."

Mary stepped aside to let him enter Clara's room. "I'll be back momentarily. Would you watch over Clara for a moment?"

"Certainly." William breathed a sigh of relief when Mary stepped away. She was too astute not to figure out his problem was more than just general discomfort with sick people if she observed him for long. He held his memories of Alice too close inside a vault of pain over her loss. The thought of sharing those was almost as anxiety-inducing as stepping into Clara's sick room.

Please, Lord. Don't make me need to bury another woman beside Alice. I know the first round of missionaries to the coast paved the way with their graves. Must this interior mission, too, add more graves before we add converts?

William felt peace and determination settle over him. Not a guarantee he wouldn't be digging another burial site beside his Alice, but peace that God was in control despite his fears.

He took a deep breath and stepped into Clara's room. She slept soundly, a slight sheen evidence of the fever cycle of the disease. He moved forward and began to pray. When he was finished, a weakened hand touched his, managing a small pat.

Her thin voice added, "Thank you, Pastor Mayweather. I'll rest so much better since you've prayed for me. Won't you stay a moment and read to me from the Psalms? Psalms are my favorite and I'm in no shape to read them for myself."

He wanted nothing more than to escape the sickroom. Compassion overrode his own needs and he pulled up a chair to be close enough for her to hear.

When she finally fell back to sleep, he stopped reading and contemplated the woman battling for her life in front of him. Would she live through this? Alice had looked so peaceful in the last few moments, but Clara seemed to be peaceful now.

He stood to go and saw Mary leaning against the door post. How long had she been listening? He'd been so engrossed in reading, he hadn't heard her return.

"I enjoyed your reading, Pastor Mayweather. You have a voice suited for the scriptures, as your evening readings on the trail often proved. Seems you also have a bedside manner suited to the infirm. Surprising given your earlier statement."

William stepped toward the door and waited for Mary to move. "Yes, well, it was Mrs. Smith's request I read to her. Discomfort or not, I had to fulfill her wishes. For all I know it will be the last time she hears the scriptures in this life. Now if you will excuse me."

The air outside breathed of freedom from the memories

stirred in the sickroom. He had a cure for his own ailment. Losing himself in the work of the compound. A busy man had less to think about. Less time to contemplate the pain of the past or its repetition in the future.

Mary pulled the linens off the bed while Anaya helped Clara to the chair. This was the first time they'd done so in the last week that Clara was able to sit out of the bed. "We'll get these clean and back on the bed in no time. I'm so glad you're feeling well enough to sit up for a while today."

Clara settled into the chair, Anaya solicitously at her side. "If I had to stay in the bed much longer, my sanity would rebel."

Mary laughed at her friend. "How about just being glad you're alive, bed or not?" Mary handed the sheets to Anaya to launder. Fortunately they would dry quickly in this heat.

After Anaya exited, Clara asked, "How are the language lessons coming?"

"Her English is surpassing my Kru. Good thing I studied medicine. I make a terrible linguist. The tonal quality of the language is giving me the hardest time."

"Stick with it. I have faith in you. Now that my strength is returning, we can learn together. I'll need something besides pantomime to help me with the students I hope to teach."

"I think I can allow you to do language lessons. But not something more strenuous. Are we clear?"

Clara's head turned to the sound of the knock on the doorway.

Hannabo stood there, grinning. "Mammy Clara is better?"

Clara nodded. "Yes, much better, thank you."

Mary asked. "Hannabo, where is Pastor Mayweather? He seemed pretty upset when he came to pray for Clara last week, but since then I've hardly seen him."

"Nana Pastor is working hard every day. He helps with all the building. He doesn't speak it, but he worries for Mammy Clara."

Clara said, "Tell him to come see me now that I'm better."

Hannabo nodded. "I will tell him. Mammies, do not be offended. Fearing a woman's death is hard for Nana Pastor. I am going now. Looking for Anaya."

Mary informed him, "She's gone to the stream for washing laundry. You'll find her down the hill."

Hannabo turned on his heel and left before Mary asked him more about William. Then she remembered his dead wife. If her death was traumatic for him it would explain a lot.

William's heart rejoiced when he caught sight of Clara sitting on the porch of the infirmary with Mary. In spite of his fears, Clara Smith had recovered quickly. Other than to lay hands and pray for her initially, he'd kept his distance while he waited to hear if she would end up like almost half the white missionaries coming to this clime, buried within the first few months. He'd prayed for her daily, but after the devastation to his Alice, he couldn't bear to see another woman in the same distress.

Even now it bothered him to think about her near death. It was safer to think on the construction progress. He surveyed the site with a swelling pride. Two weeks of dawn-to-dusk work had finally made the main house and most of the compound habitable.

The low fencing that surrounded the site had suffered the most. The white ants had found their favorite spots and feasted. New chicken wire was going round to fill in the gaps until more boards could be hewn to supply the need. Right now all the production of new boards from the saw pit went to building the school.

Their old stores of chicken wire had been, as he expected, pillaged in his absence. He was pretty sure several of the bracelets, beaded necklaces and fetishes he saw on the workmen he had hired from Nynabo village were held together with that very same chicken wire. He'd spotted his old brass cook pot now gracing a cook fire in the village. The villagers would not have let anything go to waste short of dismantling the actual buildings.

He headed to the main house to survey the final work on the floor. The stone pilings the mission house stood on had spared it much damage. Termites preferred to come directly up through their tunnels in the ground. Other than repairs to the floor in the main room and one of the bedrooms, all was well. Even the canvas mats that served as windows in the house were left undisturbed.

William climbed the steps to his home and reached for a handkerchief to mop his sweating brow. Today seemed hotter than usual to him. He would have thought he'd get used to the humid heat after the trip in and two weeks of hard labor in the Liberian sun. Instead, all it had gotten him was aching joints from being on his hands and knees setting the new boards in the floors and shoulders and arms complaining about carrying new boards overhead from the makeshift mill to the house.

Come to think of it, he ached all over. Maybe he should ask Mary for an analgesic powder. He looked toward the infirmary about ten yards off to his right.

He heard the women's soft conversation carrying from the porch without making out the actual words. He didn't have to decipher it, his imagination sufficed. Mary was probably still upset he'd vetoed her request to travel to Nynabo proper and try to treat the villagers in their own homes, even though she'd gained Anaya's trust and wanted to use their relationship as a way into the village.

Once again, she didn't realize the risk. Even though she'd insisted she would confine herself to helping women and children, he still couldn't get comfortable with the notion. She had too much to learn about this place first. Her temper had flared in her eyes when he'd said no, but she'd acquiesced. But that little spark made him rethink the old wives' tale about red hair and fiery dispositions.

He cocked his ear at the encroaching sound of Mary's voice. She must be heading out of the infirmary. He turned and proceeded off the side of the porch in the opposite direction. The woman would wear him down with her persistence. She always had a well-reasoned argument, but he was determined to protect her at all costs until her replacement arrived. He preferred to think of his avoidance of her not as cowardice but as a passive form of diplomacy. Keeping it up became harder as he squelched his natural desire for intelligent conversation and companionship. Those and other emotions he preferred not to identify were better left buried.

His long strides carried him without thinking to the back of the compound. And face-to-face with the memories he had hoped to avoid. In his haste to remove himself from any unplanned encounters with Mary, he had come straight to the crude cross under the sprawling shade of the cottonwood marking Alice's final resting place.

It was no place for him to seek refuge. But now that he faced the grave, well out of sight, and everyone else was busy with their own tasks, his grief struck as fresh as before he'd left a little over a year ago.

He bowed his head under the weight of the outpouring

of grief. A chill ran through him as he stood before the grave of the woman he'd both loved and failed. He tried to shake it off and speak. He knew Alice was beyond his hearing, yet he felt compelled to speak to her as if she stood there.

"I failed you, dearest one. I wish so much I had left you home." William closed his eyes as if that would hold the tears of his heart from spilling.

"I should never have brought you here. It was selfish. And I...I can never undo this thing I have done." William dropped to his knees. "Oh, Alice, if only you stood here so I could tell you how sorry I am. If I could hold you one more time." A breeze ruffled through the trees and his chill increased. The sun was only yet three-quarters through the day, yet goose bumps rose on his arms.

He searched the sky for any sign, but the sun only glared at him, mocking him. Mocking? The sun?

Something was wrong. William struggled to get himself upright. He started to call for help, but knew the sounds of the milling wood would drown out any cry he might make. He got one foot under himself before the sky darkened, blocked by an angelic face close to his, filled with concern. The halo around her head. Was this a visitation?

Words. Words that made no sense. Alice's voice? His vision blurred as he strained to make out the features in front of him.

Shouting now. The Alice angel shouted for help. Strong arms grasped him and he was hauled to his feet. Another chill gripped him and shook his senses. Then he knew. He would be joining Alice soon enough.

Malaria had finally struck.

Pastor Mayweather might have thought he was subtle in his obvious avoidance of her, but Mary knew every time she had a new idea and headed in his direction to discuss the possibilities he left the scene or got very, very, busy. It was almost amusing. Did he fear talking to her? William was certainly no coward, so enough of his polite but pointed avoidance of her.

He stayed so stuck on the idea that her lack of cultural understanding would endanger her, he failed to notice how much she'd learned since she arrived. Her confidence level rose after her lessons with Anaya and the many evening chats she'd had with Hannabo. This time she intended to press William to go with her to observe and see that she had learned her lessons.

Now if she could only school her face to hold on to her desire to laugh at his expression when she found him yet again. Really, in her case, he was the one without cultural understanding. A female didn't become a physician in this day and age without immeasurable persistence, something he would eventually learn as she applied a diligent pursuit of her goal.

Her short legs couldn't compete with William's long-legged strides, so when she found him at the very back of the compound, she'd paused to catch her breath from the pace. It was enough of a disadvantage to have to look up into his tall visage. She didn't want to be puffing from exertion as well.

What was he doing? Was he talking…talking to a tree? Mary took a few quiet steps forward. The heat was oppressive today. William could be in danger of heatstroke, his thinking completely addled. Her mind ran through her options for cooling him even as she crept quietly forward. The stream nearby was barely deep enough for the silt to settle when they drew drinking water to purify. Better than nothing with no ice to be had in this bastion of uncultivated forest.

A couple of strong men would have to help her get him there. More if he was combative, as victims of the heat-scorched mind could often be.

Wait, he went down on his knees. Relief flooded Mary. He was praying. Not out of his mind after all. In front of him stood a small wooden cross. Two crude pieces held together with wire. A grave.

And then she heard him. "Alice." His wife's name? *Oh, dear Father, it must be his wife's grave. Let me get out of here before I intrude on this man's grief.*

Mary had come to politely press her point assuming he was avoiding her once again. And here he'd only come to visit his dead wife's grave. Privately. She took a tentative step backward. Intruding on a man's grief? She needed to leave.

She caught the words "…how sorry I am," just as a shudder ran through him. He was visibly shaking.

All of her medical training kicked in. Not heatstroke or grief. She watched for confirmation. He was sick. When she saw him struggle to get to his feet without success, she dropped all plans to escape unseen and headed straight for him.

William's face was pale and his skin clammy to touch. She brought her face closer to his to check his eyes. They were glassy with fever.

Mary yelled for help before she realized the futility with the milling of the boards. So she waited for less than a minute, a minute that felt like an hour. When the pause she expected came during the setup for passing the next board, she yelled again.

This time someone heard her. Two men from the village, whose names she didn't know, came running. Fortunately they didn't need to understand her to see the problem. They in turn shouted for more help and grabbed the pastor under the arms, placed his arms around their necks and proceeded to carry William to the infirmary. Or at least that's where Mary hoped they were going. Her pidgin-based communication failed her in her nervous panic, so she got in front of them and marched to the steps of the clinic, where she was met by the recovering Clara.

Clara's worried face belied her calm actions. "I don't have the clinic beds ready yet."

"Then we'll use mine for now."

Mary led the men to the back room, gesturing for them to put William on her bed. "Clara, get the thermometer please."

Clara grabbed the small leather case that held the two thermometers and handed it to Mary while the men got William situated. Mary opened the leather case and looked at the set of oral and basal thermometers secured in the blue-velvet-lined holder, a gift from Jeremy when she graduated from medical school.

Mary's hand hesitated. She'd thought she could save her brother on that fateful day in Argonne. After all, why else would God have brought him to her table out of all the hundreds of casualties? She'd prayed and put her faith in both God and her skill.

Neither had proven true. Was she destined to lose another patient she cared about? Something about this prickly, overprotective missionary tapped her emotions as no other man before him had.

"Mary?" Clara's hand touched her arm in a tentative question. "Are you all right?"

Mary strengthened her resolve. If she questioned herself now, she would lose him from pure indecision. "Sorry, Clara." She handed Clara the bent basal thermometer. "He's too confused to cooperate for an accurate oral read-

ing. Let's get his shirt off and get an under-the-arm reading."

Clara removed the detachable collar and they both tack-
led the buttons of the white cotton shirt down the front.
Mary grasped his wrist and removed the cuff links while
Clara repeated the motion on her side. Hannabo entered
the room and sent the other two men out. Mary started
to lift William to finish removing the shirt, but Hannabo
stepped in and, with a surprising gentleness, lifted William effortlessly.

Mary completed her evaluation while Clara took his
temperature. Even with him this sick, his muscles reflected a man who worked alongside the men he hired
to build the compound. Nothing about him had clued her
in to his being ill. If her persistence hadn't caused him to
avoid her lately, maybe she would have noticed he was
getting sick. He was dangerously ill at this point, a state
which induced a panic in her. She pushed the feeling aside.
There was no room for anything but her professional best.
She forced herself to focus on the medicine.

His skin was already a sallow, grayish-yellow color,
so characteristic of malaria. She palpated his belly and
found the slightly enlarged spleen she was expecting. Her
hands rubbed the light scrape of a day's beard growth as
she pulled his lower lip out to check his gums. Definite
pallor. Blood under her microscope would confirm which
strain they were dealing with, but the fact that he'd lost
consciousness told her it was not the easiest one to treat.

"One hundred and three, Doctor." Clara set the thermometer on the bedside table after shaking it down.

"He must have had the chills earlier. If he'd come to me
sooner…"

Clara shook her head. "No what-ifs. Let's just move
forward."

Mary nodded at the sage advice. If he lived, she could lecture him later. "The rapid onset and severity of symptoms tell me we're going to have to go with the intravenous injections. Plus, he's in no shape to swallow a tablet."

"I wonder if he's been taking the preventative doses."

"Even if he had, quinine doesn't guarantee prevention. Have you unpacked the sterillett vials yet? I need a Pravez needle, too."

"Yes, I'll get both from the cabinet." The long skirt Clara had switched back to wearing now that travel was done swished as she turned to retrieve the supplies.

A sheen of fever covered his face and torso. God willing, the fever wouldn't climb too much higher. Crazy thoughts ran amok in her brain. Would she ever see those dimples again, the ones that came out with his rare smiles? Panic reared its ugly head again. Hannabo shifted, reminding her of his presence. *Pull yourself together. You're a professional.*

Clara returned with the supplies and Mary busied herself with the procedure, banishing all thoughts of either dimples or death as she worked. She wrapped the tourniquet, finding a promising vein bulging from the pressure. She swabbed the area with the tincture of iodine Clara provided. Filling the glass syringe with the ampoule of quinine, she injected directly into the vein. Once she removed the needle, she placed gauze over the site. "Hannabo, please put pressure here." Mary cut a piece of tape to hold the gauze in place. "Clara, would you boil the syringe in the carbolic solution? I'm afraid we may need it again in a few hours if he doesn't respond."

Mary surveyed William's unchanging pallor. Hannabo cleared his throat. "Will Nana Pastor live?"

"I don't know, Hannabo. I hope so."

"Then we must pray as Nana Pastor would do for us. The One God holds his life and it is up to Him."

Mary felt awe and shame. Awe that this relatively new convert would turn so quickly to the new God he served, and shame for not already doing the same. She'd allowed her doubts and grief to override her faith so easily after Jeremy's death. Would God listen to her prayers now?

"Yes, let's pray." When Clara returned they all bowed their heads and Hannabo spoke. "Our God, the One God, the True God, we ask you to protect Nana Pastor from this sickness. We ask that he live to spread your Word among my people that they may know you as I do. Amen."

Such simplicity in a heartfelt prayer. Mary marveled at Hannabo's open heart. His plea for William to live to spread the Word reminded her more was at stake here than just her own need for William to live.

My, when did it become a need? Mary decided to examine that later. Or maybe never. She couldn't afford to be too attached to a man who, if he lived, wasn't likely to change his opinion of her. She'd still be an unconventional woman in the world of a man of solid traditions. A gap unable to be bridged. Besides, she'd seen him at his wife's grave. He obviously still loved her. What woman could ever compete with a memory?

"Dr. Mary, I'll watch over him for now. Anaya cooked dinner. You go eat and then I will."

"Thanks, Clara, but I'm sure I won't be able to eat yet. I'm going to stay here for now. You are still recovering. You and Hannabo go eat."

"All right, but you call the minute you need anything." Clara's concern for her was obvious.

"I too am here to help for any of Nana Pastor's needs. I will be near." Hannabo's firmness reassured her she would have any help she needed. Given the vigil and care necessary, she would need it.

"Thank you both." Mary sat wearily in the chair beside William's bed. It was going to be a long night. Sweats and more chills would appear sometime in the next twelve hours. If the quinine worked, it would be obvious in the next day or so.

Would he regain consciousness? She could only hope. It would be one sign meaning he might live and not need to be buried beside his wife.

Chapter Twelve

William was shaking and couldn't stop. Faces in front of him came and went as he alternately heated and chilled. The sheet covering him was suffocating. The pillow beneath his head radiated heat. A strong arm slid beneath him and raised him up slightly. When his head came back to the pillow it was cooler. He wanted to thank the face in front of him, but his tongue refused to obey.

A cool cloth granted a short-lived relief to his forehead. Cold liquid, the smell of iodine and a burning in his left arm made no sense. He understood only one thing. He had malaria. Malaria killed Alice, and now it was his turn to die.

His mind struggled to form a prayer. If he was going to meet his Heavenly Father today, he wanted to prepare. There was so much to be forgiven.

He had failed. Failed his uncle, failed his wife, failed his Heavenly Father. All his plans to evangelize the Kru, and later the Pahn, the people who had killed his aunt and uncle, were for naught. He'd made a vow to God to carry out the work his uncle's death had left unfinished. He moaned, and a worried black face leaned down to him.

Hannabo. The only convert out of the bush and one secured not by him, but by his uncle's martyrdom.

The only thing William had accomplished was death—his wife's and now his own. A woman's face replaced Hannabo's. Fire surrounded her alabaster face and green eyes burned through to his soul. Was she here to accompany him to Heaven? She spoke, but he couldn't make out the words. Darkness eclipsed her features and he surrendered into a bliss of unconsciousness and fevered dreams.

The landscape of the darkness was jumbled. The only consistency was the earth shaking in the vined tangle of pictures flooding his mind. The oppressive jungle heat saturated him as he struggled to push through a path that kept disappearing. He'd lost his way, and no matter which direction he turned, it wasn't to be found again. His arms ached as he pushed his way through unrelenting foliage. Where was his machete? He turned and tried another way, but the result was the same. He was lost, hopelessly lost. In his exhaustion he collapsed on a fallen tree and stilled himself. *God, where are you? I can't find my way.*

After what seemed like an eternity, the earth stopped shaking and a seasonal downpour began, soaking him to the skin. Finally, a cool breeze found its way through the dense vegetation. When next he looked, the path opened up before him and then began to fade away as a bright light hit his eyes.

The light resolved into the face of a woman. It was Mary speaking to him, only this time he understood.

"William? Can you hear me? Wake up now." The beautiful melody of her voice had an insistent undertone.

His lips felt dry. They cracked and tore as he tried to speak. A slightly salty drop of blood seeped into the corner of his mouth. It was quickly replaced by the metal rim of a cup held for him as her arm snaked under him and lifted him upward.

"Drink something. Slowly. You are dehydrated, but too much too fast will make you sick."

"I think I already am." He croaked. "Sick, that is."

Mary laughed and said, "Drink, funny man."

He took a few tentative sips and the dryness of his mouth and throat eased.

Too soon Mary took away the cup and eased him back toward the pillow. "More in a few minutes. Let's be sure you can keep the water down."

"What day?" The words rasped out of his throat.

"If you're asking how long you've been cycling through the chills, fever and sweats, the answer is seven days. Your fever broke early this morning.

"Seven days?"

"Yes, and you're quite lucky to be alive. Here," she said a few minutes after he drank. She held out a thermometer. "Put this under your tongue so I can see if your fever has truly broken."

William took the glass rod and put it under his tongue as instructed. There were many questions he wanted to ask. He wondered if the work had continued on the compound, but even as he did, he caught the sing-song cadence of the work crew in the distance outside the window.

He was both relieved and worried. Relieved that work progressed with the rainy season only a couple of months away, but worried that it wouldn't be done right.

He thought of his plan, his timetable and immediately felt foolish. Malaria had proven his planning useless. He watched Mary as she fussed with his covers and folded a red blanket lying in the room's one chair. Who had slept there watching? Had Mary? She certainly appeared tired, and her face had a slightly pinched look.

As she returned to his bedside, he felt a heat rising up his neck. Not fever this time. Embarrassment. He hadn't wanted this woman anywhere near the compound. Now she'd saved his life. She made a habit of saving lives. If things had gone according to his plan, he would be dead right now.

Mary reached out and gently pulled the thermometer from his mouth. She held the rod to eye level and twisted it back and forth until she saw what she needed. Only then did her face relax. Her eyes reflected her relief as she said, "Normal. I think we can safely say you're on the mend. Hannabo will be in to tend to your needs soon. The dear man nearly exhausted himself making sure the work on the compound continued and then sat with you to spell me through the night."

Mary offered him more water before leaving the room. He lay back and listened to her movements in the other room, wondering if she ever sat still. She reminded him of a tiny hummingbird he'd once observed flitting from bush to bush, always in motion. Like the hummingbird, she'd captured his attention. Too often his thoughts wandered to her when he should have been concentrating on his plan to advance the Kingdom of God.

If he wasn't careful, she would distract him just like the hummingbird of yore. The end result of that had been a switching from his aunt when he failed to get his chores done. Now he gave himself a mental switching and put thoughts of the beautiful, busy doctor aside. He had to stay focused on the plan. He was grateful she'd saved his life, but he knew better than to get attached. It was only a matter of time before he received an answer from the Mission Board and the women found themselves leaving the dangerous interior for a safer posting.

He heard a door open and close in the other room and

then the low murmur of voices. A few seconds later, Hannabo strode into the room and his face split into a broad grin. "Nana Pastor is awake. God worked in a mighty way and saved you."

William immediately cheered at the sight of Hannabo. Hannabo was the living legacy of his uncle's work, proof a heart could be turned from the darkness of superstition and witchcraft of the bush. To make more converts like Hannabo, he would need to focus on his plan, not on the beautiful doctor. God's plan had used her to save his life, but now that he'd survived the first bout of malaria, the Mission Board's policy no longer bound him. He could man the station alone if need be. A physician was a bonus any of the stations near the coast or in the capital at Monrovia would rejoice to receive.

"Yes, I am grateful our Lord saw fit to spare my life."

"The Mammy Doctor, her medicine was strong. First she cured the evil of the sasswood and now the shaking sickness. Father God made her a powerful healer."

"Yes, well, God uses the science of man to save the body. Still," he admonished, "it is God who does the healing. It is in his hands whether we live or die."

Hannabo looked puzzled, but before he launched back into the doctor's praises, William asked the question on his mind. "The building, how is it coming?"

"The chapel is almost finished and the school walls are built and wait only on the thatching."

"I need to get out of this bed. There is so much to do." William struggled to sit up, but even his elbows refused to cooperate in lifting him.

Hannabo shook his head. "You must rest. The work will get done while you heal."

"I guess it must. I am weaker than I thought."

Hannabo reached for the metal cup with water and

easily lifted William up enough to drink. "Mammy doctor says you must drink, eat and rest. We will keep the men working."

"We? Who is helping you?"

"Mammy Doctor kept the men working. They wanted to stop and see if you would live so they would get paid." Hannabo laughed. "She told them in a loud voice they must work or when you were well, you would be displeased and then they would not get paid."

"They are taking orders from a woman? How can that be?"

"They are all a little afraid of her medicine and so they worked harder than ever before."

William felt his tongue cleave to the roof of his mouth. She was taking charge of his compound? And the men obeyed her? Hannabo seemed unaware of his distress and continued to speak.

"Without Mammy Doctor, we could not have continued. The workers were about to disappear back into the bush but she stopped them. Because of her powerful medicine they listened."

William finally found the hinge on his tongue. "Her medicine? Do they believe she is a devilman?"

"Of course, how else could she cure the sasswood or a white man of bad shaking sickness?" Hannabo pressed on. "Even though I explained it was the Father God, they know only their magic and believe that among the white man, maybe a woman can be a powerful devilman."

Apprehension grew like a mushroom on the damp jungle floor. This belief in a female devilman could undermine all he was doing. How could the Gospel compete if they believed he used magic as part of his mission? It sent the wrong message. He would have to nip this in the bud before it could do any more damage. All the more reason to get her out of here quickly. He had been right to fear having her here. He was only wrong as to why he should have feared. It wasn't just a danger to her, but to men's souls.

"Hannabo, you must continue to correct them in this belief. I will speak to Dr. O'Hara about this and get her to do the same."

Hannabo shrugged. "I will, but they do not understand the One God. Their beliefs are strong. Devilmen have a strong place from when we are born."

"You believed, Hannabo. They can too. If we continue to preach the Word, they will believe."

"But Nana Pastor, even I did not believe until Nana Joseph and Mammy Ruth. It was how they died that made me see. Will you too die that others may see?"

William felt the cold sobering of reality on his religious fervor. Would he? He'd always known it was a possibility. He carefully considered his answer. "The Father sent his Son, Jesus, to die for all of us so our sins may be forgiven. Many who believe have died for their faith since then. If He requires that of me, I hope to follow His example."

Hannabo nodded seriously, content with William's answer. "I will go now and check on the work."

William contemplated what Hannabo had asked. Would God require that of him? To become a martyr was not what he'd envisioned. He had a plan and it included many converts for the Kingdom of God. He'd focused only on his plan, yet God seemed to be altering it daily. First, Alice was taken by malaria, then he lost a year of ministry because of the difficulty booking passage with the Kaiser's attacks on shipping. Next he was sent not one, but two women—one of whom had saved his life but now endangered his very mission by the appearance of a power the tribesmen didn't understand. Nothing seemed to be going according to plan. Especially not his vow to never be responsible for another woman's life in the bush.

He might not know what God would ultimately require of him, but one thing was clear. The sooner he was out of this bed and back in charge, the better it would be. He would renew his appeal to the Mission Board as soon as another caravan delivered supplies and could take mail back to the coast. Better yet, he would try once more to convince Mary and Clara to return with them. A doctor was a luxury few missions ever received. Hopefully it was just a matter of time before her replacement arrived, physician or not.

Chapter Thirteen

Mary watched the workers come to a halt as she approached. When would she remember to wear a hat? Red hair was a mighty distraction. She'd put it up in as neat of a bun as the humidity would allow, but the color acted like a beacon for attention. The men stared until she got closer and then averted their eyes.

She surveyed the growing compound while the sun seared her cotton shirtwaist and the heavy skirt she wore left her with an unpleasant stickiness. Normal for here, but would she ever get used to the heat? The fabled rainy season said to start in May sounded like a welcome relief.

All the more reason for the work on the compound to at least get the buildings dried in before the rains started and made things twice as hard to accomplish. It was only the end of January, but three more months didn't look nearly long enough when they made each board one at a time.

Since she'd had a talk with the workers while Hannabo translated, things were back on track. She'd been surprised they'd listened to her, but didn't know what else to do when Hannabo told her they all feared William's death and that they wouldn't be paid as promised. Apparently all it took was a little reassurance and a daily walk or two around the compound to make sure the work continued.

Repairs were finished on the main house and today the thatched roof was going up on the chapel. Next, the school, and she hoped William would be well enough by that time to take over the supervision, or at least direct what needed to be done.

If he was the typical male patient, he would want to be out of bed and back at work way too soon for his body's needs. She was just as anxious, but it wouldn't do for him to relapse. Still, the appeal of being able to confine herself to building a medical practice was high.

Between caring for William and keeping the work on track with Hannabo's help, she'd had little time to run her clinic. With William out of danger her priorities would change. Clara's vast experience as an aide in the Great War proved invaluable with unpacking and organizing the medical supplies they'd brought. But soon enough Clara would have her own duties as she began a school for the children in the area.

She itched for her first new patient here at Nynabo other than Clara and William. She'd yet to see the local village despite its proximity. Maybe next week she could get Anaya and Hannabo to take her for her first meeting with the local women.

If she could get William's approval. Hmm. Maybe she should go before he was strong enough to object. No. The one thing she'd learned in the jungle was her depth of ignorance of bush ways. She'd do this the right way and hope to avoid any trouble. Enough with making avoidable mistakes. Really it was no different than learning medicine from hostile professors. Tutelage under a scornful man was survivable, bush mistakes might not be. The only difference here was she'd started to secretly long for the approval of the teacher. And that was a weakness she'd carry to her grave before revealing.

Jabo waved at her from behind the mounds of leaf stalks intended to become the roof of the chapel. His wave signaled a desire to talk to her. Every time she set foot out the door, the men sought her approval or wanted her direction in their work, especially Jabo. As if they were concerned she wouldn't be happy. Sweet of them, but the work all met standards as far as she could tell.

She went to see what Jabo needed. As she reached Jabo's side, she was dwarfed in comparison to the towering materials. Jabo pointed at the pile with some pride. Ah, approval was what he wanted. Approval and recognition. "Jabo, this is marvelous. I am so proud of how you've kept the work going while Hannabo helped me tend the pastor."

Jabo's smile gleamed. "Mammy Doctor will have new chapel. Whole compound will be done soon."

"Wonderful. Pastor Mayweather will be so pleased when he is well enough to come and see what you have accomplished."

"Yes, yes, but is Mammy Doctor happy?"

"Of course. I am very happy, Jabo."

Jabo's smile grew and rivaled the width of his face. "Good. Good." He spoke in Kru to the gathered men and they too broke out in smiles.

She smiled in return and said, "Jabo, I need to tend to the pastor. Please continue and I'll check again before dinner."

Jabo's head bounced in nods and he turned to the workers and shouted orders. She might not understand the language, but the urgent, ordering tone came through loud and clear. Men scurried back to work and she headed for the infirmary.

* * *

The clinic bed took on prison status the third day William was conscious. His own body held the key to the cell and refused to turn the lock. His legs wobbled when he was assisted to the outhouse by Hannabo or even sitting in the chair beside the bed. Mary just smiled every time he asked when he might be well enough to go back to work. Her answer always—as soon as your body tells me you're ready. Despite the frustrating end to each of her visits, he listened for the sound of her footsteps approaching with longing. Illness was making him soft.

Even using the time for prayer or study failed to occupy his mind completely. By the time he obtained parole, he'd have enough sermons to fill a theological library. Or he'd go crazy listening to the work outside and not being able to supervise.

Today, he'd try for a little variety and resume Hannabo's reading lessons. Maybe his mind would stay sufficiently distracted to pass the time. Perhaps afterward he'd convince Hannabo to help him walk outside and allow him to check the progress. If his doctor allowed.

Footsteps too heavy to be the petite physician sounded on the front porch. Even with his return to the village, Hannabo kept his new boots on constantly, a status among his unshod tribe. Hannabo's friendly face peered through the doorway. When he saw William awake, he smiled broadly.

William motioned him into the room. Hannabo carried his own Bible, a gift from Karl Jansen after his conversion. Hannabo's determination to learn the Word shone through his every action.

He pulled up a chair to the bedside. "Nana Pastor is well today?"

"I'm feeling much better. Now if only my strength would return."

"Strength will come back to you. God has been good to give you continued life. He will also give you strength."

God was also good to give him gentle reminders and encouragement through this convert who barely knew His Word yet. What did it say about his own faith that he needed the words of a newly converted bushman to give him a godly perspective? "That he will, Hannabo. Now, shall we start back in Romans eight? I believe that's where we left off."

As instructed, Hannabo read aloud, halting frequently with the unfamiliar words and concepts. The distinction between the tribal concepts of ghosts and spirits and the Holy Spirit evoked a long discussion. In the end Hannabo grasped the difference. In the end, explaining spirits proved less challenging than dealing with Romans 8:28.

Hannabo read the passage aloud. "And we know that all things work together for good to them that love God, to them who are the called according to his purpose."

"How can this be, Nana Pastor?" Hannabo looked at him quizzically. "There is much evil in the world. How can God use all things, even evil things, and make them good?"

"Sometimes it's the effect of what happens and how we grow to trust Him, or how change comes about causing other choices we may not have made in our lives."

"So, if you are a Christian man, everything works together for good, even the bad things in your life?"

"True."

"So even when Nana Joseph and Mammy Ruth were killed, their deaths were a good thing?"

Pain slammed him in the chest and his breath caught. Was it still a good thing? Did he believe, or did his faith draw a line that God had crossed in allowing Uncle Joseph and Aunt Ruth's deaths? Thoughts swarmed and doubt rose as he struggled for an acceptable answer for this young Christian. And an acceptable answer for himself. The words in front of him blurred and he broke out in a cold sweat.

"Nana Pastor, are you all right? Should I get Mammy Doctor?"

William looked up into the wide-eyed concern of Hannabo. "No. No need to get Dr. O'Hara. I'm all right. It's just the sadness I feel when I think of Joseph and Ruth."

"I am sorry for reminding you of this grief. But are they not in Heaven now, free of pain?"

"Yes, they are. I am sad because I miss seeing them, talking to them."

Hannabo took the Bible from him and sat it on the bedside table. He pulled out the pillows that propped William into a sitting position. "You should rest now."

William laid down and felt the exhaustion from deep in his bones. "Thank you, Hannabo."

"I will return later and see to your needs." Hannabo left with his Bible in hand.

William expected a discreet check from Mary shortly. Hannabo would no doubt tell her of his episode. The man's loyalty shifted in favor of the doctor where matters of health were concerned. At least he hoped it was the only area.

Dr. Mary O'Hara far outstripped him in tangible results. William had failed to produce an answer to a basic theological question. Or a single new convert.

The answers had seemed simple as a newly called preacher back in upstate New York. Nothing like the bush to help convert even a Christian pastor to a higher faith. God's Word challenged him here on every level. Other men's souls required that he get it right and quickly. He was supposed to be the one with the answers.

He sighed and rolled to his side. Answers were in short supply for him right now. What he had was too many questions of his own, some of which revolved around the beautiful doctor.

Until his talk with Hannabo, he'd been so sure that the doctor needed to leave the interior. Like a lot of things he'd just accepted without closer examination, her success and influence here made him rethink his request for her transfer. Without her, he wouldn't even be alive. He'd opposed her vehemently, and yet she was the critical piece of God's plan to keep him alive. His own vows aside, was this a case of things working to the good as God promised? He was alive to preach the Gospel and see that his uncle's sacrifice was not in vain. And yes, he could now do without her here, but was he wrong about a woman's place in the bush? With her safely confined to Nynabo, a lot of the danger declined. Should he try and rescind his request? Sleep beckoned and answers fled.

Mary returned from her morning stroll around the compound braced for the inevitable argument. Her conscience ultimately wouldn't allow her to go to Nynabo village without William's permission. Her faith might be shaky, but she knew better than to abandon basic moral precepts. Being upfront, even if it brought a refusal, was always better than deception.

William's progress the last week encouraged her. Certainly he was strong enough for a healthy discourse on the subject. She had to do something. There were only so many ways to rearrange supplies, so many times to check on the compound work when she didn't know much about construction, and only so many excuses she could make to continually check on her patient.

Clearly unless she went to the village herself, patients were not going to come to her. Throwing herself back into her work was a vital distraction. Especially when she remembered the smile he'd given her the other day. Of course, any man could be nice to you when he depended on you for his life. Soldiers in Argonne often suffered the same affliction, but all recovered from any romantic interests at discharge. So would William. She just had to make sure she did too.

He probably didn't even realize how nice he'd been to her lately. Illness and dependence worked their own magic, turning men thankful at first and, once they tired of being dependent, ill-tempered. Well, she was about to change his disposition for him a little early. She hoped her repeated request to go to the village wouldn't be the straw that broke their newfound peace. After all, she'd diligently inquired and learned from Anaya, and with her as a guide, Mary could handle a trip to Nynabo. It was no different than a lot of other firsts, especially a first surgery. You got the experience under your belt and you learned.

Deep breath, professional face. Smooth skirts. The heat of a blush traced across her cheeks. Other women wore skirts. Why shouldn't she? A feminine tactic and one she was above at this point. So why did her hands also go to her hair before she entered his room? Why did part of her hope to hear a compliment or see those dimples when he smiled?

She snorted. Couldn't help it. She had let his smiles become too important.

She knocked on the doorpost. A hanging cloth separated the rooms. Doors were a luxury for later.

"Come in."

He sounded stronger this morning. She stepped into the room and found Hannabo with a razor and water, the stubble gone from hollowed-out cheekbones. She'd thought to distract William with her feminine appearance. Instead she was caught by his clean-shaven visage and the intense brown eyes that once again burned with life instead of fever. Such a relief.

Hannabo broke into a grin as he gathered the shaving equipment and headed out of the room. "Morning, Mammy Doctor." He addressed a comment to the pastor in Kru dialect and left.

"What did he say? It's not like Hannabo to abandon using the English pidgin in front of me."

William wiped his face with a towel and looked amused.

Mary's heart skipped at the sight of those long-absent dimples. "What? Is this going to be one of those mysterious men things? Some secret you won't let me in on?"

"Well, if you must know, Hannabo speculates you'd bring many oxen to your father from a suitor. I'd guess the change in attire prompted him to comment on your beauty."

Her beauty? Did the pastor see her as beautiful, too? "Seems I'm not the only one concerned with appearance today. You've had a shave. You must be feeling better."

"Quite. And I've managed to walk around the room several times." He must have noticed her frown. "With Hannabo's help, of course. My strength is returning."

"Wonderful. You'll be back to normal in no time. Just don't push yourself too far too quickly or you'll relapse."

"I can't tell you how much I want to be out of this bed, out of this room and back to work."

"Work is a worthy goal. Keep walking with Hannabo's

help. Extend it a little each day, but listen to your body's needs. Rest is still important."

"I have a request, one that should meet your requirements."

Mary moved close to him and picked up his wrist. Pulse normal. "I too have a request. First, let me listen to your lungs and heart, see how you're doing today." She placed her stethoscope on his chest.

"I was…"

"Sssh. I can't hear with you talking." She moved the bell piece to listen to the other side. Lungs were clear. Did his pulse just jump? Or was that her own pulse confusing her judgment?

Finished, she stepped back to a safer emotional distance. "Everything seems normal."

"You have a request for me, Doctor O'Hara?"

"Mine will wait, what did you want? If it's to be released back to work, I'll have to say no. It's still too soon."

He smiled wryly and cocked one eyebrow. "No, even I can tell that for myself. However, taking strolls in the compound and placing a chair at the worksites for short intervals through the day would keep my sanity while I recover."

"An argument I can well understand. You are at the point in healing where the confinement will wear on you."

"So, can I try this? With Hannabo's help, of course."

"I'll approve. Twice a day, but you must promise to keep to short intervals and not exhaust yourself."

Dimples deepened into ravines and his eyes lit up with excitement. "Of course. Can I start today?"

Mary laughed and sat on the edge of his bed. "Yes, you can, but if I didn't know better, I'd think you hadn't been enjoying my hospitality here at the clinic."

His eyes grew serious and he reached out to clasp her

hand. "I am very grateful for your care, Dr. O'Hara. And very much aware that you saved my life."

Warmth suffused her body. A swelling of feelings blossomed at the point of his touch. She willed him to keep holding her hand, not wanting the feelings to end. The spell broke when he asked, "So what is this request of yours? How may I accommodate you?"

The warmth fled and a nervous zing vibrated in her belly. Conscious of her impropriety, she pulled her hands free and stood up. "It seems we have the same problem, Pastor Mayweather. We are both hindered from our work. In the weeks we've been here, you and Clara have been my only patients. It's clear the women and children of the village won't come to me at first, so I desire to go to them."

Dimples disappeared and the fire in his eyes banked and grew cold.

"Please listen. I've studied and learned from Anaya, Hannabo, and even from Jabo. I can do this."

"Absolutely not. I agreed to allow you to treat the women and children who come here."

"What women and children? So far only Anaya comes from the village. My skills aren't to be wasted on the occasional burn."

"Eventually they will come. Once the compound is finished, we will hold services. We'll actively recruit students for the school. The patients will be a natural outpouring of the process."

"My clinic is ready now. I'm idle, an uncomfortable state that I thought you of all people would understand. Don't preachers always say idle hands are the devil's workshop?"

He sat up straighter, putting sorely won energy into his posture as he hammered home his point. "First of all, the Bible says no such thing. Second, and most important, if it were Biblical, you'd be the exception. Trouble shows up every time you take action. Idleness is the safest state for you."

Mary lost all sense of restraint. She didn't care if the whole compound heard them. "Hands that just a few minutes ago you were happy to hold and laud their skill."

"Should I remind you of the myriad of troubles you've brought upon us? I'd think a woman of your intelligence would have a little common sense and be able to understand these limitations are for your safety."

"Limitations? That's what you call completely impeding me from using my skills to help the natives? I may have a lot to learn about the bush, but I won't learn anything in this little bubble of confinement."

"Neither will you bring trouble down on us again. No. I absolutely forbid it. You are not to leave the compound."

Mary lost all semblance of a reasonable tone. Everything she'd envisioned, her ability to atone for her brother's loss, this man held hostage. "You forbid it? How dare you? I answer to the Mission Board, not to you. My mission is to establish a clinic, a mission your stubbornness is hindering me from completing."

He matched her strident tone. "My stubbornness, as you put it, is keeping you alive in a country of which you know too little."

"I knew enough to keep you alive. All your knowledge of this country was pretty useless when you lay shaking in this bed."

Mary found her right arm in a vise-like grip. Clara had entered without her hearing her approach, a testament to their volume.

Clara wasted no time making her opinion clear. "In the name of all that's holy, what do the two of you think you're doing?"

Clara's uncharacteristic glare stopped any answer Mary might have made. "You, Dr. Mary, step out of the room and get hold of your temper."

Mary found herself steered out of the room. "I'll deal with you, Dr. Mary, after you settle down. Go take a walk or something while I talk to that one in there." Clara turned back to the pastor's room and Mary shook herself out of her shock.

Why did William bring out the worst in her? Feminine wiles and a sweet disposition were her plan. She'd even prayed God would soften the man's heart. Fat lot of good that did.

She'd better take a walk. Otherwise she'd be right back in there giving William a piece of her mind. There had to be a way to make him see reason, but she wouldn't do it by yelling.

She heard the low, hissed tones of an angry Clara and decided absence was the safest course. She'd walk the compound, find a shady spot and ruminate alone. She needed the time a walk would give her to get her perspective back.

If she was lucky, the relentless sun would burn out her addled thoughts. She'd put a skirt on for a man who rejected her skills, hoping to win him over. She'd made sure her hair was just right, and now she'd allowed her restless impatience, her panic over not being able to do some real good, to create conflict. What else could she be if not addled? The only thing she was sure of was the other possibility was unthinkable. She was emphatically not attracted to a man as tradition-bound as William Mayweather.

Chapter Fourteen

William's shock at how quickly he and Mary escalated into a shouting match was matched by his chagrin at being scolded by the normally mild-mannered widow.

"Have you ever stopped to ask yourself why your temper is such a problem around Dr. Mary?" Clara asked.

At least she wasn't scolding him anymore. She gave a tongue lashing that would have made his Aunt Ruth proud. Last time he'd felt that uncomfortable was when he was twelve and his aunt called him out on his errant behavior since his parents' deaths. Like Clara, she'd given him plenty of time to work things out on his own first, but with mercy-laden love set him back down like a lad in knee pants when he'd gone too far.

"In truth, the woman frustrates me like none other. I suppose it is my constant worry for her safety that riles me so. Whatever the case, I am ashamed I let it get so out of hand as to have an effect on the workers in the compound."

"As well you should be. When I returned from the kitchen, I saw grown men stopped in their tracks, listening to the commotion you two caused."

"I have no excuse. I'll pray and seek God for how to

make this right with them." Shame burned in him. One thing for Mary to endanger herself and the mission. Now his reaction to her endangered his witness as a messenger of the Gospel.

"Aren't you forgetting something?" Clara, schoolteacher that she was, waited while he searched hopelessly for the correct answer in an unstudied subject.

Her silence was ruthless. He gave up. "I'm not sure what you mean." He tried for as much meekness as possible.

Clara's shoulders raised and lowered with her exaggerated deep breath while she lifted eyes to heaven seeking some divine intervention. When next she fixed her gaze on him, it was with all the patience one has for a slow pupil. A very slow pupil.

"I'm talking about Dr. Mary. What are you going to do to make it right with her?"

How did she remain so still and yet imply an impatiently tapping foot? "Of course. I should apologize for my temper."

The woman actually snorted at him. "I meant what are you going to do so she is able to fulfill her mission here at Nynabo. You aren't the only one with a calling, you know. You're preventing her from doing the work God has called her to do."

Sparks flared in his banked fire of anger. He tamped them down. "Mrs. Smith, you've experienced for yourself the problems Dr. O'Hara's ignorance of the bush caused. I cannot let her run around willy-nilly and bring havoc on herself and us all."

"No, but you could instruct her now, and then take her to the village once you're well. It's not right for you to hinder her service here. I strongly doubt you came to the bush already knowing everything there was to know, now did you?"

"Of course not, but I'm a man and better..."

"Just stop right there. You have no idea what Mary O'Hara endured before now or what she is made of. I watched her deal with the horrors of the Great War, work never-ending shifts because casualties don't observe a regular workday, and she did it all under the watchful eye of male physicians who taunted her abilities and tried to relegate her to lesser duties at every step."

She paused, choked up. When she continued, Clara's eyes glistened with angry tears, her voice low but emphatic. William felt like the moneychangers in the temple when Jesus overturned their tables and called them on their unrighteousness. She knew how to be angry and sin not. *Lord, forgive me for my angry display with Mary.*

"God called Mary to medicine, something she's had to fight for every step of the way. I watched her nearly break with grief when her own brother died in that last vicious battle at Argonne Forest and couldn't be saved."

"She lost her brother? I...I didn't know. What happened?"

Clara blinked. "I've said too much. Argonne is her story to tell. But I will say this. She is a strong woman, a dedicated doctor, and the sooner you treat her like God made her, the better for all of us."

"You're right. I am ashamed of the way I've acted."

"Which brings us back to my original question, Pastor Mayweather."

"Your original question?"

"Have you ever stopped to ask yourself why your temper flares around our dear doctor?"

"I thought we'd covered that. I fear for her safety, the safety of the whole compound."

Clara's barking laugh came, straight from the belly. "And is that why you think such sparks fly between you and Dr. Mary?"

He felt like a stupid pupil whose times tables were all wrong. His tongue found no answer from his brain and sat there immobile, useless. Unable to deny her next words.

"No one gets that upset unless they care for someone. The sooner you admit that fact and stop acting like she's your enemy, the sooner we'll all have peace around here." Clara turned to leave. "You think on what I said. I've got to go talk to the other half of this temper tantrum."

With a swish of her skirts, Clara Smith left the room and left his mind in a quandary. Did he care about Mary O'Hara? He'd avoided her, protected her, yelled at her, bemoaned her very presence, but surely he'd protected himself from inappropriate feelings. Hadn't he?

Clara read too much into things. Worry and thoughts of sending both women packing as soon as possible didn't qualify as any romantic interest. He couldn't possibly have strong feelings for a woman he was sending far away. No. He couldn't.

Mary's feet took her straight to the back of the compound. She walked past startled workmen who held their tools in silence and watched her passing. She didn't have it in her to stop and admire their work or give encouragement. Discouragement weighed heavily on her spirit.

All of those men heard her argument with William. William, try as she might, he remained William to her after nursing him back to life, even though she wanted him to stay Pastor Mayweather and at arm's length. How could she ask people to trust her medical judgment if she couldn't control her temper? Would they be afraid to come to her after this? Some of the men looked fearful.

She sat on a log under the large cottonwood beside Alice Mayweather's grave. No doubt she'd been the perfect help here at the compound. But feeling as he did about endangering women in the bush, what was so special about his Alice that he brought her here?

She probably didn't have a temper that exploded all over the compound, frightening grown men and provoking her husband to wrath. Mary knew she was unsuited to be a missionary wife. Not that anyone was asking her to be one.

She sorely lacked the temperament necessary. What did William say when he first met her? Oh, yes, in a superior tone he'd judged her instantly as "so unsuitable for the position." A phrase oft repeated since she'd first tried to enter medical school. A phrase reiterated in France when she fought to do something besides sit at a male surgeon's side relegated only to anesthesia. A phrase defying all her courage to stand against it.

Absently she brushed off the beetle scurrying across the lap of her skirts. Her pathetic foray into acting like a traditional woman and dressing the part couldn't disguise what she really was underneath the outer dressing. An unholy anomaly of a woman in a position requiring more faith and less temper than she possessed. What was she thinking when she decided the Liberian jungle would be a refuge, a place to do some good in the world?

She closed her eyes. *Lord, I even foolishly thought this was a place I wouldn't be judged. Was it only the pain of Jeremy's death, my father's angry letter disowning me for the loss of his only son that made this decision for me? Do I even belong here?*

No heavenly voice rolled back clouds and answered her. Instead she heard footsteps and the unmistakable swish of a skirt.

Opening her eyes, she saw Clara coming toward her, looking less like the wrath of God than in their earlier encounter. "I wondered where you'd gotten to, Dr. Mary. Praying, I see."

"Yes, but I've received no heavenly guidance. Is God even hearing my prayers?" Mary braced herself for the rebuke to come, one she deserved.

A voice gentler than she'd expected replied, "Of course He hears you, Mary." Clara brushed off the insects and debris and sat beside her. "The question is, are you listening, believing he'll answer?"

"I try. But no, I'm not really believing. The last prayers I cried out from the depths of belief weren't answered. The one I thought was answered, what to do with my life after the Armistice, appears to be a mistake on my part." She stared at the scuff marks on the toes of her boots as she waited for the coming rebuke.

"Lift up your chin, my girl. Look at me."

The silence following pulled her into obedience. Clara's concern etched itself all over her face. No trace of rebuke was there.

"You are still stuck in your grief, Dr. Mary. Until you forgive God for Jeremy's death, you'll not move on from the pain or even be able to hear God's voice clearly. You'll miss what he has for you in this place or any other."

The pressure of building tears and unvented sobs pressed out, seeking release. Clara's arm around her shoulder broke the dam that held them back.

Clara pulled her in tight and held her while she sobbed. "There now. Let it out. All of it."

Mary's sobs wrenched her apart while Clara held her together. An eternity later, they stopped and she gradually became aware of the damp cotton where her cheek lay. She pulled herself away with a shuddering breath and apologized. "I've gotten you all wet."

"About time. Emotions we lock up have a way of leaking out anyways."

Mary accepted the kerchief Clara produced from her pocket, drying the trails down her cheeks. "Is that what I've been doing? Leaking out with my temper?"

Clara smiled. "I don't think that's the only reason you lock horns with the good pastor. Mostly I think your buried grief turned to anger at God."

Desperation flared. "But how can I not be angry? When I needed Him most, He didn't answer."

Clara shook her head slowly. "No, my girl. He didn't give the answer you wanted. God always answers, He just doesn't always follow our plans."

"Meaning it was God's plan for Jeremy to die a horrible death on my operating table?"

"God knew from before Jeremy's birth exactly what his number of days was. Jeremy made a choice to enlist. His death brought you to the choice to come here. It may not have been God's desire for Jeremy to die there, but the Father still worked everything to His good for the ones you will help here."

"Why couldn't God simply have guided me some other way to come to Nynabo?"

"I don't know, Mary. I do know God used your grief and your father's to guide you here. Without Jeremy's sacrifice, you'd be sitting in some cozy parlor worlds away from here."

Mary shuddered. "Ugh. No parlors please. But I'd have been back in the tenements where at least I would be doing some good. William has no intention of letting me practice medicine here."

"Aah, William is it now?"

"I meant Pastor Mayweather. Don't be making anything of a mere slip of the tongue, Clara. Formality is hard to maintain in these circumstances."

"The two of you can both keep lying to yourselves that way, but it's obvious to anyone with eyes in their head how you both feel about one another."

Panic threaded through Mary. She stood before Clara could continue. "It's an effect of the close quarters and constant care he's needed. There is no way I could have a life with a hidebound traditionalist like Pastor Mayweather."

Clara shook her head and stood. "Well, I'll leave you to that little bit of self-deception then. But I'm telling you God often does many things at the same time. It may be He brought you here for more than the practice of medicine."

"That's crazy. Pastor Mayweather won't even let me practice medicine except for when he's flat on his back and has no choice."

Clara dropped her chin and raised her eyebrows in silence.

"It won't ever work, Clara." Further silence only raised Mary's panicked feelings. To believe God would want her bound to a man who opposed the very heart of her, her medicine. Unthinkable. There was only one solution she saw. "In fact, I'm going to tell him now I've changed my mind about being in Nynabo. I should never have come into the jungle and expected anything to be different than it is anywhere else. When the next caravan can be arranged, I'll return to Newaka until a new posting can be found. One without a thoroughly intractable man at the helm."

Mary turned and left an astonished Clara standing under the cottonwood. Maybe leaving was an impulsive thought, but another posting would solve the impasse with William. No William to lord it over her, no impasse. She'd find a different post. A different country if need be.

Her thoughts drove her toward the clinic. Better to get it over with now. The sooner she left Nynabo, the happier they would all be.

Mary rounded the corner of the main house and saw a pale William sitting in a chair near the chapel work area speaking with Jabo. No, arguing. Hannabo stood stoically. The rest of the men were gone and there were hours left in the work day. What was going on?

All eyes turned at her approach. Jabo met her gaze and then turned back and said something to Hannabo in their native tongue before turning away and leaving.

What was the problem? Jabo's behavior was out of character. He acted afraid. But of what? The look on William's face was one of total defeat.

She stopped beside William's chair. "What's going on here? Where did all the men go? And Jabo looked like he'd seen a ghost before he ran off."

William hung his head and sat in silence. Would no one answer her? "Hannabo, what happened here?"

Hannabo looked to William who waved his hand and said, "Go on. Tell her."

"Jabo and the other men have left. They are afraid."

"Afraid of what?"

"They say Nana Pastor has angered you and it is not safe for them to stay."

"Why, that's silly. We argued, but why would they think it wasn't safe to be here?"

William started to rise and Hannabo stepped closer and took his arm to help. William said, "Because of you, Dr. O'Hara. The men believe I angered a powerful devilwoman and that it is unsafe to stay and be caught up in the curse they expect you to place on me."

"The curse? No, no, Hannabo, go explain to them. I'm not a devilwoman. I won't be cursing anyone." Suddenly it all made sense, the men's deference, constantly seeking her approval. Fear drove them. Fear of her supposed magic.

"It would be of little use for Hannabo to try. Congratulations, Dr. O'Hara. You've finally done it."

"Done what?"

"Singlehandedly shut down ministry to the Kru people here at Nynabo."

Chapter Fifteen

He was stuck with her. Again. Never mind he'd been considering allowing her to stay before this fiasco. But now... Now he couldn't run the station without the women, or at least without Mary.

William paced the confines of his home, glad to be out of the infirmary and away from the ever present Mary and all the emotions she stirred in him. He still tired easily, but only time would completely remedy that problem.

Time, however, wouldn't remedy the problem of Mary. He couldn't believe he'd debated rescinding his letter to the Board. He wished a replacement had arrived sooner. Then he wouldn't be stuck in negotiations with the men in the village to return to work. Men who feared a curse at the displeasure of Mary and who refused to return unless Nana Doctor was happy.

He'd made two trips to the village, the first in a hammock chair because of his weakness. The second time he'd walked, hoping to show he was alive, well and not cursed. Both visits met with skepticism and no volunteers to work at the mission.

With rains only a few short months out, he desperately needed to get the buildings finished. But who was he kidding? The buildings would remain empty if he couldn't convince the villagers there was no danger. How did you convince men who'd lived their whole lives around the teachings of the bush school? Who'd been indoctrinated from an early age in witchcraft, devilmen and all the animistic beliefs of their country.

Only one way out of this mess. Take Mary to the village. Let them see for themselves their Nana Doctor wasn't angry with him and no curses would be forthcoming. If that didn't solve the problem, he might as well pack up and go home. He'd have no ministry here.

"Nana Pastor, your meal is ready."

William startled. He hadn't heard Hannabo enter. Hannabo's cooking alone was enough reason to pursue his idea. Losing Anaya's cooking had been a powerful blow to his stomach. Hannabo's limited repertoire manifested as spicy or indistinguishable food.

"Thank you, Hannabo. Just put it on the table."

"You were deep in thought."

"Yes. I may have an answer to our problem."

"You can convince the men to come back?"

"Yes, I was thinking if I took Dr. O'Hara to the village, then the men would see for themselves she is happy and isn't placing curses."

"This idea might work, but for one problem."

"You don't think the village will feel better after they see her?"

"No, they will be very happy. The problem is how to make Mammy Doctor happy with you, Nana Pastor."

"Well, my friend. We have to convince Dr. O'Hara she's happy with me."

Hannabo shook his head. "It will be just as one of the miracles in the Bible we read about. That Mammy will take some mighty convincing."

"Yes she will, my friend. She told me last week if I didn't let her go to the village to doctor the people, she would leave on the next caravan back to Newaka."

Hannabo's eyes lit up. "Aaah. So you will let her go to Nynabo and she will stay and be happy with you."

"Exactly. She gets to do what she wants, the men return and the ministry goes forward. I'll accompany her and keep her out of trouble."

"This is a good plan. But one part is not so good."

"What part is that?"

"How are you going to keep Mammy Doctor out of trouble?"

The argument had been worth it. She was finally on her way to the village. William took the lead, for once in a cheerful mood. She'd thought he'd be angry or feel outmaneuvered. For all her understanding of the human body, she'd never understand William Mayweather and his moods.

Cultivated fields spread before her like a welcome mat to the village entrance below. Unlike Nana Bolo's village, where tightly packed conical huts created a claustrophobic maze, this one contained four large open areas, with long rectangular huts, neatly thatched and arranged around their perimeters.

It was too far to make out anything in the village itself, but the fields before her contained women scattered throughout the neat rows. They actively harvested what, from this distance, looked like melons and squash. On the path from where she knew a small river to be, women carried tall, clay jars balanced on their heads.

In contrast, the few men traveling the same direction walked unencumbered. Mary turned to Clara, whose eyes busily took in the sights as well. "Did you notice only the women seem to be carrying loads?"

Clara snorted. "Isn't that the way it always works?"

Mary's laughter joined Clara's exclamation. "Maybe in the medical profession. A lot of those men in the field hospital avoided work they believed beneath them. Nurses carried such a load. But back home, good manners dictate basic courtesy. Is it not polite here for a man to offer help?"

"There's Hannabo. Let's ask." Hannabo responded to Clara's wave and joined them.

Mary pointed to one woman walking in step behind a tribesman with her balanced load. "Why doesn't that man carry the jar for her?"

Hannabo looked at her as if she told the funniest joke. "Men do not do women's work, Mammy Doctor. Women carry the water for drinking, baths, everything."

Mary pressed in, gesturing to the porter behind them. "These men carry my things."

Hannabo giggled at the apparent absurdity. "You are a Mammy."

"But I am a woman."

The commonality was lost on Hannabo. "Men only carry for work. To be paid. A woman of the bush plants and gathers food, carries firewood, gets the water."

"But wouldn't it be polite for a man to help her? Look," Clara pointed at a small group of men talking and laughing together. "Their hands are free and she has a full load."

"No woman of the bush would expect a man to carry for her. She would be beaten if she asked."

Clara's shock probably found its twin on Mary's own face. Hannabo's jovial look went flat, his eyebrows pressed together in question. "Is it not this way in the white bush? Do all Mammies have special status like you?"

Mary thought carefully. Thought about what it took to have achieved her "special status" and how she was still treated by the male medical community. Faces of battered women she'd treated before she'd enlisted with the Red Cross sprang to mind. She shook her head. "No, Hannabo, most Mammies in the white bush do not have special status. The ones who do have fought hard for it."

Hannabo nodded and seemed appeased. "So the white bush is not so different."

She and Clara exchanged glances. Mary broke the silence for them. "No, I guess some things are the same in any bush."

They wound their way down the well-worn path to the village in silent companionship. When the walk leveled off, Mary turned to Clara. At the entrance to the village was a welcoming arch, with a miniature conical hut decorated...were those monkey tails?

Hannabo had gone ahead, so Mary had no one to ask about its significance. As she got closer, she realized it looked like a shrine of some sort.

William and Hannabo waited just ahead, William's foot tapping an impatient rhythm in the dust. In the middle of the dry season, he was a storm cloud brewing. Patience definitely wasn't his main virtue.

They drew near and he started in on her. "Remember what I told you. This tribe may not be as hostile as Nana Bolo's, but that doesn't mean they don't have strict rules and customs. You will be received by the head wife."

"Do any of the women here speak English, or am I going to be left to pantomime?"

"I'll leave Jabo here with you to translate. The head wife will entertain you and Mrs. Smith. Keep things social. Jabo carries your gifts for Mammy Lehbo. Be sure to receive anything she gives you cheerfully."

When he turned his back and departed, Clara looked at her and said, "If you keep rolling your eyes, they're going to get stuck that way."

"Now you sound like my mother. Really, Pastor Mayweather acts like I can't be trusted out of his sight."

"He does know more about the customs here than we do. Remember that, please."

"Well, I'm learning as fast as I can. Maybe if he'd take the time to teach me instead of being upset when I break one of his unwritten rules, I'd not make so many mistakes. Of course, then he wouldn't have anything to complain over."

Jabo approached, cutting off any further discussion. Mary dismissed her irritation and focused on the hope the head wife would like her enough to allow Mary to treat the village women and children.

Jabo gestured. "This way. Mammy Lehbo's hut is this way."

She and Clara followed Jabo to the other side of the village. Other than wandering fowl, Mary noticed few roaming animals. The paths were all clean and no sanitation smells were apparent. The village was in cleaner shape than some of the tenements she'd worked in after medical school.

Mammy Lehbo's hut stood larger and taller than the others nearby, her prominence displayed by its size. Several young girls ran inside the structure at their approach.

A smiling young woman whose eyes roamed over all of Mary and Clara's features unabashedly appeared at the doorway and motioned for them to come inside. Unlike their guest hut at Nana Bolo's village, this one had several windows. At the far end sat a majestic older woman with a colorful red cloth wrapped around her waist and hanging across one shoulder. Each finger was adorned with a ring of some sort, and she sported iron and brass bangles on both arms. Her neat cornrows were partially covered by the same cloth as her dress. Her nose was narrow by tribal standards and her lips full and lush. Her keen brown eyes spoke of the intelligence within. By her sides sat six young girls flanking her. A queen and her court.

Mary waited while Jabo introduced her and Clara. They were offered intricately carved wooden seats. After many polite exchanges, Mammy Lehbo gestured and two of the girls began to serve them each a small rice-filled gourd with peppers and other vegetables dotted throughout. Giggling, one of the girls sat a wooden cup in front of Mary and Clara.

Mary leaned toward Jabo, who sat on the ground beside her sans food and beverage and said, "Tell our hostess thank you. And what are the dish and drink called?"

"The rice gourd is called a calabash. The drink is palm wine."

Mary kept a smile on her face. "Jabo, missionaries can't drink wine. What do I do?"

"No problem. I will tell her you're not allowed."

Mary turned to Clara, who had her cup in hand, sniffing.

"It's fermented, Dr. Mary."

"Jabo says it is palm wine. He is telling Mammy Lehbo now that we can't drink it."

"By the frown on her face, I think he just did."

Jabo turned from talking with their hostess. "Mammy Lehbo is not happy. But she decided not to insist after I told her about your medicine. She wants to see your black bag."

"You did tell her I was a doctor and not a devilwoman, right?"

He shrugged. "I told her, but she does not believe me."

Clara nudged her. "Humor her. Show her the items in your bag. You want to get permission to treat patients first. You can argue the other later."

Pragmatic but true. Mary reached for the bag sitting at her feet and pulled out her stethoscope, a Ford Bell model. She inserted the tips and rose. "Jabo, ask if I can listen to her heart."

At the translation, Mammy Lehbo paled and shook her head violently.

No further translation necessary. "Jabo, ask her if she would like to listen to mine instead."

By the look on her face, the idea was quite a relief. Mary approached carefully and offered the earpieces to her hostess. Mammy Lehbo took them and put them in her ears, imitating Mary. Mary moved closer and placed the bell on her own chest, finger resting on the top.

She waited. The light in Mammy Lehbo's eyes and the upturned corners of her mouth told Mary the precise moment the heartbeat came through. The earpieces came right out and were offered in turn to all of the women present. They then took turns listening to each other's hearts.

Clara stood beside her. "Do you think you're going to get your equipment back?

"Let's just say that I'm going to leave my blood pressure cuff and its explanation to another time."

"I think we'll need a second meeting to even talk about the school."

"We'll see. Jabo knows his chief's wife. Maybe he can talk to her about the school."

"Oh, looks like Mammy Lehbo is trying to get your attention."

Mary turned to face the stately woman, who retrieved her stethoscope from a reluctant user. The chief's wife held it out to Mary.

"Jabo, thank her for me. And see if she will allow me to examine any of the women or children who are sick today."

Jabo translated and there were nods all around. If the reaction to the stethoscope was any indication, a long clinic day lay ahead. Finally, despite the roadblocks William stationed at every turn, she'd get to practice medicine again.

Chapter Sixteen

William looked up from his preparation of Sunday's sermon. Having invited the chief and his tribe to visit the finished station, he wanted to weigh every word carefully. Normally he preached in small groups at the palaver houses or by a campfire, but he knew the crowd would be larger tomorrow.

Curiosity would bring most of the tribe here to see the finished compound. A good impression would go a long way to having parents send their children to school at the mission. The Gospel imbued to a young generation was easier than correcting a lifetime of false beliefs.

Mary proved to be quite a draw. With Jabo and sometimes Anaya at Mary's side to translate and smooth over any cultural issues, her travels to the village qualified as uneventful on his front. Maybe the good doctor had learned a little restraint. Not to run headlong into trouble.

She involved herself so thoroughly with her patients, she didn't notice those times he watched her. A gentle spirit surrounded her and reassured even the most frightened of little ones. The children loved her. She was the kind of woman who should have a house full of her own. Not a suggestion he'd make for fear of another lecture on his traditional ways. The woman said tradition as if it was a sin of some kind.

He wasn't sure what had interrupted his train of thought. The noise level hadn't risen. In fact, it had dropped. Quiet when he should have been hearing all the final preparations for tomorrow's big day got his attention.

Pushing back his chair from the desk, he went to the window and peered out. A group of workers were gathered at the southern edge of the compound looking expectant. Hannabo was among them. Hannabo looked in his direction, then gestured to another worker and sent him toward William.

The sturdy young man ran toward the main house. William stepped onto the porch to meet him. Eagerness plastered itself all over his face. "Nana Pastor, a caravan. A caravan is coming."

William's breakfast turned to iron in his stomach. "Thank you. I'll be out shortly." He waved the young man on his way. The worker needed no further encouragement. He ran so he wouldn't miss any of the excitement.

Could it be? Now, as things began to work out for the good, had replacements arrived? Replacement for the request he'd failed to rescind. *Please, Lord, let it only be the supplies I ordered before I left Newaka.*

How would things continue if Mary suddenly left now? He wanted to run and see too, but decided a little dignity was in order. He waited until the caravan topped the hill and entered the compound.

Four men came laden with packs. Not a single one of them was a white missionary. William wanted to fall to his knees in gratitude. The villagers would have been upset if Mary left now.

Hannabo quickly went about getting the porters' needs met. Drinking water, rice and fresh fruit were offered.

The supply train's leader stepped over and brought a small pouch to William. *Mail!*

A slight catch pinged his chest. Although no replacements arrived with the small caravan, had the Mission Board answered him about rescinding the women's assignment here? So much had changed since he first wrote that letter.

He took the pouch with some trepidation, wondering at his mixed feelings. Disloyal, that's what he felt. Dr. O'Hara had been instrumental in saving him from death. Because of her, he was still able to complete the call of God on his life. The village children and their mothers loved the woman. She drew a crowd every time she entered the village. Gatherings he'd taken advantage of from time to time to preach the Gospel. Large numbers of converts still lacked, but it was only a matter of time.

But maybe it was for the best. The jungle interior was still a dangerous place, and although he intended to confine her activities to the mission and the Nynabo village where she'd be safer, his actions might not be enough to protect her and Clara overall.

He felt more mercenary than missionary as he contemplated her reaction to being sent home.

He took the oilskin pouch and examined its contents. A letter to him from Karl and Hannah, one from his home church, a newspaper from the capital, two letters for Clara. Nothing from the Mission Board and not a single thing for Dr. O'Hara. He was pretty sure she had family, so why no letter?

When he looked up, both women exited the infirmary and headed toward the supplies. Like kids at Christmas, they looked through some of the packs. Clara found slates, chalk and the few primers they'd been able to get.

Mary's delight at more gauze and other basics was apparent. He joined them, wondering if his favorite tins of meat were included. Native cooking aside, he found a good tin of corned beef kept the homesickness at bay.

"Well, I see you ladies discovered the joys of packages from afar. Mrs. Smith, there are two letters for you."

"Oh, wonderful." She took the letters and studied the return addresses. "My sister and her oldest daughter. They've both sent me news of home. This is better than all the tins of meat put together."

"Well, knowing how you felt about monkey on the trail and now the goat since you got here, that's really saying something."

Mary's back had been turned ever since he mentioned mail. Surely she wasn't immune to a missionary's best salve for homesickness. He hated to say there was nothing, but worse, she seemed to be resigned there wouldn't be anything for her.

"Doctor O'Hara, the mail has neglected you today. Maybe there will be something on the next run.

She never stopped what she was doing, just tossed a remark off her shoulder. "I wasn't expecting any."

He'd have to ask Clara privately why there were no letters from home for Mary. Better yet, why she didn't expect any.

The object of his musings suddenly stood straight with a small tube held triumphantly in her hand. "Hallelujah, my new ointment is here. Now if you'll excuse me, I have a patient in the village who needs this."

He watched her trim figure run to the infirmary and exit, bag in hand. After motioning to Jabo, the two set off down the hill to the village. His gaze held until her flaming locks disappeared from view. She always did forget her pith helmet.

After the packs and the porters had all been sorted out,

William headed back to the main house to read his letters in private. Nothing from the Mission Board, but maybe the letter from Karl and Hannah would have news. He opened an oversized envelope and pulled out two letters. One from Karl and the other… It was his own handwriting, the letter he'd left with Karl to send to the Mission Board. But why had Karl not sent it? Frustration mixed with a strange, unexpected relief. He'd begun to doubt his first hasty reaction to Dr. O'Hara and Mrs. Smith. Recent events had certainly proved their worth. Neither woman had proven too frail for the arduous trip and the daily hard work at the compound. And without Dr. O'Hara he never would have survived to preach the Gospel.

The spidery handwriting of Karl Jansen filled the page with well wishes and news of recent converts and an upcoming evangelistic trip to a village west of Newaka. He raced to the end for an explanation of why Karl had returned this letter to him instead of sending his missive on to the Mission Board.

William, I know your initial distress at being assigned not one, but two women to work beside you in the bush. I do not wish to make light of your feelings, but I am concerned that the loss of your dear Alice profoundly affected your judgment in this area. After our talk and much prayer on my part later, I elected not to send your letter to the Mission Board, but instead I return it to your care. It is my deepest prayer that this missive finds you well and in a different frame of mind regarding your coworkers' suitability for the work they are called by God to do. I hope that the time you have spent together has given you an understanding of their need in this work of God. However, if you have indeed not had a

change of heart, then do as God leads you with your original letter. But, my boy, please pray carefully and thoughtfully before you decide. I feel strongly that both Dr. O'Hara and Mrs. Smith will be strong allies in the work of Christ. Do not lightly put them aside.
Yours in Christ,
Karl Jansen

Shock. That had to be the term. Karl Jansen had never sent the letter. What he thought already accomplished with no undoing was now a matter in which he once again had a choice to make.

And what choice should that be? His old, blazing vow now burned in low embers. While the dangers to both women were still great, they had more than proven themselves. Was he overreacting to a vow born of pain, one he should never have made?

Would sending the women away ultimately hurt the ministry here? He didn't need a repeat of the boycott of the mission when the village workers thought he'd angered Mary. It could end any possibility of reaching the village for Christ.

So far, the women had accomplished more than he had since arriving. Clara Smith had recruited new pupils for the school after their most recent visit to the village. Village women allowed Mary to treat them in their homes and some were slowly making their way up the hill. And after Sunday's gathering, more would be comfortable coming here for treatment, once they'd seen the clinic for themselves.

Karl had been the wiser man. Why William would ever doubt that, he wasn't sure. He'd let his fears rule his judgment. While it had been a rocky start for all, to all appearances, it was working. Mary O'Hara belonged here, and the more he dwelt on that idea, the more the picture of her at his side grew on him.

Chapter Seventeen

William followed the noise outside in the compound and found a very pregnant woman being helped to the clinic. He listened to Mary's explanation and Jabo's heart-stomping proclamation concerning the identity of Mary's new patient. Mary had gone to the village to treat a rash with her new ointment and she'd brought back a death warrant for them all.

William stared with both compassion and horror at the laboring woman entering the infirmary. "I can't believe I'm saying this again. You're going to get us all killed."

"I intend to treat this woman, whether you like it or not. Treating this woman falls under our original agreement. This is not a Bethlehem reenactment with no room at the inn. Are you going to turn away a pregnant woman?"

"Of course you should treat her. Do you think me so callous I would suggest you leave her and her baby to die when you could possibly help?"

"Yes, as a matter of fact, I do."

William staggered back as if she'd slapped him in the face. He tried to temper the hurt he felt over her low opinion of him when he spoke. "I cannot adjust your poor opinion of me, but treating her is not my objection."

"Well, what is the problem?"

"According to Jabo, she belongs to Nana Mala. He's a Pahn speaker and not exactly a man known for his compassion."

"You know, there's far too many Nanas around here for me to keep track of. And then, one is friendly, one is not. And now one is Pahn, whatever that means. The only thing these Nanas have in common is they are hard on the women in their lives."

"This girl is a runaway. From Nana Mala no less. She is here without his permission.

"I still don't understand the problem."

"Then let me simplify things for you. If you had left her in the village, one full of armed warriors, and treated her, none of us would be in any danger. Nana Mala would not risk a confrontation with such a large tribe when he would have her back simply for the asking. By her presence here, he can attack us, recover his wayward wife and risk nothing."

"Why would he attack us? He can see for himself that she is here and safe. We're not keeping her against her will."

"Nana Mala won't care. His runaway pregnant wife in the compound of white missionaries will be all the excuse he needs to feed his hatred."

"He hates missionaries?"

"Nana Mala believes we are all tools of the government in Monrovia, sent to pacify them with the white man's religion so the government can eventually control the bush tribes."

"But if we explain I was only trying to help her medically…"

"Nana Mala won't believe your explanation. He will kill like he's done before."

"He's killed missionaries?"

"Nana Mala is the chief who killed my aunt and uncle four years ago."

Fear snaked like a tightening vine around Mary's stomach and took up permanent residence. What had she done? "Do we know for sure he's coming? Maybe I can deliver the baby and return her to Nynabo village before he even arrives."

William shook his head. "Have you been listening to the drums the last couple of days?"

"Drums are almost constant around here and I don't speak drum."

"Hannabo does, and he told me they signal Nana Mala is on his way. He'll be here soon."

"Then you better spend some time in the chapel, because her labor is too advanced and not progressing. If there is any chance of her living at all, she can't return to the village at this stage."

He looked stricken. "Then do what you can. There's a slim chance if you deliver a healthy infant he will be appeased. I will pray, but I'll do it while I get the men in the compound armed. That is, if they haven't all fled."

"Pastor Mayweather, I've delivered babies before, but this is a difficult case. So if you'll excuse me, I'll tend to my patient."

She turned her back and headed into the infirmary to examine the young mother. Clara nodded at her entrance but kept her attention on the young woman in front of her, valiantly trying to calm the wailing jabber between contractions.

"Clara, go take care of your students, and if you spot Jabo on the way, send him in here to translate. I'd prefer she was calmer to help with the delivery."

Clara headed off and Mary used her most soothing tone as she approached the young woman and tentatively placed a hand on her belly. All she knew from the women at the village was their visitor had two previous failed births. The girl's stomach muscles tightened as Mary saw the spasm of pain cross the girl's face. She waited till the movement passed.

After the contraction, she once again felt the girl's abdomen to determine the baby's position. The infant was breech, as she'd feared when she first heard the story of how long the labor had been active. While not related to losing other babies early in their terms, it was the reason her labor was failing to progress. She'd have to turn the baby manually if she could.

Mary chided herself. If only she'd understood the risk when the village women tried to persuade her to stay and deliver the baby there. No, she wanted to be sure she had everything she needed at hand.

Would she have done any differently if she'd known? Here in the infirmary she could have cleaner conditions and access to ether if necessary for delivery. It was the better place for their survival. Or, with an irate chief, maybe not.

Once again, she'd proven William to be right about her. She might know medicine, but she didn't know the bush. Would this be the time her ignorance cost them their lives?

The unmistakable wail of a newborn distracted William's attention from his lookout. The strong lusty cry of a baby angry at being pulled from his mother's comfort and into the great, wide world. Breech, Jabo had told him, and a girl. It was a miracle, and she'd pulled it off.

The short-lived relief fled when a worried Hannabo came toward him. "Nana Pastor, warriors are coming."

"Nana Mala's men?"

"They are still too far to see their face tattoos, but yes, it looks so."

"Prepare to greet our guests, Hannabo. I'm having Anaya set out food."

"Nana Pastor, they intend war on us, not eating dinner. They are too large for a friendly party. They mean serious trouble on us."

"I hear you, Hannabo. Keep your weapon at the ready. But if we can stop them from attacking us before they have time to see the girl child she delivered, we may be saved. We'll have to pray that God delivers us in this time of need."

"Nana Mala is not a patient man like Nana Pastor. He will use spears before he talks. But he will be happy it is a girl. Much girls are much wealth in the bush."

"Let's hope he's grateful. Tell the men to help cook set up the food as if we were feasting in honor of their coming. To act like honored guests are arriving when they get here and hope they go along. Once we can be sure spears won't fly, we can bring out the girl and the babe."

"What about the children in Mammy Clara's school? If he decides not to be an honored guest."

"Is his approach all from the north? Or did they circle us around?"

"Yes, they all come from the same direction. They avoid my village so as not to stir the warriors there."

"Then just to be safe, send Mammy Clara with the children out to the south to your village."

Hannabo shuffled his feet and hesitated. "What about Mammy Doctor?"

William shook his head. "If I know anything about her, she won't run away and leave her patient."

"This is true. She is hard in the head, that Mammy.

She has no husband to beat her. Men of the white bush are probably too afraid."

"If this wasn't so serious, I'd laugh with you about that. Tell Mammy Doctor that Nana Mala is coming and to wait indoors until it's safe to come out with the baby."

"I will tell her, but it is up to her to do."

William put his hand on the faithful man's shoulder. "Make sure Jabo stays with her to see that she does. If things don't go well, try to get her to safety in your village. Nana Mala didn't come prepared to make war on your tribe. She should be safe there."

Hannabo nodded grimly. "It will be as Nana Pastor says. I will carry her myself if she won't leave."

"If she obeys, it would be the first time. I hope I live to see it."

Mary sponged the squalling infant. The mother lay exhausted but smiling, watching her child's every move. After losing the last two babies, Mary couldn't blame her. It probably didn't seem real. But there was nothing imaginary about those lusty squalls of indignation. This little one had a strong set of lungs and she wasn't afraid to use them.

The baby's mother frowned when Mary took out her stethoscope and tried to place it on the little one's chest.

"It's okay, Mother. Oh, I wish I'd gotten someone to ask your name." At the woman's quizzical look, Mary abandoned the attempt. "Never mind, I know what will fix your anxiety."

Mary hastily wrapped the squalling infant in a small cloth and held her out for her mother to hold. The woman broke into a big smile and took the infant, eyes brimming with tears. While she held her, Mary pantomimed and was allowed to listen to her heart. Everything looked and sounded normal.

Mary tensed at the sound of hoarse shouts from the compound. The new mother pressed her baby closer.

Mary held up a hand for the woman to stay there while she went to see what was wrong. Hannabo met her as she reached the outer doorway.

"Mammy Doctor stay here. Nana Pastor says do not come outside."

"What's going on, Hannabo?" Her attempts to peer past him were blocked by his maneuvering.

"Nana Mala and his warriors have come. Mammy Clara and the children have escaped to the village. If there is trouble, you must follow Jabo and go out the back window and run for the village. It is your only safety."

"Jabo went to get more water for me. What about the woman and the baby?"

"Nana Mala will not hurt the child."

She didn't like what he was leaving unsaid. "And his wife?"

Hannabo shrugged. "He may decide to punish her for leaving him. Nana Mala cannot be known."

She struggled with the last sentence. "You mean you can't predict what he will do?"

Hannabo nodded. "I will protect you. But you must stay here, out of sight until Nana Pastor talks with the chief."

"Assuming the man will talk."

"Nana Mala is smart like the leopard. He will circle his prey, watching to see the best time to strike."

"But will he listen to reason?"

"I cannot say. That he came himself with warriors speaks to his anger with the woman."

"What will make that better?"

"He may only beat her as a lesson. It's hard to say."

"He will beat her? That's barbaric."

"It is his right as a husband. Because she ran away, she must be made an example for the other wives of the village."

"What about the warriors from your village? Will they help protect her?"

Hannabo looked sternly at her. "Mammy Doctor, no one can stop this. The men of my village will expect him to discipline her for running away. It is the way of the bush. She knew this when she ran."

"And us? Will they move to protect us?"

"If we seek refuge in the village, we will not be bothered. Nana Mala does not want war with the Kru. But from here?" Hannabo shook his head. "We are on our own."

"But the child is safe?"

"Mammy, do not worry. He will not harm the child. Now, please step away from the door. It is better if you are not seen while Nana Mala is here."

Mary went back inside to check her patient. Doing her job was the only way she knew to keep the fear from winning a foothold in her heart. Hannabo followed her and spoke with the woman in her Pahn dialect.

Presently, he turned to Mary and said, "Nana Mala's wife wishes to thank you for taking care of her and the baby. After two babies died, it is a joy to hold this little one."

"She seems so calm. Does she know her husband is coming?"

Hannabo nodded. "She is a lesser wife with no children. She says it was worth a beating to have the child alive. She heard of your medicine and came for you to save this baby."

"My medicine? Does she think I am a devilwoman?"

Hannabo shrugged an apology. "It is the story of the bush. Even the drums have carried it."

"Pastor Mayweather will not be happy."

"Nana Pastor is too busy to have it through his head now."

A shudder of fear ran down her spine practically through her toes. To think that hostile tribesmen were at their doorstep, something that was again her doing. William was right. She brought nothing but trouble. Time and again. While she was busy doing one thing right, saving a child and its mother, she was doing another thing wrong. Missionary medicine was so different than she'd expected. All her knowledge was useless to stop a mob of angry warriors with spears.

Hannabo interrupted her mental fugue, placing a hand on her shoulder. "We will pray. If it is our time to die, then be it so. But Father God can do many miracles. Pray, Mammy Doctor."

Mary nodded her agreement and turned away. The combination of fear and Hannabo's simple faith brought tears to her eyes. Tears she was embarrassed to have him see.

She silently sent up a prayer. Every time she glanced at the new mother and her infant daughter, she knew she'd done the right thing, only the wrong way. Would it end in disaster?

Maybe… "Hannabo, ask the mother was she running away from her husband or simply coming here for the baby's sake."

"Mammy, why does this matter? She left the village without permission."

"Just ask."

Mary waited for the answer. Hannabo translated. "She says she came because she feared this baby would die like the others. Not running away."

"Does Nana Mala have other children?"

After the brief exchange, Hannabo said, "Yes, he has one son from his first wife. A warrior already grown. No girls."

"So how important is this child to Nana Mala?"

Hannabo gave her a look questioning her sanity. "All children are important to the tribe, Mammy Doctor. But girls bring much wealth in their bridal purchase, especially the daughter of a chief."

Mary was sure her grin left Hannabo wondering about her sanity. "The one time being a girl matters in the bush."

"What?"

"Never mind, Hannabo. I think I may have a way to fix this."

"Mammy, I do not like that look. It looks like trouble."

"Maybe, but maybe it is a way out of trouble."

William stood in the middle of the compound to greet the arriving warriors. He'd left his rifle on a nearby chair where the table of food he requested had been placed. In truth, his defenses were too paltry to withstand a full assault. The weapon was in reach, but it would only slow them down.

So instead of barricading himself and the others in the main house and hoping to prevail against hopeless odds, he stood with the unlimited ammunition of prayer next to a tense Jabo, who waited to translate or die. Or maybe both.

The drums from Nynabo village went silent. William felt a strange peace even though his knees were not the sturdy fellows he'd hoped for in a crisis. He and the rest of the compound would die this day or God would do a mighty work. The irony of dying at the hands of the same man who'd murdered his aunt and uncle wasn't lost on him.

Nothing in this country had gone as he'd planned. This, too, his uncle must have known.

William had judged his uncle for dying in this place. For getting both himself and his aunt Ruth killed. William had been in such grief, he'd denied the anger. Then he'd turned around and done the same thing. First Alice from malaria and now these few loyal workers and Mary. He couldn't prevent it any more than Uncle Joseph could have. Funny how facing death made a lot of things very clear. *Father, forgive me my judgment. I have become as I have judged. Save us this day, Lord, from the wrath of man. But Lord, whether we live or die, don't let it be in vain. Use this situation to your Glory, Father.*

William looked up. Twenty armed men rose up from the hill and entered the compound with spears in hand and countenances that spoke of death. And in the center as warriors parted, the chief who haunted his thoughts and dreams, Nana Mala.

Nana Mala was surprisingly short. Under the slight hint of corpulence to come were honed muscles. His hair hung in long braids glistening with palm oil, his face unsmiling.

His stern look broke, but only for a moment, when he caught sight of the table behind William. The look was gone as quickly as it came and a mask of ill will settled over his countenance.

"Jabo, please welcome the revered chief to our humble mission. Tell him we prepared a feast in honor of his visit."

To his credit, Jabo delivered the translation with nary a stutter. Silence was the only answer.

This guy could stare down the best of them. William prayed ceaselessly as he tried to maintain a placid look. Nana Mala's jaw tightened, his eyes narrowed and his gaze quickly swept the compound and returned to William.

Harsh, guttural sounds proceeded from his mouth and William turned to Jabo.

"Nana Mala demands his wife be presented to him immediately."

"Tell Nana Mala that his wife is here and kept safe for him. She and the baby are in good health. Ask if he will join us for a meal in celebration of the child's birth." William stalled for time while he thought how to keep Mary out of this. If he took the chief to see his wife, Mary would be seen. Was the new mother in any shape to come out on her own?

Jabo complied. The chief crossed his arms over his chest, puffing it as he did. More guttural words poured forth.

"Nana Mala says no delay is acceptable. Present the woman or he will find her himself and it will not go well with you for keeping her from him."

William decided to retrieve the chief's wife and child from the infirmary. Mary must be kept out of this at all costs. If only he could calm the man…

Apparently not. Patience was not the chief's strong suit. The fierce adversary began issuing orders and warriors surrounded William before he had a chance to even think about getting his rifle. Jabo translated his shouting. "He says no hand of the government will take what is his. Tell him where his wife is or die."

Before William could reply, a door opened. The infirmary door. He shot a fervent prayer to heaven that it was the runaway wife and Mary was safely out of sight. Nana Mala would not kill her. Mary and he were another matter entirely.

Red hair, that beacon of impending trouble, capped the face that peered out the open door. Mary walked out of the infirmary with a small bundle in hand and a worried Hannabo behind her.

Shouts went up and warriors rushed the trio. Mary kept coming, baby in arms, Hannabo trailing. Despite being surrounded by the fierce tribesmen, she kept walking forward, a vision of calm in men's trousers and a white shirt. The child was clutched to her chest, but when she got close to Nana Mala she stopped and spoke, holding the infant extended toward him. William tried to move toward Mary, but the warriors blocked his passage. All he could do was watch helplessly while Mary tried to win over one of the worst cannibal leaders known to the bush.

Through Hannabo Mary instructed the young woman to wait until she'd placed the baby in his father's arms before coming out. The mother had nodded her understanding, and handed the newborn to Mary. Her lack of fear for the child's safety reassured Mary. At least the mother believed the baby to be safe.

Mary wished she could be so sure of herself and the others. But either the sight of the child would soften the warrior's heart or it wouldn't. All she could do was try. Well, pray and try. Was this how Esther felt when she headed for the king's court unbidden? All she knew was, if she lived through this, William would probably kill her himself.

He would be upset to see her. Once again, she wasn't following his plan. But she couldn't cower in fear waiting to see if the compound would be slaughtered. She was the one who'd brought the trouble in the first place.

Hannabo's objections had gone so far as to include blocking the doorway. She'd waited, unmoving, with the baby in hand until he relented. He walked beside her as every eye in the compound turned toward her.

Within seconds warriors rushed her, stopped only by the shout of a grim, stodgy man near William. Nana Mala in the flesh.

She lowered her eyes and kept walking, the babe sleeping peacefully in her arms. Mary's arms trembled as if she carried a much heavier weight.

Everything was so quiet. Dust settled silently from the warriors' charge. It was as if the whole jungle held its breath to see the outcome.

Two feet from the chief, she stopped, afraid to take a breath. As their eyes met, the baby stirred and let out a high piercing wail. Mary startled, as did the chief. Then the most amazing thing happened. His face split into a wide grin, revealing two rows of teeth filed to ominous points. The incongruity of the grin and the deadly teeth drove home the reality of a cannibal standing before her. But apparently proud papa existed in every culture. He thumped his chest and shouted to the compound, pointing to his daughter, and Mary dared take a breath.

Hannabo leaned in and translated, whispering in her ear. "He's naming her Wonlay. It means we are tired of our troubles. The name is given when you've lost many children in childbirth. He's bragging how healthy the child is already. How strong, and you haven't even applied the pepper yet."

That was too strange to let pass. "The pepper?"

"Babies are rubbed with pepper after their baths to make them cry and gain strength."

Mary stood flabbergasted with the crying baby in her arms while the chief beamed his pride, soliciting responses from all his warriors. A gentle hand at her elbow let her know the child's mother had come out. She gratefully handed the child to her mother and watched the family reunion. It seemed to consist of chastisement and pride in equal parts, at least that was her best guess.

Mary started to back away when the chief and his wife both looked to her. The new mother was beaming and pointing to her. The chief narrowed his eyes and surveyed Mary until she felt like a pork chop at the neighborhood butcher shop. Finally he grunted and nodded and she moved toward a much-relieved William.

She'd only chanced one look in his direction when she'd come out. He'd paled at her appearance. He'd been afraid for her. Well, she'd been terrified too.

Humor, however inappropriate the response at the time, were the first words out of her mouth when she reached his side. "Well, I guess we're not on the dinner menu anymore."

William shook his head in resignation. "Dr. O'Hara, I don't know whether to strangle you or kiss you right now."

"I get that a lot."

"I can't say I'm surprised."

Mary asked, "So which will it be?"

"Huh? Oh." And then he felt himself blush. "It was a figure of speech, Dr. O'Hara."

"Of course it was, William. By the way, don't you think it's time you called me Mary? After living through this together, it's a little silly to stand on formality."

"Yes, I guess it is. Well then, Mary, shall we see if we can feed our guests? God has worked a mighty miracle here and I intend to take every advantage of it I can. Perhaps before the day is out, Nana Mala will allow me to speak to him about God."

"It is a day of miracles. Maybe your cannibal chief will come to God."

"I doubt it will be that easy, but let's pray it's so. One

baby saved the day today, maybe he'll be open to the story of another who saved the world."

He held out a chair for her at the table, marveling all the while at how God worked. What he left unsaid was the clarity it had given him about the good doctor's position at the mission. Just when he'd thought everything was working out, he'd been provided a strong reminder of how dangerous this place could be. Mary seemed determined to experience every danger she could, even though it had been her compassion driving her decision.

He'd send a sole courier in the morning with his revised letter to the Mission Board outlining the danger of Dr. Mary O'Hara continuing in the interior. Hopefully a replacement would come soon. If not, he'd settle for orders moving her to one of the more civilized towns on the coast.

Watching her now, he knew Clara was right. How could he not care for such a strong, compassionate woman? He would miss her, but for the safety of all concerned, especially Mary, the women were leaving Nynabo.

Chapter Eighteen

Mary hurried up the steps to the main house and scurried into the dining area. "Sorry I'm late. I'm starved. The clinic stayed so busy today that I barely had time for a banana around lunch."

"Cook saved you dinner, Dr. Mary. With Anaya cooking, you'll never have to worry about missing a meal again." Clara laughed.

Mary noticed William's uncharacteristic quiet mood. Normally he joined in with the day's events. Seeing as how he just returned from preaching in Nynabo village, it was surprising. Maybe things didn't go as well as he'd hoped. He'd seemed a little discouraged ever since Nana Mala hadn't been receptive to the Gospel.

Although the chief had hinted that they could visit the Pahn village to preach, William failed to commit to a specific time. She didn't blame him. Nana Mala gave her the willies.

She probably wasn't the best person to try and draw William out anyway. He'd been a little distant toward her since Nana Mala had left. Maybe he'd chime in on his own later. "Well, now that we know my day was too busy, how was yours, Clara?"

"Those little ones are so smart. A couple of them can say their entire alphabet and will be reading in no time."

Mary asked. "How many do you have now?"

"Seven—six boys and one girl."

"That's a great start."

"True." Clara dabbed her dinner from her mouth. "Still, I wish I could get more girls to balance things out. Not that I don't love all my little boys."

William took the small knife supplied to him with dinner and began to peel and eat a mango. "For the most part, you'll have to buy them."

Clara dropped her fork and shot him a look of total shock.

Mary couldn't believe what she was hearing. Was he deliberately provoking them? "That's a pretty outrageous idea coming from one of the most traditional men I know. It does fit with the patriarchal attitude you and half the world have, but slavery isn't something I'd expect the Mission Board to approve."

"And that, Mary, is yet another proof of how little you know of how things work around here."

Mary stood to her feet. She didn't know what was bothering him, but she didn't intend to take this sudden return to formality and ill-temper without protest. Clara's eyes shifted from Mary to see William's response.

When he only looked up lazily, Mary's Irish got the best of her. "So are you back to keeping a running tally of all the ways I don't measure up to your standards, William? You must have a whole book by now."

Her anger finally stirred him and he rose, slowly, deliberately and took one step toward her.

She craned her neck rather than give him the satisfaction of stepping back. "At least I know enough to know slavery is wrong. One cannot condone the owning of human beings."

"Of course not. It is Mission Board policy to facilitate the ultimate freedom of the young women of Liberia by purchasing them from their fathers."

"To facilitate their freedom?"

"Yes. If no one buys them, makes a dowry-like payment to their fathers, then they will be subject to any offer made by someone with the power to force the family's hand. Bound, mind you, for the duration of their natural lives. In cases where the father no longer lives, they can simply be claimed against their will."

"How horrible," Clara murmured.

William continued. "Yes, indeed, how horrible. I would think after the incident with Nana Mala you would see more clearly a woman's position here in the bush." William bore in on Mary and held her gaze mercilessly.

Uncomfortable at what truly was her lack of understanding and her moral accusations of the man, she would have loved to look away. Something in her couldn't. He wasn't only angry, he was hurt. And she couldn't help but feel it was her fault.

Mary persisted. "So, it's better if we own them? Is that the philosophy behind this policy?"

"We take the girls in, educate them, prepare them for life, ministry or marriage depending on their own desires. But they are always free to leave with no obligations. Because she's been once purchased, our so-called slave will henceforth have a choice in a matter she didn't have before."

Mary found herself at a loss for words. The apology she knew she owed him stuck itself to the roof of her dry mouth and refused to exit. After a few uncomfortable seconds, William turned his back and headed outside to his favorite evening rest spot on the porch, leaving Mary standing with her indignation in shreds.

"Well?" Clara asked.

"Well, what?"

"Dr. Mary, you owe that man an apology."

Shame bled all the tension from Mary's shoulders and they sagged. "I know, I don't know what comes over me sometimes. I really don't. But in all fairness, he's in a prickly mood over something and taking it out on me."

"Sometimes, my fiery lass, you two are like the trails we took to get here."

"What do you mean, Clara?"

"Well, we could hardly walk down them without briars reaching out to grab us. It's like that with the two of you. You go for a conversational stroll with him and you both run smack into each others' briars. And what do you both do? Like the trail, you get out your machetes and clear the way."

"You're right. He did carve me up so well I could be a proper dinner fowl, ready for the table."

"And now you're going to go serve yourself up on a platter and offer him your best slice of humble pie. Go apologize. Maybe then you'll be able to get him to talk about whatever it is that's really bothering him."

William barely noticed when Mary slipped quietly onto the porch. He was angry with himself for losing his temper with Mary once again. The chair rocked him into intro-spection.

What was his problem, or perhaps his sin, that he let his temper fly in her presence so quickly? His Aunt Ruth would have had a thing or two to say about his lack of courtesy towards Mary. She'd instilled in him from an early age that women were to be treated with the utmost courtesy by a man. He was failing miserably in that regard.

Dear Aunt Ruth. She and Uncle Joseph would be so disappointed to know that he had made so little progress spreading the Gospel. Their blood was spilled to ensure a rich crop of converts, but he couldn't seem to manage the harvest to save his own soul.

He had a mere handful of converts, including Hannabo, and most recently Jabo at last Sunday's sparsely attended service. Of course, Hannabo wasn't even his convert. Uncle Joseph's example and prayers had brought him to the Lord. William was only reaping the benefit of their work with him.

William sat there, rocking with a vengeance. Mary cleared her throat and his rhythm broke. "William, I came to say I'm sorry."

"No need, Mary. I'm not sure why we rub each other the wrong way, but we do."

"I'm not sure either. It's one case I have no diagnosis to explain."

"It could be worse."

"I don't see how."

"If we were married instead of just serving here together, we'd never be free of each other."

Is that how he saw her? As someone to aspire to be free from? Disappointment pushed through her quick mental denial of hurt.

"Please, Doctor, have a seat. They're not as comfortable as Karl's handmade rockers back at Newaka, but then I'm not much of a woodworker. Frankly, I'm not half the missionary that man of God is either."

So she hadn't misjudged his earlier mood. He was despondent. And his comparison to Karl Jansen? Did he feel like a failure? She kept her voice neutral and asked, "Why would you say that about yourself?"

"Well, it's true. I'm no hand at woodcrafting."

"That's not what I mean. Why do you think you're less a missionary than Pastor Karl?"

"Truth be told, Mary, you're a bigger crowd draw out here than I am. They all come for you. Out of medical need, curiosity, to find hope their devilmen's fetishes haven't given them. Let's not kid ourselves. You're the main attraction here and I'm the sideshow."

"You exaggerate. They come for your preaching." Well, mostly. "And what about those nights in the village you preached in the palaver house?"

"The palaver house? I'm beginning to think they only like a good story. What I'm saying isn't getting through to them."

"Have you thought about trying to relate to them a little more?"

"What do you mean, relate a little more?"

"Well," Mary paused. This was a problem she could help solve. "I've noticed that you're a little aloof. Paternalistic in your preaching. It comes across as if they were children and you're the adult. If you'd try to relate more on their level, not sound so superior, for example, they'd probably flock to you and the Gospel. Isn't that what we all want, someone to relate to and identify with before we give them authority to speak into our lives?"

"Like you do, for example?"

Mary felt the chill of his words. For the life of her, what did she say wrong this time? Actually it felt like the first real conversation they'd had in a while.

"Not exactly, William. I'm not suggesting you be like me. That wouldn't be genuine. They need someone genuine to relate to, respond to and to draw them in to the truth."

His quiet response surprised her. "Are you trying to lecture me on how to preach and reach a lost, heathen people?"

"What? I'm not trying to lecture you! I thought we were discussing problem solving together."

"That's what you thought you were doing?"

Now he was deliberately trying to provoke her. "Well, I don't claim to be a preacher, but I know not to treat grown men and women like they're little children."

"I do no such thing. I deal with ignorance, that's all. They need correction from their heathen ways. If that sounds a little like a parent talking to a child, disciplining them, correcting their mistakes, so be it."

She snorted. There was no such thing as a simple conversation with him. She'd come to extend an apology and now this? The two of them would never be on the same page of any book, Bible or not. "What next, William, are you going to send them to their room, take away their favorite toys to get them to listen to you?"

"How I preach the Word is no concern of yours. Do I tell you how to fix the maladies that present themselves in your clinic? No, I don't. Now if you'll excuse me, I'm going to spend time preparing for tomorrow's sermon."

William crossed paths with Clara as she exited the main house. "Clara, I bid you goodnight."

A startled Clara replied while he went off to do his evening devotions. He was still fuming, but in the midst of his indignation, he realized something. The good doctor may have seen things all wrong, but she'd still given him an idea.

Maybe he should take away all their toys. Well, not

exactly toys and not directly take them away. But shine a light on their deception. The fetish houses were an affront to God. A stronger man of God would have challenged them long ago. It took a thorn-in-his-flesh redhead to get him to see what he should have all along. He should preach against the fetish.

It was time he took more direct action. But how to go about it? They had to be made to see they'd put their trust in false idols before they would ever be free of the super-stition and fear of the devilmen's society.

He sat at the small table in his room, studying the Bible and taking notes while the daylight still prevailed. Oil lamps were precious, but the mission of salvation even more so. He kept his lamp going until well into the night.

Tomorrow's sermon would be the start of a new evange-listic push. He'd begin a campaign of preaching about the one true God and build toward Elijah's story and recount the scripture on what happened to false prophets. Then he'd seek the chief's permission to preach to the village as a whole. People would be freed from the superstition that held them in thrall.

Finally, he was getting somewhere. Who would have thought Dr. Mary O'Hara would have become his muse, the inspiration for his strongest evangelical campaign yet? He would sorely miss her. Arguments and all.

Chapter Nineteen

Morning crept into Mary's window like a thief to steal her dreams. Sounds of men in the early-dawn compound brought her exhausted body fully awake. Yesterday had been no exception to the weeks of patients flooding her infirmary following the birth of Nana Mala's daughter. Her complaints of nothing to do fled. She'd even been allowed to treat the occasional man.

She got up quietly so as not to disturb the soft snores of Clara and moved the curtain out of the way to see what was going on. William was outside with a small group of tribesmen. Was he preaching? Jabo stood, hanging on his every word. Since the service where he'd given his heart to God, Jabo followed William around with constant questions. She missed her former shadow, since William now garnered all Jabo's attention.

She was almost jealous of Jabo's newfound fervor for God. She felt the sparks of faith returning, a slow spiritual healing taking place in her heart, but nothing like the experience of a new convert.

All the talk of false gods lately made her examine her own heart for things she placed above God in her life. Jabo's interest focused more on the literal idols of his culture. His fervor to free others from the superstitions he but recently embraced grew daily.

Well, whatever kind of palaver the men were having, Jabo's excitement was evident. Hannabo, on the other hand, stood to one side with arms crossed. Now her curiosity was piqued. What were the men up to so early?

Not likely to find out from here. Mary moved to dress. Trousers and a white shirt went on swiftly. She reached for the all-necessary boots. If she wanted to know anything around here, she'd have to find out for herself.

She laced one of her boots, pulling it snugly. Maybe William was negotiating for help on a trek to one of the outlying villages. He definitely would have kept something like a new village trip from her. His more relaxed demeanor didn't extend to the idea of further travel for her.

She slid the second boot over a sock and questioned her own reasoning. If he went somewhere new, she wanted to join him. A new village would broaden her experience. Besides, the medicine drew in crowds and William always had a ready-made congregation when they went down into Nynabo village. Instead of being grateful though, it bothered him somehow.

Men and their egos. No medicine to cure that problem.

She stood and cast one more glance at the still sleeping Clara. She'd let her rest a little longer. Saturdays meant no school and a well-earned break for Clara. Mary pulled the door open and headed for the compound.

She would never completely understand William Mayweather. One minute he seemed to be a tradition-bound Bible thumper, and the next, he risked life and limb to confront a dangerous warrior to save her from a deadly mistake and ensure a new mother and baby would be all right. His overbearing attitude with her disappeared into the campfire smoke when he played with the village children. He would make a good father someday.

She swatted the insect lying in wait outside the clinic door a little harder than necessary. Why would she even be considering him as father material? Sure he was, but for some sweet little missionary wife.

As she stepped further out into the faint morning sunlight, the only really cool time of the day, Mary figured out who the tribesmen with William were. Nynabo's chief and two of the village elders gesticulated and shook their heads.

William caught sight of her and he put up a hand to ward her off. Must be man talk, women's opinions not needed. She changed course and headed for the main house, hoping Anaya might already have breakfast ready. The boys could palaver all they wanted, she'd hear about it eventually from one of the men around the compound.

Her stomach gave a rumble. Definitely food first. Pounding from the kitchen drew her toward her objective.

More rice. She found Arway, the girl who often substituted for Anaya, kneeling on the ground pounding the grains for uji, a thin gruel of cassava and rice that reminded her a little of wintery breakfast foods she'd eaten as a child before her father fired the cook. It was an acquired taste her tongue hadn't caught yet.

The only consolation to the regimented breakfast was a lack of red pepper. Mary grabbed fruit off a platter and proceeded to peel a banana while eyeing a mottled green butter pear.

Arway smiled and stood with her pounded rice. "Mammy Doctor is early this morning. Breakfast is coming."

Mary tried to drum up enthusiasm. The cook turned in

profile and Mary smiled. "Arway, you've got belly," she said, proud of remembering the native term for pregnancy.

"Yes, yes. Baby coming."

"Come by the clinic and let me check you."

Arway smiled shyly and shook her head. "No, no. I am good. I eat many lizards."

"Lizards? Whatever for?"

Arway laughed. "The lizard is quick. If I eat lizards then baby will come quick like a lizard."

"Oh. A fast delivery." Hard to argue with bush logic. Better to nod, accept the belief and try to introduce some Western medicine along side. Besides, what harm came from eating lizards? Extra protein in a rice-based diet would help the baby. "Still, let me check the baby and see if both of you are healthy."

Arway looked eager. "Will Mammy Doctor make me a gree-gree bag for the baby?" Arway clutched the pouch hung around her own neck, purchased, no doubt, from her local devilman.

Better set her straight before another lecture comes my way from William. "No, Arway. I am not a devilwoman. I use science, knowledge of how things work, to help make people healthier. Not magic."

The young woman's head hung in disappointment, but it soon came back up and Arway stared at Mary, her mouth tight. "I do not understand. You have magic. Why will you not use it for me?" Her lip came out in a remarkable pout. "You and Nana Pastor are both selfish. Surely your God cannot mind to protect a baby. Is He more jealous than the other gods? Is that why Nana Pastor goes to preach against the devilmen today?"

Mary's understanding of anatomy warred the way her heart fell to her feet. "What do you mean, Arway?"

Arway waved toward the village impatiently. "Nana

Pastor asked the chief to tear down the fetishes. My chief said no. He is not convinced your God is powerful to protect him from the spirits who would seek vengeance. Or from the devilmen."

Well, at least the man asked permission. Maybe that was an end to it. Something about his countenance this morning still worried her. It was like the little itch between your shoulder blades you couldn't quite get at. "Arway, I'll take breakfast later. I'm going to have a word with the pastor first."

"You had better hurry then. He will go to the village soon for his big palaver."

This is what all those sermons were leading to? Preaching against fetishes and devilmen in their own village. And he called *her* trouble.

"But you said the chief refused to pull down the fetishes."

"Yes, yes. Nana Pastor goes to palaver with the whole village. That is why I came in Anaya's place. It is big doings there. I go listen after I finish making uji."

William was treading on dangerous ground. Still, if it was only preaching and the chief allowed the meeting, nothing bad would come of it. William must be sure of himself and the outcome of his message. After all, he was the one constantly harping on safety.

Mary took a full breath of relief. No, the king of jungle safety would not deliberately do something dangerous. It would go against everything he'd lectured her.

"Mammy Doctor, if there is nothing more you wish, I go to see if bluff boy is true."

"Yes, you may go, Arway. But what is a bluff boy? I do not savvy this expression."

Arway thought hard on an explanation. "Bluff boy is one who promises many big things. Big, big things."

"Oh, maybe someone who brags. Can they do these big things?"

Arway shook her head.

"Then definitely. We call a person who promises big a bragger."

Arway nodded in understanding. "So, Jabo is a bragger! We have both learned new words today."

"Jabo is a bragger? I mean a bluff boy?"

"Yes. He bluffs he will pull down the fetish houses himself as a surprise for Nana Pastor. This is a crazy thing. I savvy he is a bluff boy."

"Oh, no." Mary whirled and took off running to the spot where she'd last seen the men palavering. She had to tell William. Jabo's plan was misguided, disastrous. She rounded the corner of the mission house.

Not a single man in sight. She checked the chapel and the school and then ran for the infirmary.

"Clara," she shouted for her friend as she burst in the door. "Clara, come quickly."

She almost collided with the now awake and fully dressed Clara. Worry lined Clara's face. "Doctor Mary, what's wrong?"

"It's William, he's gone to Nynabo village."

"Stop a minute and catch your breath, dear. Now why exactly is that a problem?"

"He…" Mary gulped for air. "He's gone to preach against fetishes."

"Wonderful news. Do you think the villagers will be receptive?"

"No, yes. I don't know. You don't understand. He doesn't know."

"Doesn't know what? Dr. Mary, get a hold of yourself and speak straight." Clara took her by the arms as if to shake some sense in her.

Mary steadied herself and took a couple of deep breaths. "Arway told me Jabo bragged he would pull down the fetish houses when William preaches. William doesn't know."

"Oh, my. Jabo should know better. Destroying something symbolizing their ancestors, their go-betweens to God will only make his people angry."

"They could all be killed."

Clara's serious face conveyed understanding. "You run ahead. Maybe you can get to William before Jabo acts. I'll follow with your medical bag."

William's party of men quickly broke apart when they reached the village. The chief disappeared like cook-fire smoke on a windy day. Only Jabo and Hannabo followed, Jabo stalwart and as determined as he was, and Hannabo solemn and serious.

William had spent hours in prayer and the Word leading up to this sermon. He knew what he wanted to say.

God would certainly prevail this day. He prayed the people would see God was stronger than the curses they believed would follow those who challenged the fetishes. The chief feared the magic of his devilmen, and even though he'd given permission, he remained on the sidelines. If the people responded to William's message today and accepted Christ, the chief would come around.

William chose to preach at the village entrance where the fetish house stood guard. It was a small mudded and thatched structure covering the idol. The idol was clay sculpted into the semblance of a squat, misshapen little man with no legs, a symbol of the ancestral spirits. Remnants of rice, kola nuts and other food offerings lay nearby, placed nightly to appease the spirits and eaten by roaming animals. Fetish bags and other charms hung from the house's walls, and the tails of white monkeys adorned its sides.

To think people believed an inanimate object gave power. Well, no more. Before this day was out, they'd finally see where true power lay. Not in some idol of clay in its garish hut to guard the village from harm, but in the One God who created the Heavens and the earth.

A crowd began to gather. William turned to Hannabo. "Start the way we discussed. Tell them we mean no harm. No disrespect. Everything the way we discussed."

Hannabo nodded. "Nana Pastor, I will speak it this way. But the devilmen will not like you preaching against the fetish. If they stir the crowd, we should leave."

"I agree. If it becomes a problem, we will cease and return to the compound. I'm not risking our lives today. I merely wish to bring this word to all of the village. Not just the few coming to the chapel."

William laid his heart bare. "You of all people, Hannabo, know the truth, how the devilmen enslave your people with the belief in the fetish's power. I must try and set them free, make them see the truth."

"It may take more than the words, Nana Pastor. I, too, heard many words and did not believe."

William cast a glance at the growing crowd. Rumors of the chief's earlier palaver at the compound brought out the curious. When enough of a crowd had gathered, he opened his Bible, waited till Hannabo prefaced his message and began paraphrasing the scriptures from the King James English into a translatable form for Hannabo.

It was the sermon of his life. The crowd was nodding. He had them. Then murmurs from behind arose. The crowd parted from the back. The devilmen had come to hear the threat to their rule.

Three of them, they'd all come in force. Their garish

tattoos made quite a spectacle, but today they'd pulled on the full regalia. Leopard's teeth on necklaces and medicine bags hanging from the vine rope holding their beaten-bark loincloths were their principal adornment. Iron-pointed spears in their hands completed the effect.

Mothers pulled small children behind them. Some at the edges quietly sought to glide back from the crowd toward the village or the jungle, whichever was closer.

The chief had sidled up to the outside of the crowd, waiting on the outcome of this power play. Politicians. The same in every culture.

Many who'd stood ready, maybe on the verge to answer his call, moved back. The crowd now held a line behind the devilmen. If he didn't do something, the danger those three radiated would carry the day.

He nodded to Hannabo to continue for now. William kept one eye on the potential threat and recited scripture from memory. Both he and Hannabo watched for any sign they should stop. Jabo fidgeted at his side. An agitation rose from him the minute the devilmen arrived on the scene. As William neared the end, Jabo tried to confront individual members of the crowd. One of the devilmen turned and began to shout at Jabo.

What was he saying? William glanced at Hannabo, who'd stopped translating, but got no answer. Jabo stiffened as the man shook his spear at him, finally bringing the point within a foot of Jabo's chest.

William ordered. "Jabo, don't provoke them. Walk away and come to my side. We've done all we can today."

Jabo stared back to William. The intensity of Jabo's study made the hairs on William's arm stand up. Jabo reached out and calmly pushed the spear to one side.

He turned his back on the devilmen and walked away. William breathed a sigh of relief and instructed Hannabo to thank the people for allowing him to speak and to invite them to the chapel on Sunday to learn more. William watched the crowd's reaction. Relieved expressions quickly turned to horror. They yelled and pointed. Hannabo turned to determine what they were gesticulating about.

Jabo stood at the fetish house, transfixed in a heavenly stare with his machete drawn.

William yelled. "Jabo, no. This is not the way."

Jabo didn't hesitate. The crowd collectively drew a loud breath. The devilmen yelled, egging on the crowd. The spear pointer ran at Jabo.

Jabo's machete came down in the center of the idol's clay head, sending pieces everywhere. The devilmen's shouts and roars turned the crowd into their arms, their feet, their deliverers of vengeance.

William ran for Jabo. Out of the corner of William's eye he saw the fast-moving figures and heard the shouts. Hannabo tried to push through the melee. William used the surge of energy rushing through his system and sent it all to his feet, hopelessly trying to reach Jabo before the devilmen and the crowd.

Everything happened at once. Devilmen ran toward Jabo waving their spears. Hannabo cried out and attempted to block the devilmen.

As Jabo raised his machete a second time to attack the structure, one of the devilmen reached him. The yelling reached a roar, or was that him? The triumphant look on Jabo's face turned blank and his eyes glazed before he fell to the ground, the hilt of a spear extending from his back.

The devilman had stabbed him. No, this wasn't supposed to happen. William dropped his Bible and reached for his fallen convert. Evil in greased braids and a face of implacable hatred glared at him when William lifted Jabo.

William's only thought was if he could get Jabo back to Mary, maybe he could be saved.

The first blow staggered him before he made a step in the direction of the mission. Mary was coming down the hill, shouting his name. Hands firmly planted in his back shoved him down, Jabo slipped from his arms and William fell with him, their limbs tangling together.

Blows rained down on his head, his legs, his back, as an enraged mob attacked. He tried to roll to escape, but only managed to cover Jabo's inert body. He chanced a look and saw a pair of painted feet. A face leered down, one of the devilman grinning at his accomplishment. He heard Mary shouting and lifted his head, then saw Hannabo restraining her. Good, she shouldn't die too.

The shouting was awful. The rage of the village mob carried on the wind reached her well before she had it in sight. Her heart pounded from fear as much as from running. She rounded the bend and saw William holding a limp brown body, staggering away from the village, a mob pressing in behind him. Hannabo ran to his rescue.

"William." What good shouting his name was supposed to do she didn't know. She desperately wanted to get his attention, to let him know she was coming. For whatever good that would do.

The figure William carried hit the ground as he tilted in the same direction. Blue cloth. Jabo wore the trader's blue cloth. "Noooo."

A burst of icy fear coursed through her veins and propelled her toward William. She couldn't see him because of the crowd surrounding him, clubs and sticks rising and falling. They would kill him if she couldn't stop this.

He lifted his head as a strong pair of arms grabbed her,

stopping her forward motion. "No, Mammy Doctor, you must stay back. They will kill any who get in their way."

Tears flowed freely as she looked up and saw a bloody Hannabo. "They'll kill him. Hannabo, we must stop them."

"I can try, but you must stay here. Nana Pastor would want you safe above all. Only the devilmen can stop them now. Or the chief, but he fears them too greatly."

"If only a devilman can stop them, translate for me. Maybe a devilwoman can do the same. William can't take much more of a beating."

"I will do it."

He released her and Mary stepped closer and shouted close to the face of one of the devilmen, Hannabo at her side. Her shrill voice pitched above the guttural grunts of the mob. "Stop this at once. You must stop this, now. You will kill him. I will be very unhappy if this man dies."

The head devilman looked up, startled at her presence. Most of the mob quieted. Hannabo took advantage of the silence and translated what she had said. One of the devilmen stepped toward her, waggling his tongue and gyrating. His superior barked an order and he stepped back, glaring. She'd made no friends today.

The head devilman raised a hand and shouted to the crowd. The frenzy slowed for all but one determined soul, but the devilman put an end to his action with a glancing blow from the staff of his spear to the unfortunate fellow's head. He then glared at her in challenge. As long as he didn't make another move to harm William, he could glare all he wanted. She glared right back, the stare-down interrupted by Clara's appearance with her black satchel.

With her medical bag in her hand, she moved toward William. The crowd dropped their eyes and parted. The devilmen continued to glare, but stepped back as she drew near. They were afraid of the bag or her, and right now she couldn't care which. If having them think her bag was a powerful fetish saved the lives of Jabo and William, she'd use whatever worked. She'd ask forgiveness of God later, if forgiveness was indeed needed.

She examined William quickly. Everyone took a further step back when she pulled out her stethoscope and hung it around her neck for effect.

Hannabo was at her side. "Does he live?"

"Barely. Tell them I want both men carried back to the mission immediately or I will be very angry."

Hannabo barely suppressed his grin. "You are a smart Mammy. They are afraid of the white devilwoman's anger."

"Just get them to do it."

The translation went out and the crowd murmured.

"What's their problem now?"

"They are still afraid of your anger. They fear getting near you now."

"Tell them whatever you need to say. Reassure them I will be happy with the men who do this for me."

Hannabo complied and four tribesmen stepped forward to carry William. She moved to Jabo, fearing what she would find. He hadn't moved since she seen him fall from William's arms.

She checked for a pulse. Nothing. She put her stethoscope to use and couldn't hear a heartbeat no matter how faint, no matter where she moved it. Her heart froze in the tropic heat. Jabo couldn't be dead.

Hannabo loomed, an anxious look on his face. "Is he living, Mammy?"

Mary shook her head and suppressed the threatening tears before she lifted her head. She couldn't afford to show any weakness lest the devilmen see it and challenge her. She had no real magic, and what little medicine she had wouldn't raise a man from the dead.

Hannabo bent down and spoke softly. "They will not take your word for his death without sitting vigil. Even if they did, his death will upset them more. Maybe even start the violence once again. We should take him back to the compound with us."

"Won't the men carrying him know?"

"They will suspect, but until his mouth spoils and his tongue hangs out, they will not accept it as true."

Mary didn't even want to know what that meant. Getting William to safety was the only drum rhythm in her head. "Then take him, too. We'll give him a Christian burial in the graveyard William started behind the compound."

Mary stood and brushed off her pants. Mustering as much dignity and authority as she could, she turned her back on the murmuring mob and followed the small troupe back up the hill to the infirmary, praying as she went for William to live. Wondering as she walked, *William, what have you done?* She held on to the tears for her dead friend and the one about to die until they were safe to shed.

Chapter Twenty

Mary left the room where William still lay unconscious and told the waiting Clara, "His life is in his own hands now. And God's. There's nothing more medicine can do. Three days unconscious with a head injury isn't good." Weariness had latched on to the very marrow of Mary's bones and seeped into her words. Jabo's funeral had leeched her last vestiges of hope.

"We'll keep praying. It's always been in God's hands. Come, sit down and eat something, Mary. Cook made you fufu." Clara looked as exhausted as Mary, yet she had a small smile on her face.

"I don't know if I can face more cassava this morning. Maybe something out of a tin if we have any left. Wish I knew your secret to happiness today. You're practically humming."

"The children came back." Elation highlighted the worry that had gone before. Mary's conscience pinged. She'd failed to give thought to how Clara had handled the last few days. She loved those kids. No one who saw her with them would doubt Clara Smith had found her calling.

When the children didn't show on Monday, it wasn't clear to Mary if the mission was still viable. "That's good news. If the children are back, maybe we can all get a good night's sleep. No more guard duty."

Clara nodded. "They would never send the children if harming us were on the agenda. Now, if you don't need me, I've got to go start class. I'm going to get Hannabo to help me with the chapel since Pastor..."

Clara's hitched breath sharpened Mary's focus on her friend's distress. "What's wrong?"

Mary couldn't remember ever seeing Clara cry except at Jabo's funeral. "Clara. Tell me. What is it?"

Clara pulled out a handkerchief from the pocket at the side of her skirt and dried her tears. "I'm sorry. It's just the stress of the last couple of days. Burying our dear Jabo, William hovering near death."

Mary moved to console her friend, wrapping an arm around her. "Grief is like that. One minute you're fine and the next all the pain comes flooding back."

"I know. I'll be all right. The children will distract me. It will be a good chapel with Hannabo leading. He's come so far in his studies," she said, nodding and wiping away her tears.

Clara smoothed her skirts and headed for the door. When she opened it, a startled Hannabo, hand raised to knock, stood on the other side. "Ah, here he is now. Hannabo, I need you to help me this morning at the school."

"What do you need, Mammy Clara?"

"Come with me and I'll explain on the way."

Hannabo closed the door behind them and Mary sought the nearest chair, exhaustion weighing heavily. She was only going to sit for a minute or two. But her eyelids were awfully heavy.

A loud thud startled her and shook the building. What... was she asleep? Something woke her. Something falling. She bolted upright, the crick in her neck giving her a short pause before she headed for the room where William lay. She found him face-down on the floor beside his bed.

He'd woken up. At least enough to move and throw himself out of bed. Now what? He was a little big to move on her own, and Hannabo hadn't returned.

She grabbed the pillow off the bed and managed to roll him over, placing his head on the pillow as she did. Whatever woke him was short-lived. Still, movement on his own provided hope, even if he did fall to the floor.

As long as he was already safely on the floor, he couldn't fall again. She'd be quick and go get Hannabo.

She stood and headed out the door only to stop short at the sound of William's voice.

"You should have let me die too."

She turned back. Incredulity oozed out of her every available pore. Hearing his voice again answered her prayers these last long nights. She had never thought to pray for what he'd speak. "What did you say?"

He struggled to get the words out. "I'd be better dead. You shouldn't have saved me. At least as a martyr I might have done some good in this place."

"Oh, you'd like the easy way, wouldn't you? Then you wouldn't have to face the facts."

He whispered. "The facts?"

The memory of a fresh grave and the days of wailing in the village over Jabo's death drove her to speak. Her anger came out in a hiss. "From the beginning you've tried to keep me in my place to protect me. Lectured me on how I'd get us all killed. But it wasn't me that was the danger. It was you. You're the one who got someone killed."

The sounds of children streaming out of school brought William to attention. He'd sat on the porch and stared at the same page in his Bible for he didn't know how long.

Despite the bright March sun, he surrounded himself with gloom and only watched life go by from the safety of his porch chair.

Little ones chattered as they left and headed for the village. Dormitories. Another thing he failed to accomplish.

Did dormitories matter when the Word seemed as dead to him right now as Jabo's body lying cold in the grave for the last three weeks? The basic work of the mission went on without him. Hannabo took over morning chapel with the children, the school was growing, and Mary's practice still thrived. She'd even been back to the village, although she didn't come to tell him about her trips.

Couldn't blame her for not speaking to him. She was right. The real danger at Nynabo had proved to be him. The irony. He'd kept her out of the jungle, adamant about not putting another woman in harm's way. Instead he'd never recognized the misguided zeal his preaching inspired in Jabo. He'd protected Mary and failed Jabo.

How did one go forward when the last sermon you preached resulted in a new convert's death? Three weeks and he still had no answer. The only thing he knew was his own failure. Mary, Clara and Hannabo accomplished the real work.

He was pathetic. Venturing out on the porch at times, he might catch a glimpse of her. Trying to be satisfied with just the sight of her while all along missing her company. Nothing would ever come of a relationship between them. He didn't deserve love. *Not even yours, God.*

God didn't answer. He too didn't seem to be speaking to William these days. Small wonder. The only one who insisted on still speaking to him was Hannabo.

Movement by the school caught his attention. He saw Clara, in a faded blue skirt and white shirtwaist, with her arm around a skinny young man in the khaki drawstring

pants that Clara had sewn for her students. They stood
outside the school door, the young man's serious face and
nods as Clara spoke to him, total rapport.

Clara managed to reach more for Christ in her school
than he had in his entire mission career. Daily reports from
Hannabo kept him up-to-date on the progress there. Several of the older boys came to salvation during their morning chapel. Boys who would soon be facing a challenge
to their faith, since they were almost the age when young
men entered the devilmen's bush school. There they were
indoctrinated in the practices and religion of the devilmen.
Only yesterday Hannabo had expressed his concern over
the pressure the boys would face if they followed tradition
and entered the school or the ostracism if they didn't. Hannabo pointed out the dormitories were the solution and it
would allow boys from outlying villages to come as well.

William knew he was supposed to care. He did. But
what help could he offer them? His advice was deadly.

Aromas from the kitchen wafted through the open windows of the house. Anaya bringing his lunch. Hannabo
wouldn't be far behind. You could set a watch by the man,
if you had one to set. No timepiece ran for long in this
overly humid climate. Maybe Hannabo had his own inter-
nal clock. His regular appearances suggested it. Showing
up three times a day was Hannabo's version of a compro-
mise after William recovered enough to refuse his hovering care. Hannabo had been by his side exclusively while
he healed from his injuries.

Anaya came out on the porch and placed a bowl of soup
in front of him. The rising steam carried the distinctive
scent of cooked goat and stirred his dormant appetite.

"You eat, Nana Pastor. You must get your strength
back."

He tried for a smile. The quizzical look he got in response made him wonder what he'd managed with his facial muscles. "Thank you, Anaya. The soup smells wonderful. I'll do my best with it."

Anaya returned to the kitchen just as Hannabo's head appeared coming up the hill from the village path. They must have a silent choreography going to keep him under observation. The only one not participating in this little dance was Mary. She came only when Hannabo brought her.

William raised the spoon to give the appearance of interest in his food and try to satisfy the faint rumble of his stomach and the louder rumble to come from Hannabo and Anaya if he didn't eat. Mary would make little comment beyond a bland statement of how nourishment was a key to getting well. No amount of nourishment would heal his heart. His clothes hanging off of him didn't concern him in the least.

The spicy broth of the goat soup made his eyes water. Anaya was going all out to try and stir his appetite. This was traditionally a dish served for celebrations. There was nothing to celebrate that he knew. Through his watering eyes, he saw Hannabo wave in his direction. He nodded and watched him knock at the clinic, waiting for Mary.

Mary stepped out of the clinic. She was in her usual peg-leg trousers and white shirt, her fiery hair swept back in a neat bun with the usual small tendrils escaping with the humidity.

He kept eating, more for something to do as they stepped on the porch than any real hunger.

"I am glad to see you well and eating, Nana Pastor."

He started to reply but choked as the soup went down the wrong way.

Mary moved behind him and raised his arms. The

coughing cleared quickly. "It opens up your airway," she said, almost apologizing for assisting him.

"Thanks, I swallowed wrong."

"Other than eating, are you having any other difficulties or problems at this time?"

"No, I…"

"Any swelling or remaining tenderness?"

"No…"

"Are you getting the exercise we talked about?"

"Hannabo makes sure of it."

"And how's that going?

A fourth question. Positively loquacious today. Could she be thawing toward him?

"William, I asked how the exercise is going."

Okay, maybe not thawing exactly. "I find myself still quite tired at the end of a walk, but it is getting better."

"Eat more. You'll have more energy. Time is the only other cure. I'll check again tomorrow. Send for me if there is anything you need." Mary turned and headed down the porch. Definitely not thawing.

Hannabo noticed his nearly empty soup bowl. "May I get Nana Pastor more?" The man's determined cheeriness was as welcome as the bugabugs on a wood-eating rampage.

"No, I've had quite enough for now." William stood. The sooner they got the exercise portion of the day over, the sooner he could plead fatigue and go lie down. "Let's go on and get this walking business out of the way."

Hannabo took him by the arm, but once down the steps, William pulled away. "I think I can manage."

"I will stay close in case you are unsteady on your feet."

Three times around the compound. Three times to see Jabo's absence in every location they passed. It ate at him, a festering sore growing on his heart and threatening to take it over.

The first day they'd walked, Hannabo suggested he might want to go and see the grave where his friend was laid. William made his feelings clear. Hannabo hadn't pressed him since. Now, as they neared their turnaround point for the final lap of the day, his heart's pain pressed in on him, pressuring him.

Instead of turning, his feet took their own path to the small graveyard. Maybe it was just another way of punishing himself. Whatever it was, he couldn't avoid the tangible evidence of what he'd caused any longer.

A pressure on his elbow stopped him. Hannabo. "Are you strong enough now?"

Emotion choked William's throat and he stuck to nodding.

Together they followed the path from the back of the house to the cottonwood at the far end. A new cross, earth still mounded, in a display next to Alice's grave. His knees threatened to buckle, but somehow he made it as far as the log beside the graves and sat.

Both crosses stood straight, silent, mocking him. Hannabo took a seat beside him and waited.

"The village agreed to his burial here?"

"Yes, his brothers came and his mother. They laid him on the mat and poured the palm wine in his mouth to keep it from spoiling. I thought you would not object."

"No, of course not. The custom is nothing to go against his conversion."

Hannabo nodded. "His mother first sat vigil to take care he was dead. Then the villagers came in turn to say the traditional words, give the kola nuts. After the third day, we buried him with Christian songs and prayers."

"You did well, then."

"I watched you and Nana Joseph. I've learned much."

Like how not to represent the Gospel? William's example fell far from that of his uncle. The proof lay in front of him under a mound of earth. No, two mounds.

"Pastor. I have something important to ask."

"Anything, Hannabo."

"I wish to go to school to learn to be a pastor to my people and others in the bush. I wish to go to the white man's bush and learn more of the Bible and how to speak God's Word so more of my people might know Him. Like you and Nana Joseph."

Hannabo's words impaled him more than any spear of the bush could. He choked out his words. "The school in Monrovia prepares young men. I will make inquiries. Desiring to serve your people is wonderful, but how can you want to be like me? How do you even still believe after you watched Jabo die because of my mistake?"

"My belief is not in you, Nana Pastor. It is in the God who saved me."

No words came. William stood dumbfounded.

"How can I not believe? Jabo was my friend, and even if he was foolish, he died for what he believed. Since this time, many of his family ask me about the God Jabo served, they want to know how he lost his fear of the fetish."

"I would have thought they wanted vengeance."

"They saw you pick him up in your arms and try to save him. They ask what can make a white missionary want to protect him when you could have run away and saved yourself."

Hannabo stood and pointed to his friend's grave. "So, it is as you say. As the Word says."

William tried to shake the fuzz from his brain. "What Word? What are you talking about?"

"The part about all things."

"All things?"

Eagerness and fervor swept over Hannabo's face. "In the book Nana Paul wrote to the Roman bush. All things work for good to those who are called to Christ Jesus. Remember, we studied this. Jabo's family, my tribe, they ask to hear the story of the One True God. Even out of his foolishness God has brought good."

If he hadn't been sitting, his legs wouldn't have held him at this revelation. This primitive bush man believed. Really believed. Believed in a way William didn't. *Oh, God, forgive me. What Mary's said to me is all true. I have felt superior and acted like a detached father instead of just another man like the one in front of me. For all my learning, it is one with a childlike faith who teaches me.*

Hannabo pressed on, oblivious to William's stunned silence. "From Nana Joseph and Mammy Ruth's death I came to know God, and you came here to serve in their place. Because of that, Jabo believed. Because of Jabo's death, many more are now hearing the Word."

It was like a hand from the grave reaching out to him through Hannabo, piercing the cold indifference he'd felt since he'd learned the young convert was dead. Gentle warmth suffused his body.

His body still denied the experience when he stood, but he felt the renewal taking place. His heart beat once again. The rhythm for God. All his own plans, his thoughts, worked for naught but God.

But God, that was as far as his mind could even travel. When the sobs racked his body, he gave free rein and he gave his will, his direction, his calling back to God where it belonged.

Hannabo held silent vigil. Then he clasped William's

hand and began to pray. "Father God, comfort my brother. His heart breaks with sorrow."

The simple prayer left him with peace. He looked up to find gentle concern.

William reached out and clapped Hannabo on the back. Hannabo's startle changed to a toothy grin as he saw his friend smile for the first time in weeks. "Hannabo, you will make a strong missionary to the bush. You've already made one here."

They headed back to the house. Hannabo monitored him, but William's steps never faltered. How could they? He floated with relief and renewed faith the entire walk back to the house. The only hitch in his step was Mary. He needed to make things right. Given her anger, it would take another miracle of God.

Chapter Twenty-One

Mary couldn't miss the spring in William's step and the smile on his face as he headed to the school for his first chapel time with the children since his recovery. Everything Clara and Hannabo had told her was right before her eyes. William was the proverbial new man.

She dropped the curtain when he turned his gaze toward the infirmary. Silly woman, what does it matter if he sees you looking out your window? It was a perfectly normal thing to do. Look out your window to see if any patients were coming to your unusually empty clinic.

A perfectly normal thing that proved Clara and Hannabo's thesis right. She was avoiding him. She'd been using work, nonstop, daily work, inventing work if necessary, just to justify being too busy to seek out his company. So what if she missed communal mealtimes and had food brought to her at the infirmary? She was a busy woman, right?

No, she was an angry woman. Jabo, a sweet, gentle man was dead and it was William Mayweather's fault. If the good pastor hadn't preached his fateful sermon, one that inspired a new convert to the unalterable consequences of the actions he took, Jabo would still be alive.

Like her brother would be alive if she hadn't gone to war first. So who was she really angry with here? She had more in common with William than she'd realized. Except he seemed to be able to move on. The man was cheerful even. It wasn't right.

Footsteps pounded on the steps to the porch, interrupting her self-flagellation. She stepped to the side, barely avoiding the nut-brown body that propelled itself through the doorway. It was Tulie, one of Clara's students. His real name was substantially longer, but they'd all taken to calling him Tulie. She caught him by the arm. "Whoa, there, Tulie. What's wrong?"

"Mammy Clara says come quick. Bring your bag." Tulie turned to leave.

Mary held fast to his arm. "What's happened? Who's hurt?"

Tulie pulled free, saying, "Come quick. Come quick." He disappeared in a streak toward the school.

What kind of trouble could have happened during chapel? On second thought, she didn't want to dwell on the possibilities. Look what William's last sermon had provoked.

Mary grabbed her bag and headed for the chapel.

The location of the problem was easy to find. Fourteen children, William and Clara ringed a writhing body on the floor.

Mary ordered, "Everybody step back. Give me room."

Most complied. Clara and William herded the more curious children back to their seats on the benches.

A beautiful little girl, adorned in country cloth woven in the village and with many rows of braids glistening with palm oil, lay on the ground clutching her stomach and moaning.

"What's her name, Clara?"

"Sonlee. She's Tulie's little sister. She looked fine when she came in this morning. Then she yelped and fell on the ground holding her stomach."

Mary knelt down beside her and used her best nice doctor face. "I'm going to need one of you to hold her. I need to check her abdomen and I can't do it while she's curled up like a little porcupine."

William squatted on the other side of Sonlee and nodded his head toward the benches. "Maybe we should take her to the infirmary while you examine her."

Mary saw fourteen sets of eyes riveted to the spectacle. "Definitely. Clara, tell them she's going to be all right. William, take my bag and I'll carry her."

Before she could react, William had scooped the child into his arms and was murmuring soothing sounds in the child's dialect. He headed out of the school, leaving her to trail in his wake.

At the doorway, Mary paused to ask Clara, "Can I take Tulie with me?"

Clara assented and instructed him to go with Mary.

William had already laid the squirming child in the infirmary bed by the time she caught up with him. He stroked Sonlee's head and continued his soft patter. This was a side of William she hadn't seen in a while. At least not since before Jabo's death.

It made her uncomfortable. Easier to keep him distant as a stern villain. Acting tender like a father to a sick child made him harder to vilify.

"William, can you ask Tulie if anyone else in the family is sick?" While she waited, she attempted to press on the child's belly, searching for any clue as to what was giving her such pain. Sonlee resisted all her attempts.

"He says no, only Sonlee."

"Well, that's good. Maybe it's something simple, like

what she ate. Hold her arms, see if her brother can help with her legs while I try to check her belly more thoroughly."

As soon as they grasped Sonlee's limbs, Mary began a careful palpation of her belly. After a few seconds, she knew what was wrong.

"Ask Tulie if his sister has eaten a lot of fruit lately."

The words barely left William's mouth before the boy's face split into a wide grin and he nodded.

William looked back at Mary. "So this was a case of a bad tummy ache?"

Mary straightened. "Unless I miss my guess, our little one here is a tiny bit dramatic with her physical problems. Maybe she's trying to gather sympathy for when her mother finds she'd been in the food stores."

"Can you be sure it's not something more serious?"

On cue, like the little actress she was destined to be, Sonlee rolled over toward William and promptly threw up off the side of the bed. William jumped back, but from the look on his face, didn't quite clear the incoming fire.

Mary tried to suppress a laugh. She failed. Sonlee sat straight up and smiled, obviously relieved of her burden. The brother giggled when he peeked around the bed at the pastor's clothes.

William tried for stern, but gave up and shrugged. "Good diagnosis, Doctor. Now do you have a cloth so I can wipe off my shoes? I didn't move quite fast enough."

Oblivious to the problem, Sonlee hopped up and ran out the door with her brother.

"Another crisis averted. Now let me see if I can get you a damp cloth for your shoes while I clean up the floor."

William finished cleaning and helped her get the rest of the floor. "So how's the glamorous life of a missionary doctor working out for you?"

Mary shot him a grin before she remembered her anger. The question hung in the air. The man was tender with children and attempting humor to boot. Maybe the blow to his head did more good than damage. Still didn't absolve him of Jabo's death, though.

She stepped outside and deposited the soiled cloths in a basket so the smell wouldn't pervade the small clinic. She had no choice but to walk back into the clinic where he was. She could have used another little emergency right about now. *Face him and get it over with, woman.* She turned to go in and walked smack into his broad chest as he was attempting to exit. For a second, she froze, her senses assaulted by his sheer masculine nearness.

He gently lifted her chin with his hand, saying, "I owe you an apology."

The tenderness in his eyes scared her. One look and her anger fled. She knew how to battle a man's prejudices. How did you battle his affections?

She wasn't going to stay close enough to engage the enemy in hand-to-hand combat. She turned her head and ducked around him, firing the only salvo she knew might work. "You owe me a lot of apologies. What say we just move forward?"

Mary stared at the shelves in front of her, desperately wishing they weren't already so well organized. Giving up, she turned back to face him.

William closed the clinic door and leaned against it, his hands in his pockets, effectively blocking any run for freedom. "I've found it's the things we don't face or try to ignore out of existence that are the most destructive. Better to get it out quickly and let it heal."

"Fine." Oh, anything but fine. The newer, gentler William was a terrifying proposition. "What is it you believe needs to be said?"

"I was wrong."

In all her life, she'd never heard those words cross a man's lips. Was this some new trick? Erupting anger still to come? "About what?"

He laughed, a light sound in heavy atmosphere. "Um… everything for starters."

"Care to elaborate?" Mary asked. He sounded sincere. Trust held itself in abeyance for now.

"Not giving the enemy any quarter?"

"Do you deserve for me to make this easy on you?" She hated the hitch in her voice. "You got my friend killed."

Pain flashed its stabs through his eyes. His jaw tightened. Silence held a beat. "No, I don't deserve anything. It is entirely my fault Jabo is dead."

Tears threatened. She stomped them down even as the waterworks of grief tried to breech the damn. "Why? Why did you do it? How could you preach a message and fail to see its effect on Jabo?"

He looked at her without flinching. "I've had a lot of time alone lately asking myself that question. It took Hannabo to help me see it."

She crossed her arms and waited.

"I was jealous."

"Jealous of what? Jabo?"

"You."

Would the floor open up now and take her? Was he going to blame this on her? "Explain yourself."

He ran a hand through his thick black mane, brushing a stray lock from his forehead. "When I first came here with my wife, I was full of both grief and idealism. I had something to prove to the aunt and uncle who raised me."

"The ones who died here?"

"Yes. I wasn't going to let their deaths be in vain. So I dragged my wife, my fragile little Alice, to a country she never should have come to in the first place. After she died, I felt, well…"

"Guilty. I'm well acquainted with the feeling."

Surprise lit his eyes as they crinkled in consideration of her insight. "Exactly. And out of guilt, I vowed never to endanger another woman in the interior again."

"Let me ask you something, William."

"Anything."

"Did Alice believe in the mission or was she only being a dutiful wife?"

"At first duty propelled her, but after she prayed, she caught the vision for the country too."

"So your wife understood what she committed to doing?"

William gave a rueful smile. "As much as anyone coming here ever can."

"Then why do you say you dragged her here?"

William shook her head. "My enthusiasm carried the day. I passionately believed I could win the hearts of the heathen to Christ, become an evangelist to the unplowed fields of Africa, one my uncle would have been proud he'd raised."

"What does this have to do with Jabo's death?" Don't cry. Don't cry.

"I let my vow blind me to what God's plans really might be."

Could anyone change this much? "What do you think those plans might be?"

"It's pretty clear to me nothing I thought or tried to do was right. God sent you and Clara here and I blocked you at every turn. But without you, I would have died. Twice."

She laughed, nerves flushing out the sound. "I don't think anyone gets to die twice actually."

He grinned and her knees weakened. "Probably not. Although with you around to revive them and God in charge, I'm not so sure of any hard-and-fast rules anymore."

"That's a big change in attitude. Given our history, I'm still waiting for the 'but' or for both our tempers to fly."

"There is no exception here. I am sorry for the way I've treated you. The way I've failed to value God's plan in your life for Nynabo Mission."

Oh, my. This was an emotional minefield. "This is all very touching, but I still don't understand how any of this relates to Jabo's death."

"I had this picture of myself, the great white evangelist preaching to the natives. But who do the natives hold in high esteem here?"

The whisper tried to catch in her throat. "Me." Oh, God, no.

"Exactly. All I could see was the crowds lined up to see you, your medicine. My message was sincere, I truly felt God had called me to preach it." William hung his head. "But I also felt I had to do something to take back control."

What could she say to any of this? Suspicion that it really was her fault grew like mushrooms on the forest floor after the rain. If she'd never come here, Jabo would still be alive.

He must have caught the emotions she tried to hide. "None of this is you. My ego, my flesh as the Bible puts it, couldn't handle it."

She nodded, but her mind screamed, *my fault.*

"I got it in my head I could be a modern-day Elijah, taking on the prophets of Baal. I'd talked about it so much Jabo…"

Were those tears she saw?

He cleared his throat and continued. "Jabo's fervor as a new convert was inflamed by my rhetoric." He shook his head, eyes downward. "I believed we could be there and safely preach. I never meant it to go that far. What happened that day will be with me forever."

His repentant spirit was contagious. "Well, as long as we're clearing the air, I'm sorry too," she said.

William straightened and closed the distance between them. Taking her by the arms, he looked earnestly into her eyes. "You have done nothing that requires an apology."

"I put you in that position. I should have tried harder to make the people I treated understand I wasn't some kind of magical devilwoman."

"In the end, it was what saved my life. The devilmen were afraid of you." He laughed, a short bark.

"Humor? I don't find any of this funny."

"No, not funny. Ironic. Hannabo pointed it out to me. God really does work all things to His good."

"What good could you possibly be talking about now?"

"The thing I made such a hindrance in my mind, their fear and respect for you, was the very thing that saved me. I doubt little else could have stopped that mob in its tracks."

"But I wasn't in time to save Jabo." She stepped back from his hold. Put up a wall with her eyes.

"Another thing I've come to understand since my talks with Hannabo and spending time alone with God and in his Word. Jabo made his own choice…" He put his hand up to stop her protest.

"I'm not absolving myself, but we are all responsible for our own actions. Hannabo reports that many in the village have been asking questions about the missionary's God as they put it. Jabo's actions and his death have stirred something all my preaching and teaching never did."

"It's a high price."

"One Jabo knew he risked paying. I saw his face before

he attacked the fetish. He was resolved to die for what he believed."

"But why? Did he not understand there was another way?"

"Was there? I certainly would have counseled him against what he did if I'd known beforehand. And I might have been wrong."

"How can you even say that? Jabo's death was wrong."

"But out of his death comes a valuable lesson. For me, I've been so busy trying to be sure we're all safe, I forgot that sometimes an ultimate price is paid to advance the Gospel. God himself provided the example when he gave his only Son over to die so we might live."

Silence laced the air. Mary's protests all died before they formed. How could you argue with the ultimate source of salvation?

And in the silence, awareness grew. Not exactly Godly in nature. The small space, the nearness of the man, his repentant heart all fertilized the tender feelings she'd been so ruthlessly pruning.

And then he took two fatal steps and put his hands on her arms again. "We've declared truce before, but I really mean it this time. I see God's call on your life here. I won't interfere with it again."

She tried to laugh it off. God's call? She'd not been thinking too closely about God when she signed the contract with the Mission Board. Just her own guilt. "You mean God called me to allow these people to be deceived into believing I have some form of magic? Seems to me false belief is part of the problem here."

Since she was avoiding looking up at him, she studied the button on his shirt in front of her as if she were back in medical school and there would be a final exam on it any minute.

"Mary?"

She raised her eyes up two more buttons, an open collar and a chin, not stopping till she met the depths of his liquid brown eyes. "Yes?"

In answer his lips moved toward hers and captured them with a tender kiss.

She'd never had a more thorough apology.

He lingered close. She waited in case he wanted to repeat the apology.

He did. Only verbally.

William dropped his hands and took a step back. "I'm sorry."

"So I gathered."

"No. I mean for the kiss. I didn't mean to take advantage of you. I'm not sure what came over me."

He was apologizing for kissing her? Now that was insulting. So much for letting her guard down. She responded with the only safe answer available for a woman who'd had her heart stolen with a kiss and handed right back to her. "Be sure it doesn't happen again."

Chapter Twenty-Two

He was such a liar. William climbed the hill from an early-evening palaver with the elders, one that had turned into a pressing invitation to a late-night celebration with drums and dancing. He'd stayed and spoken of God at every opportunity. Now, swinging the torch to light the path back to his bed, the truth that he'd stayed busy to avoid burned within him. It had ever since he told Mary he hadn't meant to kiss her.

Kissing her had been in the back of his mind since the night on the banks of the river after she saved Anaya from the sasswood. Her exhausted determination, strength and presence of mind had touched something deep within him even then.

He was newly freed of the blind prejudice and lack of vision that had kept those feelings suppressed. Now he found countless excuses to be around her. Watching her work with the children and adults that came to the clinic was sheer pleasure. He'd learned a little more of medicine, seen a few more gory sights than he'd wanted, but it was all worth it.

He'd like to think he was having an effect on her too. Except it was all spiritual. After hearing his approach to the Gospel when he assisted her with a patient, she'd begun a few conversations with her charges that weren't strictly medical in nature. She never seemed really comfortable with it though.

What kind of minister wanted the influence to be more romantic instead? If it wasn't for new converts in the village, he'd think he was striking out spiritually too. It was pretty clear he'd never get closer than the length of her arm if her demeanor was an indication. Completely professional.

He topped the hill and glanced toward the infirmary. No lights. The women had long acclimated to sleeping with the nightly drums. He'd hoped for a light. An excuse.

He turned his hopes to his bed. It, at least, would be more welcoming.

What did he expect? He'd kissed the woman and those soft lips had kissed him back. And instead of telling her how he felt, he up and apologized for kissing her.

He grabbed an oil lamp hanging from the nail on the porch and lit it before extinguishing the torch next to its predecessors in a bucket of dirt.

Once inside he quickly readied himself for bed. But even as his head hit the pillow, thoughts of soft red hair, soft pink lips, intruded. He fluffed the pillow viciously and tried changing positions. Rolling over wasn't the answer, but maybe he was on the right track with changing positions.

This time he slipped out of bed and onto his knees beside it. *Father in Heaven. You know my heart. If this woman is meant to be more in my life than a colleague, a fellow missionary, then give me the opportunity to express my love. Let me see the perfect time and place. Until then, help me to focus on You and the reason you brought*

*me here. And Lord, whatever this is that holds her back
spiritually, free her Lord, as you've freed me.*

Wearily, William climbed back in his bed and found
sleep. Love he would leave to God.

Her jump in awareness never failed to remind her of
the feelings she suppressed every time William walked
into the room. The common breakfast Clara had chided
her into this morning was no exception. Fortunately, the
handsome preacher couldn't know the longing beat he set
off when he appeared.

This morning it was a different beat disturbing her. She
hadn't slept well. The celebration drums last night had
kept her from an easy rest. And now drums were going
again this morning.

She recognized the low timbre of the talking drum used
in the bush like a telegraph. Something was going on.
More tribal troubles? Every few days brought more news
of fighting, sometimes with the smallest of provocations.
More than once local villages had called on William to
come and settle disputes that would have led to bloodshed.

"Good morning, ladies."

Cheerful too. He must have slept through the drums.
Not fair. She nodded her reply while she finished chewing.

Clara asked, "Pastor, any idea what the drums are
saying? Could we be about to get mail or supplies?"

"Sorry, ladies. I'm not an expert on the drums. Master-
ing the various tones of the language is enough of a challenge for me."

"Well, I guess we'll hear something soon enough. Mail
would be nice." Clara looked wistfully out the window,
trying to conjure up a caravan. "Look, there's Hannabo

up from the village. Maybe he can tell us." Clara got up and went to greet him.

Mary thought Clara must be homesick. For her sake, Mary hoped mail would come soon. Even if it meant facing the fact that her own family still hadn't written her. "Maybe Hannabo can tell us when they'll stop."

"Not feeling well, Mary?" William's focused attention brought her back to ground.

"I'm tired this morning. I didn't sleep well and my clinic hours have fallen off, so I'm a little ragged."

"Be grateful things are a little boring right now. There's always the alternative."

"I know. At the hospital we all learned never to complain about it being too quiet. It was sure to start the next wave of causalities."

"Superstitious nonsense."

"Maybe so," she said, rising to take her dishes back to the kitchen. When she returned she found a trio of serious faces. "Why the long faces? No mail after all?"

"No," William said. "Hannabo brought us a message from the drums. Nana Mala has sent word asking for you. His infant daughter is sick and his devilmen have no cure. He also wishes for me to come and preach."

There was only one answer possible. "When do we leave?"

William's machete arm was exhausted, the blade dulled. The three porters with them, each with a forty-pound pack of supplies, necessities and gifts for the village, had given up the usual singing as they traveled by the third day, reduced to grunts and groans the last two as they crawled over or under yet another log in the path. If you could call it a path. Most places were barely wide enough for the placement of a single foot. How did a pregnant woman manage the trip from the Pahn village to Nynabo in the first place? Desperation must have been a powerful motivator.

The porters sprawled in the small clearing, and Mary sat on a fallen log, taking a much-needed break. The dark circles under her eyes worried him. The tightness around her mouth, the limited conversation at the campfires. None of it good.

She looked up. Caught studying her again.

"How much farther, William?"

"The village is situated a short distance from the mountain, and we're almost on top of it. Our guide, Pennon, claims we will be there today. Closer in to the village, we should make good time. The paths will be more traveled."

"Five days is a long time, medically speaking."

She was worried about the baby. No telling if the child was still alive at this point. "There's no helping it. Even if we could have cut time off our trip by pushing harder, arriving too exhausted or making ourselves ill wouldn't help anyone."

"The baby may not still be alive."

"Or she may be. Worrying before you know won't help her."

"I know. It's just that Wonlay was the first baby I'd delivered since before the war. Bringing life after so much death, especially Jeremy's, really got me attached to her."

"Who's Jeremy?"

Mary's face shuttered. "My brother."

"Clara mentioned you had a brother who died in the war, but I didn't know his name. What happened to him?"

"The Great War happened. And his sister's bad example." Mary stood and brushed off the decaying wood that clung to her trousers. "Now, assuming the baby is still alive, there is someone I can save."

The carriers groaned when he called an end to the rest. Mary cut off any further conversation. He was frustrated not to be able to talk more and take advantage of that tiny crack into her personal life.

He took his frustration all out on the next area that needed clearing. Dull machete or not, he got the job done.

The long trek to the side of the mountain finally paid off in a dramatic view of the Pahn village. Nana Bolo's home and the Nynabo village were both small in comparison.

Two distinct paths bisected the village; judging by the sun's position overhead, they ran like compass points, east to west and north to south. From the hub came the sound of the village telegraph. The talking drum announced their arrival after they exited the jungle. Back at Nynabo, Hannabo would get the relayed message, know of their safety, and reassure Clara, who'd stayed behind because of the school.

Even if he hadn't known the Pahns' warlike nature, the construction made it apparent. A solid stockade of timbers surrounded a compound holding a tightly placed warren of conical huts. The walls they circled to get to the main gate were hung with fetishes, skulls adorning some of the poles.

The usually vocal doctor whispered, "From a distance, I thought the skulls were monkey. They're human. I know you told me what to expect, but this is pretty intimidating."

"It's designed to scare their enemies."

"Well, it's doing a good job of scaring me right now." Mary shuddered.

"It's part of their culture. They believe that if they consume their enemy, they also take on his power. They keep body parts to help hold the power and as a deterrent to any enemies."

"William, are they all as warlike as Nana Mala?"

"Some more than others, but a lot are easily provoked."

"Why hasn't the government put a stop to the cannibalism?"

"It's life here. You saw the trails we just traveled. As far as I know we're only the second set of missionaries to ever see this village. Can you imagine trying to bring troops and vehicles through the bush?"

Mary got quiet as they passed through the main gate and were directed toward an open area on their right.

He asked himself for the umpteenth time if he'd done the right thing by bringing Mary to this hostile tribe. He'd promised to trust God with her calling, but he still couldn't stop himself from worrying about her. The harder he tried to ignore his growing attachment to her, the more it interrupted his thought life.

Nana Mala would give anyone a basis for concern. He was a whimsical man. His actions at Nynabo proved that. How could William trust a chief who might have his own aunt's and uncle's skulls adorning the stockade walls?

Pennon stepped up and translated with the village representative. William arranged for Mary to meet with the head wife, observing all the protocols before she examined the baby. He would go to the palaver house and meet with Nana Mala and the elders.

Separation from Mary filled him with trepidation. He masked it as best he could and watched Mary's retreating back as she was led to her audience with the head wife. One last glimpse, then he followed their guide and prepared to be greeted by the man who'd ordered his uncle's and aunt's deaths and who could just as easily order Mary's if the baby died.

Chapter Twenty-Three

Mary wound her way through the huts, following her guide. It was hard to say what was so different here. She'd been in a tightly packed village before. But the demeanor of the people was not the same at all. Children reached out to touch her and their mothers yanked them back as if she had a contagion.

What were they afraid of?

The passage widened and opened around a larger hut. Must be the head wife's home. Some would call her a queen, but it was hard for Mary to think of it that way.

Her guide turned and spoke in pidgin to her. "Mammy Tarloh will see you now. She savvies none of the white man's palavering. I will speak for you."

"Thank you, but when will I see Jayplo and her baby?"

"Soon. The baby is well. Do not worry."

The baby is well? Had Mary worried for nothing? Mary bent and stepped through the low doorway. There were a few windows, so the light was easy to adjust to. At the far end of the room sat an enormous woman. She had to be at least three hundred pounds. Bright colorful county cloth, the kind woven in the bush, covered her with its immense yardage.

Jewelry and fetishes abounded. Beads and bones mixed together around her neck. She had feathers in her hair, including one enormous red one, from a bird Mary had not seen before. Bangles of iron and brass covered her arms from the elbows to the wrists. Each finger and toe contained a ring.

The queen had put on all her finery for this meeting. Mary was honored, but unsure what was expected of her.

Her hostess spoke first and Mary's guide translated. "Welcome. I am honored to meet the white devilwoman."

Oh, no. Her reputation had gone before her. Apparently the tales had traveled and the chief's wife had heard them. Now she would spend longer explaining science and dispelling the idea of magic than she would establishing any medical care.

Inwardly she sighed and got down to business. There was no helping it. All she could do was hope to dispel the myths quickly so she could do some good while she was here.

"Please tell Mammy Tarloh I am honored to be here. I am a woman of science and medicine, but not magic." Mary waited and watched her hostess as her guide translated.

The woman's eyes narrowed, her lips firmed. Not the answer she wanted. "Please tell Mammy Tarloh I am much concerned for the welfare of the child Wonlay and my spirit will not rest until I can see the child for myself."

This time a gleam of something Mary couldn't identify shone in Mammy Tarloh's eyes. Mary's suspicions rose.

The translator's answer didn't help deflate them. "Mammy Tarloh says Jayplo and the baby will be here soon. She offers you refreshment while you wait."

Hospitality reigned, and Mary squirmed inwardly through the entire visit. If she examined baby Wonlay and the little girl appeared healthy, she would lobby William to leave as soon as possible. This place gave her the creeps.

Mary heard the slight rustle at the hut entrance and was relieved to see Jayplo with a sleeping Wonlay in her arms. She mimed to Jayplo to let her hold the baby to examine. Jayplo's eyes flitted to Mammy Tarloh, who nodded. Only then did Jayplo hand over the child.

Ten minutes and an exam later, Mary had her answer. The baby was healthy with no obvious signs of distress. Every question she'd asked his mother filtered through Mammy Tarloh's approval first. Mary had examined many babies in Nynabo, but never with this much direct supervision from the head wife.

Finally, she handed Wonlay back to her mother and for a fraction of a second locked eyes with Jayplo. Fear. With her back to Mammy Tarloh, Jayplo showed her fear. Of what? The young mother obviously wanted to say more, but getting her alone might prove impossible.

She put on her best professional mask and turned back to her hostess. Smiling, she told her translator, "I am very tired after the long journey and would like to speak with my companion, but I don't wish to offend Mammy Tarloh. Perhaps Jayplo could escort me to a place where I can rest."

"I will ask."

Whatever he said worked to get her a place to rest. Mammy Tarloh frowned at the mention of Jayplo's name. It didn't take a translator to know she wouldn't be escorting Mary. She found herself ushered out by her translator and taken to a guest hut while the young mother and child remained with the head wife.

Her translator told her, "You rest here please, Mammy Doctor. Someone will come and get you before the sun is all the way down. There is a feast and celebration in honor of our guests tonight."

"And my companion. Where is he?"

"He is in the palaver house. You will be with him at the feast." With that he turned and left.

Mary surveyed her surroundings. They obviously meant for her to be comfortable. Skins and traders' blankets sat on a wooden sleep pallet. There was water in a large jar with a wooden cup beside it.

Temptation reared. Did she dare go look for William on her own? One quick look outside the door of her hut gave her an answer. A spear-laden warrior stood guard. When he saw her, he gestured for her to go back inside.

Mary complied and tried to ignore the gorge of fear rising. What had they gotten themselves into? Was William all right?

Had they voluntarily walked into a village that meant them harm? She sat on the blanketed pallet and began to pray. The only thing that came to mind was Psalm 23, a scripture she'd memorized as a child in Sunday school. *The Lord is my shepherd, I shall not want...* She prayed the words. Her nerves calmed, but she couldn't help but think that the valley of the shadow of death seemed an apt description of the Pahn village right now.

The drums of feasting and celebration beat out their rhythm with the setting sun. Young women danced while the men played the instruments or clapped their hands. The rhythm matched William's accelerated heart beat, a steadier beat now that Mary and her escort picked their way through the crowd toward him.

The corners of her eyes pinched in worry. She'd picked up on it too. Something wasn't right here. No, maybe it was the baby's condition. His nerves were getting to him.

To pray without ceasing had been his goal since they entered this place.

His palaver with Nana Mala and his leaders held sway in his thoughts. He'd preached the power of a risen God, the greatest miracle of all, and yet Nana Mala's questions always wound their way back to one subject—sly questions about Mary's medicine.

In the morning, he would make their excuses and get Mary out of here, provided the baby was well enough. The faster their feet hit the trail the better. *Lord, is it my part to water the seeds my family planted in their blood? I'm trying not to go by sight, but none of this reads like a spiritual harvest is imminent.*

He'd try and secure another invitation. Maybe pave the way for a future mission station or see if some parents would send their children to the school. *Lord, I know you have a plan for this people. Show me that plan, Father.*

Mary was brought to his side and seated in front of the low dais with Nana Mala and the elders of the tribe. She said, "I was beginning to wonder if they'd eaten you."

"Don't even joke about that," William admonished.

"Sorry, inappropriate humor is a tradition among doctors for relieving stress. This situation is certainly stressful."

"I'm not sure things are as they appear. Nana Mala's interest was more in hearing tales of you. Not the Gospel he supposedly wanted to hear."

They both went quiet when several calabashes replete with rice and palm butter were placed in front of them. Despite her nerves, Mary managed a smile and nod of thanks to her servers.

The same smile strained her face when she turned to him and said, "The baby is fine. It took some time for them to finally produce her, but when they did she was healthy."

"So she recovered on her own?"

She shook her head. "No, I don't think she was ever sick in the first place. Her mother tried to communicate with me, but was cut off by the head wife. The mother just looked afraid."

It was a trap. Lord, what have we walked into? "Just keep smiling, accept their hospitality and we'll make excuses to leave in the morning. If we leave before most of the revelers are up, we might be able to slip out without a confrontation."

"What will you say?"

"I will tell the truth, that the mission needs me and I am concerned to be gone too long when a woman was left in charge."

"But Clara is more than capable."

"True, and Hannabo is at her side. But they will understand my haste to return if I tell them Clara is left behind."

"But what about spreading the Gospel here?"

"I've preached, but Nana Mala wasn't receptive. I suspect he only wanted to meet the devilwoman on his own territory."

She rubbed her forehead. "Please don't call me that. I've spent all day trying to live down my reputation here."

"Sorry, but that's what he thinks."

"Well, I'm all for leaving. Since they confined me to a guest hut after the meeting with the head wife, I wasn't even able to treat any patients."

"They're probably a little afraid of you."

"I could do without the fear. It's worse than the constant disrespect I used to get from men outside the bush."

"I do believe I resemble that remark."

Mary favored him with one of her winning smiles. "You

came around. And you weren't any more arrogant at first than the male doctors I've worked with in the war or at home."

"It took the death of someone we both cared about to do it."

Mary's reply lost itself in the sound of the drums. He leaned in closer. She yelled, "You learned a valuable lesson…" The drums silenced, leaving her next words unaccompanied, hanging in the silence. "…one you'll never repeat."

When a cadre of devilmen approached in full regalia, William feared she was wrong. Dead wrong.

Mary felt William tense beside her. Her hand instinctively sought his to hold as she looked at the spectacle of devilment in front of her.

The obvious leader stepped forward and spoke and a shaken Pennon translated. "The devil challenges you to use your magic now. He says Nyesoa is the true creator and gives him power."

Mary shivered in defiance of the heat as fear leeched onto her. She looked to William. "What do I tell him?"

"You can only speak the truth here. That you have no magic, that Jesus is the true God and all power belongs to him."

Mary turned to the listening Pennon. "Tell him what William said. Tell him also that my ability to heal the sick is not magic, but medicine that was learned after many years of study."

The head devil snarled at the translation and shouted his reply to Nana Mala.

"What did he say, Pennon?"

The quaver in her translator's voice was obvious. "He tells Nana Mala that you have magic, but you are keeping it from him. He feels your magic is not as strong as his, but by taking yours, his may be strengthened."

The leering smile from the devilman and his crew exposed the pointed, razor-sharp teeth within. His narrow eyes conveyed one message. Her imminent death.

The only question was if Nana Mala would grant his wish.

Nana Mala barked harsh orders and two warriors grabbed William under his arms and began to haul him away. Before a protest left her lips, cruel fingers circled her arms and she was hauled in the same direction. Pennon remained, unable to tell her what had been said. Where were they taking them and why?

A short distance away, she was thrown to the ground in a small, windowless clay hut. William was already there, picking himself off the ground and hurrying to her.

"William, what's going on?" she asked as she got her feet back under her.

"Best I can tell, Nana Mala is deciding our fate. Are you hurt?"

"Just a little banged up, but I'm okay." Nana Mala's anger when she denied she had magic to give him replayed through her mind. Her only consolation was William was with her while they waited to hear whatever fate the furious sovereign decided.

William paced. "I'm so sorry. I had no business bringing you here."

"I don't recall being dragged through the jungle. I wanted to come as much as you did. We were tricked, plain and simple."

"No matter, it was my job to protect you. I've made the very mistake I condemned my Uncle Joseph for making."

"William, I am responsible for myself. The mistake is ours equally, if indeed it was a mistake."

"Of course it was a mistake. We're about to be sacrificed so a misguided heathen chief can try to appropriate your magic."

"You planted the seeds of the Gospel, like your uncle before you. You can't know what it will mean in the future. Isn't that what you said about what came from Jabo's death?"

William grew solemn. "Yes, but my own words still don't alleviate my culpability in your death."

"Hey, I'm not dead yet." Mary took hold of William's hand. "We're not dead yet." Despite her attempt at bravery, tears welled up and she began to shiver.

He gave her hand a gentle squeeze and released it. He opened his arms to her, giving an invitation for comfort, one she quickly accepted. He pulled her close and held her tightly. She let his strong warmth seep through her, and pretended for a time that there was nothing but this moment between them. Whether he loved her or only acted from compassion, Mary didn't care. His arms were the only place she wanted to be.

After a few moments, he disengaged his arms and spoke. "We must pray. Only God can deliver us now."

They knelt together on the packed dirt floor and clasped both hands. Mary tried to quell her fears as William prayed.

"Heavenly Father, we come to you in this time of need. Our greatest need, Lord. We pray for your deliverance, much as you gave Paul and Silas in jail that night. Your word says a ruler's heart is in your hands. Hold sway over Nana Mala's heart, Father, and let the words I've spoken reach him for you. Spare our lives that more good may be done in your Kingdom."

William's prayer gave Mary the opening she'd needed.

"William, what if the greater good comes through our

deaths?" She leveled a steady gaze at his startled countenance.

"Then we can only pray for His grace when the time comes. My only regret is that I failed to protect you."

"I was in danger long before I met you, William. The Great War wasn't exactly a safe place to be."

"But you are my responsibility."

"I've given it some thought since we last talked about Jabo in Nynabo. Perhaps our deaths will bring more missionaries, inspire them. Or maybe I will finally atone for my own mistakes. If I've learned one thing since hearing you preach, it's that you can't always know how God is working."

"What do you mean, this is finally how you can atone? What do you have to atone for?"

Mary paused. What did it matter now? The truth might as well be told. "You were right all along. I'm not the kind of missionary God needs in the bush. I didn't come to preach the Gospel. I came because I had nowhere else to go."

William's voice gentled and his hand cupped her cheek. "Whatever you think brought you here, Mary O'Hara, you're wrong. I've seen God use you time and again in ways no one else could have managed."

Mary pressed her cheek into his hand and looked up into his eyes. "You carried guilt over Jabo's death. I understand that guilt. I managed to get my own little brother killed, and for my own selfish reasons."

"I thought he died in the war."

"A German ordnance may have killed him, but if not for me, he would be alive and well. I've carried that guilt and let it drive me. If anyone has made a mistake, it's me, acting out of false guilt instead of depending on God's guidance."

"Tell me what happened."

His soft tone was almost her undoing. She pushed back tears to continue. "It's simple really. When I signed on with the Red Cross, it was because I was tired of the restrictions the medical profession and the patients put on me." Mary laughed in irony. "My brother Jeremy looked up to me as a role model. After I left for France, he defied our father and joined the army."

"You can't know he wouldn't have joined the army anyway, Mary. Jeremy and Jabo both made choices themselves."

"Oh, there's more." Mary took a deep breath and continued. "He was wounded at the battle in the Argonne Forest. Ironically, he ended up at my hospital and I took his case from a surgeon I considered a big blowhard. I held his hand and spoke with him, assured him he'd be all right. He just looked at me with complete faith that I would do what I said. Instead, he died on my operating table. His wounds were just too great. I've come to realize that my own ego may have cost him his life. Maybe he would have survived if I'd let another surgeon operate."

"And maybe he was there, on your table, for that last bit of comfort he would receive on this side on heaven. The sight of the sister he loved before he died. How many soldiers were ever granted a last wish to see someone they loved before they died?"

Mary's tears fell hot and sudden. "Do you think so?" William's arms encompassed her and she wept over the revelation.

When her sobbing ceased, she pulled back, wiping her tears with the backs of her arms as best she could. "I've never seen it that way. That I was a comfort to him before he died. I so focused on my own feelings of guilt that I didn't see it through his eyes."

William said, "Much like me right now. I've been so focused on my own guilt over bringing you here that I failed
to focus on a higher perspective. I've let myself dwell on
my own feelings and not on God."

"Clara tried to tell me I had it all wrong. I guess for
those of us who are so hardheaded, it takes something
pretty major to get through."

"But it did, for both of us. Now we must move forward
and see what God will do in this situation."

"William, I don't think that an earthquake will split our
prison walls."

"Even if there is no deliverance for us, we can take
comfort from God and each other. I know this much now
with clarity I didn't possess before. Whatever happens
here today is in God's hands, not ours. We must continue
to pray that he will give us the words to speak that will
deliver us or the strength to withstand our fate."

"I'm in agreement with you on that prayer. Strangely
enough, I've never felt so free. Or expectant, even though
I'm still terrified about what will actually happen."

"Me too. But we'll face it together with the strength and
inner peace that God provides."

They both went back to their knees, holding hands together in prayer until the warriors came and dragged them
out of the hut.

William called out his reassurance. "We're both in
God's hands now, Mary. Remember that."

It was a hard thought to hold, but somehow she managed as she was dropped in front of Nana Mala and his
devilmen.

His demanding tones were translated by her original
interpreter. "I'll give you one more chance. Tell me the
secret to how your magic works."

Scattered remnants of her medical bag were on the

ground. Her prized stethoscope was around the neck of the tallest devilman, the last gift she'd received from her father. It made her mad to see it there. Despite her fear, her anger came through. "I've told you before. I have no magic."

The translation met with harsh guttural tones, and a hand from behind shoved her in the back and forced her to all fours. Another grabbed her hair, baring her neck. There were a pair of feet in front of her flanking a wicked machete.

Fear coursed through her veins. They were going to behead her. "Oh God. Give me strength."

She could hear William arguing, pleading with Nana Mala for her life. Offering himself in her place. The words ran together, drowned out in the roar of fear. *Father, I need your peace. Give me peace to die as you would have me. Let me at least be a witness for you.*

Mary steeled herself, felt the flood of God's peace and waited for the inevitable.

Chapter Twenty-Four

William went hoarse from shouting to be heard. His pleas fell on ears long deafened by evil. He was about to watch another woman he loved die and there was once again nothing he could do about it.

He strained over and over against the arms holding him in place, desperate to go to her. He begged Nana Mala to take him instead. *Oh Lord, don't make me watch the woman I love die this horrible death. Is there no deliverance here for us?*

Mary was on her knees, her executioner standing over her. *Lord, I never told her I loved her. Lord, let me have one more minute, to at least tell her I love her.*

A terrible and loud wail rose from behind the gathered crowd, staying the hand of Mary's executioner. William's gaze stayed firmly on Mary until she was hauled to her feet, safe for the moment. Visibly shaken, she looked as if she would fall if the warriors relaxed their grip.

Her head lifted and she searched the crowd till she found him. She smiled weakly. Shouting voices, warriors' voices parted the crowd behind her. Even without a translator, William knew something major had happened. No warrior who wanted to avoid the fetters and a beating, or even death, would interrupt an execution.

Mary twisted in her captors' arms to see what was happening. William tore his gaze from her when six warriors, bloody and beaten, carried in the body of a seventh. The injured warriors laid the body with reverence at Nana Mala's feet.

No, not a body, he could see his chest rise and fall. The young man, he couldn't have been more than eighteen, was still alive. William didn't need Mary's medical knowledge for a diagnosis. The injured man's side was bleeding. He was dying.

A woman's wail and then the head wife pushed through the ranks, moving faster than William would have thought possible for a woman of her bulk. Several women followed her and she prostrated herself over the young man and continued her loud grief. The others joined in, all clamoring to be the loudest.

Suddenly William understood. This was her son. Hers and Nana Mala's.

Oh, Lord. Not a reprieve at the expense of another's life. Maybe an opportunity? Could it be? God's timing was impeccable.

William took advantage of the chaos and stepped forward to Nana Mala, pointing to Mary. "If you would have your son to live, you must not kill this woman. She can treat his wound and, God willing, he will live. But I must have your promise that she goes free first."

This was the proverbial earthquake, the miracle, the way he might save Mary. She just had to save the boy's life.

Mary could hardly stop her hands from shaking as she examined the wound on Nana Mala's son. William had reclaimed the contents of her medical bag and knelt beside her. Runners had gone to her guest hut to retrieve the other supplies she'd brought.

The iron tip of a spear was lodged deep within his side. She could only imagine the force necessary for it to have broken. This required surgery, surgery she could not do. Keeping her eyes on the patient, she whispered to William, "Are you crazy? You may have bought us a short reprieve, but as soon as he dies, we will too."

"We prayed, Mary, and this is what happened. Even as we were kneeling to ask God for a miracle, he already knew this young man was being carried back here."

"Are you saying that God caused this boy to be hurt so our lives could be spared? What kind of theology is that?"

"No, God didn't cause it. Their own tribal aggressions did this. But the timing is such that God can use it for our good."

Mary motioned for more light to be brought. "I can't save him."

"With God's help I believe you can."

"No, the wound's too great. I've stopped most of the bleeding, but he needs surgery. He'll die and then Nana Mala will turn his wrath back on us. Believe me, I know about a father's anger when he loses his son. My own father has declared me dead to him for what happened to my brother. This father will actually take both our lives."

"Mary, your father's reaction was horrible, but you can't give up here. You have a real chance. Not only to live, but to soften this man's heart to the Gospel."

"But I can't. This requires operating and that's something I swore never to do after my brother died under my scalpel. I just can't do it."

* * *

As if to contradict her refusal, two men dropped her
supplies beside her, heaving for breath from their run.
Nana Mala stepped forward and their translator relayed
his message.

"What more does the white devilwoman need? Save
my son and I shall consider sparing your life. Work now,
or I will kill the missionary man in front of you."

What choice did she have? None. Mary swallowed
the knot of fear that hampered her speech. She stood and
willed the trembling to stop as she faced the formidable
foe. "If I save him, you must promise to let the pastor go.
He must not be harmed. I must have your word."

William stood, "Mary, no. It is you who must live
through this. I love you. I could never live without you."

He loved her? The chief's answer and the boy's condition left no room to even think about William's declara-
tion. "Heal him now or you both die."

Mary made a quick decision. "Palm wine. I need palm
wine that has set to vinegar to clean this wound. And my
Army field surgical kit. Strong men must hold him still.
He cannot move while I work."

The translator saw to it and Mary began the process of
removing the spear tip from her patient. William paced
nearby and prayed, encouraging her the entire time. Mary
could only hope God had a plan. As her fingers worked,
she prayed. *Lord, the last time I used these skills, my own
brother died. I need Your help. I need a miracle.*

William never ceased his prayers while he watched
Mary work. Several of the women watching had shrieked
in horror when Mary had incised the wound further, ex-
posing more of the warrior's interior chest to view.

After she removed the spear tip, she began the arduous process of stitching. He'd lost count of just how many stitches it had taken to close the wound completely.

When she was finally finished, an exhausted Mary lifted her gaze to him. Her eyes reflected a bleak despair. "I've done all I can for him, but this wound is still likely to kill him. I don't think he will live through the next day. Not with all the damage I had to repair."

PRAY. The imperative came through loud and clear.

But Lord, my prayers have not ceased this whole time. What more can I pray?

PRAY FOR HIM.

William felt like a fool. Of course. "Mary, I'm going to lay hands on him and pray. Will you join me?"

Mary looked startled, but nodded and complied.

William spoke to the half-asleep Pennon, who'd stayed to translate any needs. "Translate my prayer, Pennon. I want everyone to know what I'm saying."

Pennon shook himself awake and nodded and William began to pray. "Heavenly Father, I come to you now, seeking your power to be made known in this place. The devilmen here say they hold the greater power, but I ask that you make the truth known."

William waited while the translation was made. Murmurs arose when Pennon paused. William continued. "Man's medicine has done all it can, Lord. I pray instead for your healing power to anoint this young man and save his life. Not for our glory, Lord. But that your power, the power of the true Lord of the universe, be made known to these people that they may believe."

When Pennon finished, many observing stared as if expecting the injured man to suddenly rise. When it was not immediate, they slowly filtered away, talking among themselves and shaking their heads.

Mary stretched and yawned. "It will truly be an act of

God if this man lives, William. There's no way my surgery, or any doctor's surgical skills, can save him. If God doesn't intervene, it's only a matter of time before he dies."

William hated to wake her. Mary had cared for Nana Mala's son for two days with hardly a break. She'd finally fallen asleep on the ground beside the now-recovering warrior. God had answered all their prayers and the cannibal chief was openly asking to hear more about the Gospel. It wasn't a conversion, but it was a start.

William reached down and brushed Mary's hair from her face, whispering her name. "Mary. Mary. It's time to wake."

Mary dragged heavy lids open and then came fully alert. "What's wrong?" She glanced toward her sleeping patient.

"He's still doing fine. Nana Mala has kept his word. He's releasing us both to go back to Nynabo. I figured we better leave quickly, lest he change his mind."

"I need to check his dressing and give some instructions for his continued care, but other than that, I'm ready to leave now."

"I'll get our packs and carriers. We can eat on the trail. Can you be ready in about thirty minutes?"

"Definitely."

William headed to get their gear. He met one of his porters near the village center and gave him instructions. No sooner had he turned to go back to Mary than he heard the talking drums relaying a message across the miles. Maybe he should ask the village drummer here to relay a message to Nynabo that they were on their way home. No, he didn't want to take the time. Getting Mary out of here was his first priority.

Pennon, his translator and guide, met him halfway back

to the hut where Mary cared for the injured warrior. "Nana Pastor, the drums bring a message for you."

Drums bringing him a message couldn't be a good thing. He listened with a heavy heart while they walked back to get Mary.

Mary felt so much lighter as soon as the Pahn village was out of sight. The only distress she now felt was when she saw the worry on William's face.

"I promise to keep out of trouble on the way home, William. Please don't worry, Pennon will get me back safely."

"I don't like leaving you, Mary. I almost lost you in the village. Your safety means a lot to me."

"What choice do you have? If Nynabo's chief is marching to make war on another village over an accidental death, of course you have to try and stop them."

"If Hannabo couldn't talk sense to his chief, I'm not sure what good I'll do, but I can't let Hannabo down. He expects me to meet them before they get there and butcher unsuspecting people."

"I'll never understand this belief that witchcraft is responsible for every death. A snake bite is a natural occurrence."

"And that's what I'll try to explain. Pray for me that my words will bring peace. This is where we part. Be careful."

Mary looked into the depths of his worried brown eyes. "I'll be all right. The trail back will be faster since we already forged it a few days ago. I'll be home before you know it and waiting for you there."

William grasped her hand and gave it a squeeze. "I had intended to talk to you in our time on the trail. There's something I must say. But now, it will have to wait till I return." William adjusted his pack and forged off.

Mary called out to his retreating back. "Then hurry, and stay safe. I'll see you in Nynabo."

Pennon waited patiently through the exchange. As soon as Mary signaled, he forged ahead with her close behind.

Mary topped the ridge to the compound. The trip home had only taken three days, since all the brush was so newly hacked on the trip there. She spotted two strangers talking with Clara at the entrance of the school. One of them a white man. News from the outside world would be great, but now her fondest desires to bathe, eat and sleep weren't going to happen. Not for a while.

Clara spotted her and waved, but with less enthusiasm than Mary expected. She looked worried. The visitors stayed put and Clara rushed forward. "Mary, I was so worried. Are you all right?"

Mary hugged her friend and said, "God has worked many things in the Pahn village. I'll tell you all about it over dinner, but first I need to greet our visitors and then go clean up."

"I'll take care of our visitor. There's something you should know." Clara's hand went to the pocket of her voluminous skirt and she pulled out a missive.

Mary hadn't seen such a serious look on Clara's face since the War. This couldn't be good. Had someone died? "What's wrong?"

"Our visitor says he's here to replace you."

Mary went numb. "I don't understand. I didn't request a replacement."

"I know, dear. Don't worry, we'll get this all straightened out. The Mission Board must have made a mistake."

Mary hadn't just faced down death to be replaced by a clerical error. Not when William had declared his love and left her on the trail with a promise to talk to her when he returned. "I can't leave Nynabo, Clara. Not now. My life is finally coming together."

Clara took her by the arm to lead her to the infirmary. "And you won't. I'm sure this is a mistake, dear. Why don't you go get cleaned up, read the letter, and I'll settle our guest in the main house."

Mary nodded, unable to say any more. Her agitation level rose with each step toward the infirmary. Once inside, she shut the door firmly behind her and sought the privacy and safety of her own room. Her hands shook as she opened the letter.

Stop it. You've faced Liberian cannibals and German artillery. This is only a letter; mere words.

Who was she kidding? This piece of paper could disrupt her life completely just as it was finally getting on course. William had told her very clearly before they parted on the trail that they needed to talk. Wait, even if the Mission Board was trying to reassign her, if she and William married, well, they couldn't be separated then. Her post and her life would be secure.

She took a deep breath and exhaled. Opening the letter gave her a frisson of unease. But knowing William's intentions placated her dread.

She read and hurt supplanted her dread. There was a mistake all right. The letter was intended for William.

It acknowledged his request for a replacement on the grounds of unsuitability for missionary work in the interior.

He had gone behind her back and had her replaced. All those words he spoke of God's call on her life, going so far as to declare his love when it looked like they might die. Their last conversation on the trail took on a whole new perspective. He didn't mean they had to talk about a future together. He intended to tell her he was having her replaced.

It was all clear now. She'd been a complete and utter fool. She wanted to wail like the frantic night cries of the jungle lemurs. Instead, she crumpled the letter and let it drop where she stood. Then she lay on her bed and cried for the life and love she'd thought were hers, the ones that only existed in her imagination.

When the daylight began to dim, she picked herself up off her bed and dried her tears. She toyed with the idea of returning home, but there was no going home for her. Her father didn't want her, and this beautifully dangerous country and its people had captured her heart. There were any number of places she could serve, all far from Nynabo and William Mayweather.

If she traveled back to Newaka, Karl and Hannah would take her in while she waited for a new posting. Pennon could guide her so they'd avoid Nana Bolo on the way. She'd leave the supplies for the mission, just take her own personal items and medical bag.

Mary packed her clothes and gear and then went to tell her dear friend goodbye. She'd make arrangements and leave at first light.

William and Hannabo entered the compound. "Home never looked so good, Hannabo."

"To me too, Nana Pastor. Still, our trip was good. You stopped the war, we saw much fruit and many came to know God."

"God stopped the war. I've come to see how much I am just an instrument, a tool in his hands. Before I was like a pot unfit for use. Just like your potters in Nynabo when the clay is not working, God is remaking me to be fit for Him to use in His way."

"As our brother Jeremiah says in the Word. It is true for me as well, I see the Father God changing me into His shape to hold whatever is necessary for me as his pot. This, too, I am learning."

"I am humbled by how much God is teaching us both, Hannabo. But I'm also sorely ready for a rest from crisis."

Hannabo grinned at William. "Now that there is no crisis, how much longer will you wait?"

"Wait for what?" They reached the porch of the main house and disgorged their packs.

"To arrange your marriage. With no father here, how will you manage the bride price?"

"Bride price?"

"For Mammy Doctor. She is going to be your wife, right?"

"What gave me away, Hannabo? I thought I'd been careful to keep my feelings from being too obvious."

"Anyone who watches you knows."

"So much for keeping a secret. To answer your question, in the white bush, it used to be that a wife would come to a marriage with money for her husband. It was called a dowry."

Hannabo's eyes grew in astonishment. Then narrowed as he tried to figure out if this was a joke. "Nana Pastor is true? The fathers would pay the husbands? How can this be?"

He patted Hannabo on the shoulder before heading out to the compound to check on Mary and Clara. "It's a very different world, my friend."

Hannabo nodded sagely. "I would like to see the white bush someday. A world where fathers pay the men to take the wives must be very different."

"That it is. I meant to ask her after we left the Pahn. I didn't count on this crisis. We will have to travel back to

Newaka to be married, and I want to do that before the rains."

"Why can you not be married here?"

"It takes another pastor to perform the marriage ceremony, and the closest one is Pastor Karl back in Newaka."

The two walked back out of the house. Children were already streaming out of the schoolhouse, chattering brown bodies in white cotton shirts and drawstring pants, bare feet deliberately stirring up dust as they headed out of the compound to their home down the hill. By his count, Clara had added five new students in the two weeks he'd been gone.

He headed for the school building, but stopped at Hannabo's words.

"Nana Pastor, there is a white man talking to Mammy Clara."

William saw Clara through the stick-built walls, walls he'd meant to get mudded before the month was out. Hannabo was right. They had a guest. Who had come to…oh, no. *Father, no.*

Mary must be livid. Of all the times for the Mission Board to be efficient. He'd planned to rescind his request for a replacement. Now it was too late.

Clara caught sight of him and, by her stiff posture when he arrived at the school entrance, was none too happy. He didn't blame her. The young man hung back. William tried to shake off the dread coursing through his veins.

Where was Mary? He had to straighten this out, and fast. Clara could chew him out to her heart's content, but he had to make things right with Mary.

"Clara, I can explain, there's been a mistake. Well, not a mistake exactly, but I didn't have time to get word to the Mission Board."

"Seems to me you got word to the Mission Board all

right. Now how are you going to fix this mess you've created?"

He deserved her ire. All of it. "I'm going to apologize to Mary. This was a mistake on my part. I've come to love Mary and don't want her to go anywhere."

Clara's intent gaze made him squirm. "You're a little late."

"You don't think she'll forgive me?"

Clara gave him a stern look and shook her head. "Mary left three days ago for Newaka. She's gone."

Hannah Jansen served Mary a wonderful breakfast without an ounce of red pepper to be found anywhere near her eggs and biscuits. But even though biscuits had been unavailable to her for so long, everything seemed dry and tasteless since she'd left Nynabo. Kind of like she pictured her life without William was going to be.

Hannah asked, "Are you going to keep pushing that food around on your plate? You need to eat something, dear."

"Sorry, Hannah. My appetite is just a little off."

"Love has a way of doing that to a body."

"It's not really love, Hannah. Almost dying with someone just has a powerful effect on the emotions. The feelings will pass."

Hannah looked at Mary like she could see right through her. "Well, whatever it is, eat your food or give it to the livestock. You're going to wear the fork and plate out if you keep moving your eggs around. Afterward, you can see about the children. They have all the usual complaints that need tending."

"I appreciate the chance to keep busy. You and Karl are so sweet to put me up while I write to the Board to see about a different posting."

Hannah picked up Mary's abandoned breakfast. "You're welcome to stay here as long as you like. You don't actually need permission beyond your first posting. The Board expects reports but assumes you'll follow God's guidance while you're in country."

"That's good to know. I'd really like to talk and pray with both you and Karl this evening about where God would have me to serve. Will he be back today?"

"I expect him before lunch, but with Karl, you can never tell." Hannah laughed. "Or maybe I should say with God you can never tell. His palaver with the elders was supposed to be just for the day and last night. Karl and I have long ago learned God doesn't always keep our schedule."

Or follow our personal plans, Mary silently added. "We can do it anytime once he's back. I'm not in a hurry. However, I think I'll head to the school now and check on the children."

"You do that. I'll be here if you need anything."

Mary stepped out into the early-morning heat and humidity. The sky was the same clear blue it had been for all the months she'd been in the jungle despite what she'd been told about the imminent rainy season. It was the jungle itself that seemed different. Rather, the noise.

The amplified sounds of the jungle caught Mary's attention as soon as she stepped out the front door. The monkeys' chatter rose to a high pitch, signaling their displeasure at someone or something entering their territory. Karl must be almost home from his overnight foray to the nearby village.

She took a moment before crossing the compound to the school and leaned on the railing, waiting to see. If Karl was indeed home, she'd tell Hannah before she went to do exams.

Karl and Hannah's encouraging words had comforted her when she'd arrived. Karl especially had encouraged her to see God's hand in all of this. She was trying, but her hurt over William's betrayal was still too raw for her to embrace that promise just yet.

Hannah stepped out onto the porch just as a flock of birds squawked their distress and took flight. "I thought I heard the jungle alert system. I may not understand the drum telegraph, but there's no mistaking it when the animals get set off."

"Karl must have made good time."

"Could be, but it's awful early. He would have had to have walked through the night. My Karl gave up jungle walks by torchlight after he tried one and almost fell and broke a leg."

"I can't imagine anyone wanting to travel through the jungle by night. You'd have to be crazy. Or desperate."

Hannah laughed and pointed. "I think *he* might qualify as both. I'll be inside if you need me."

Mary followed Hannah's pointing finger before she left the porch, only to see two men emerge from the jungle and enter the welcoming arch of Newaka. Hannabo and William. A very bedraggled-looking William at that.

Was someone so sick he'd come to get her? Had he come to apologize? Mary hated the way her heart soared at the possibility. There was no point in getting her hopes up over a man who'd made it perfectly clear he wanted her gone. Part of her wanted to turn and run away all over again. The other part wanted to fall into his arms and hear any explanation he had to offer as a salve to the pain she felt.

Love was making her weak. She'd have to be strong to deal with whatever had brought him here.

* * *

Besides Hannabo, William's constant jungle companion had been his fear. What if he was too late? She could already be on a freighter for Monrovia by this time if she'd gone straight through to Garraway on the coast. The chances of catching up with her at that point would be almost nonexistent. The thought hammered his fears home as he and Hannabo walked through the night with kola nuts to sustain their flagging energy and torches to find their way.

When they finally exited the jungle, the first thing William had seen was Mary, standing on the Jansens' front porch and without a hat to cover all that glorious red hair. He was in time.

Now the only question was whether she would forgive him.

As he drew near, Mary crossed her arms and called out, "William Mayweather, are you crazy? Did you walk through the jungle at night? Even I remember the danger of nocturnal leopards you were so quick to lecture me about on that first night on the trail."

William stopped at the bottom of the steps and looked up at her. "Not crazy. Just in love. You left before I got back."

"You had me replaced, William. Of course I left."

William took the porches steps two at a time until he stood beside Mary and took both her hands in his. "I'd like a chance to explain, like I'd planned to on the trail before we got separated by another crisis."

Hannabo discreetly wandered off to give them privacy.

Mary pulled away and sat in one of the porch rockers. "William, I saw the letter and it was pretty clear. You asked for a replacement. Your judgment of me was apparent. And you never told me."

Lord, I've hurt her deeply. Please give me the words to heal her heart. My words have caused nothing but pain.

William took a seat in the rocker next to her. "Mary, dear one, I wrote that letter after Nana Mala stormed our compound looking for his wife. I was so terrified for you, that something like that would happen again, I did the only thing I knew to keep you safe."

"For a man who says he loves me, that's an awful backwards way of showing it."

"Because I've been going at things backwards, trying to do them as I thought was best instead of in God's power."

Mary just rocked with eyes downcast.

"I was going to tell you after we left the Pahn. Losing Jabo brought about a lot of change in me, but it was at the moment of our near deaths, when I watched how God works all things to the good, that I really understood. I never expected to have anything but time on the trail to tell you my heart. And to tell you what I'd done."

For a moment, William wasn't sure Mary was going to answer him. Not until she looked up with tear tracks running down her face.

"What is it you want from me, William? Did you come all this way just to explain or justify your actions?"

William reached out to brush a tear away from her cheek. "No, I came all this way to tell you I was wrong and because I can't live my life here without you." William went to one knee. "Mary O'Hara, will you do me the honor of becoming my wife?"

Mary swiped at her tears and said, "That's Dr. O'Hara to you. Soon to be Dr. Mayweather."

William jumped to his feet and lifted her straight out of the rocker, embracing her until the porch door opened and a smiling Hannah stepped out with the missing Hannabo. "Sounds like Karl has a wedding to perform when he gets home."

William grinned and gazed deep into Mary's eyes. "The sooner the better. I want to spend the rest of my life with you, Mary."

"And I can't wait to become your wife, William, but you might need to put me down before then."

William heard Hannah's chuckle as their audience slipped quietly back into the house. He swung Mary around one more time. "Do I have to? I'm not sure I want to ever let you go again."

Mary blushed. "I'm not sure I want you to let me go either, but now that I understand how you really feel, I'm not going anywhere, my darling William. Except back to Nynabo with my husband."

Epilogue

William stood in the compound with Mary and Hannabo, watching the children. "I can't believe this day has come."

Mary agreed. "Hannabo, I know you've wanted your own posting since your ordination, but I will miss you and Anaya."

Hannabo said, "We will return to visit our dear friends."

William laughed. "You'd better. Our three-year-old is going to be unhappy when you take your son away." William pointed to newborn Joseph being rocked in the cradle by their own little Ruth.

Mary patted her burgeoning belly. "Any day now she'll have a new little distraction of her own to ease the separation."

Anaya stepped out from the main house and announced lunch. Hannabo took Joseph from his cradle, earning a small glare from Ruth, who held out her hands to hold the baby.

William scooped up his daughter. "You're still too little to carry the baby, Ruth."

Mary wagged her finger at William. "Restrictions

didn't work too well with me. I'd watch her carefully if I were you."

William said, "No doubt God has many lessons for me on trusting Him with my daughter. Hopefully, I've learned from trusting Him with her mother. Now come, darling wife, before Anaya stops trusting that we'll come to lunch."

*   *   *   *   *

Dear Reader,

One day my daughter and son-in-law brought me a book written by one of his relatives, a former missionary to cannibal tribes in Liberia. Months went by before I read it, but when I did, I knew I had to create a missionary romance set in Liberia.

On a three-day lakeside writing retreat, I typed nonstop. The result was the first three chapters of Pastor Mayweather's and Dr. O'Hara's love story. Afterward, I heard no one would buy a book set in Liberia.

But sometimes God directs us in unexpected ways, ones that make others doubt our good sense. When that happens, the best thing is to simply obey and watch the adventure unfold.

I love hearing from readers. You can find me at www.debbiekaufman.com, on Facebook and Twitter. Or email me at debbiekaufmanauthor@gmail.com.

Blessings,

Debbie Kaufman

Questions for Discussion

1. In the opening scenes we learn of William's tragic loss of his young wife to malaria. His response is not only feelings of guilt, but a vow to never endanger another woman while fulfilling God's call on his life. Have you ever made an impulsive vow in an emotionally charged situation? How did that vow get broken or does it still guide your actions today?

2. Her brother's death and her father's rejection leave Mary feeling as though she must atone for having done something wrong. How does this line up with what God's Word has to say about grace and forgiveness in our lives? Have you ever felt the need to do something to receive forgiveness?

3. Unable to dissuade Mary from a dangerous jungle trek, William steps into the role of protector, hoping to keep her safe until she can be replaced. How do you feel about the step he takes to ask the Mission Board to replace her? Has anyone ever done something for "your own good" that caused trouble in your life? How did you handle it?

4. The real missionaries to West Africa in William's fictional era knew that up to half of them would die of malaria within the first six months. What does this say about their determination to spread the Gospel? Do you think you could go into a similar situation with such dire odds?

5. Mary and William encounter many dangers in the jungle's interior. What do we risk today when we share the Gospel with people in our own community? Does it have to be life or death to be an actual risk to us?

6. William's actions repeatedly thwart Mary's attempts to minister medically in the jungle, all in the name of keeping her safe. Have you ever had to release someone you love to a risky situation and allow them to do what God has called them to do? How did it make you feel? How did you do it?

7. All of William's theological training gets called into question by the simple faith of Hannabo when he challenges William regarding his aunt's and uncle's deaths. Have you ever found a specific scripture easier to quote than to live? Which one stands out to you the most in your life? Did you finally find a way to live it?

8. The lesson both Mary and William must come to terms with is found in Romans 8:28, where God says He works all things to the good. As you look back through your life, can you find some examples of how He has done this for you?

9. What character's struggle or reaction did you most relate to and why?

10. Have you ever been far from home with unfamiliar people, languages and food? If so, how did you cope? If not, how do you think you would cope and adjust?

11. What roles do Hannabo and Clara play in William's and Mary's lives? Have you ever had a friend speak a difficult truth to you? How did you receive it when they did?

12. Do you know any real missionaries today? How important is it in our technological age for individuals and families to uproot their lives for a calling to spread the Gospel?

INSPIRATIONAL

Wholesome romances that touch the heart and soul.

Love Inspired.
HISTORICAL

COMING NEXT MONTH
AVAILABLE DECEMBER 6, 2011

MAIL-ORDER CHRISTMAS BRIDES
Jillian Hart and Janet Tronstad

THE CAPTAIN'S CHRISTMAS FAMILY
Glass Slipper Brides
Deborah Hale

THE EARL'S MISTAKEN BRIDE
The Parson's Daughters
Abby Gaines

HER REBEL HEART
Shannon Farrington

REQUEST YOUR FREE BOOKS!

2 FREE INSPIRATIONAL NOVELS
PLUS 2
FREE
MYSTERY GIFTS

Love Inspired
HISTORICAL
INSPIRATIONAL HISTORICAL ROMANCE

YES! Please send me 2 FREE Love Inspired® Historical novels and my 2 FREE mystery gifts (gifts are worth about $10). After receiving them, if I don't wish to receive any more books, I can return the shipping statement marked "cancel." If I don't cancel, I will receive 4 brand-new novels every month and be billed just $4.49 per book in the U.S. or $4.99 per book in Canada. That's a saving of at least 22% off the cover price. It's quite a bargain! Shipping and handling is just 50¢ per book in the U.S. and 75¢ per book in Canada.* I understand that accepting the 2 free books and gifts places me under no obligation to buy anything. I can always return a shipment and cancel at any time. Even if I never buy another book, the two free books and gifts are mine to keep forever.

102/302 IDN FEHF

Name	(PLEASE PRINT)	
Address		Apt. #
City	State/Prov.	Zip/Postal Code

Signature (if under 18, a parent or guardian must sign)

Mail to the **Reader Service:**
IN U.S.A.: P.O. Box 1867, Buffalo, NY 14240-1867
IN CANADA: P.O. Box 609, Fort Erie, Ontario L2A 5X3

Not valid for current subscribers to Love Inspired Historical books.

Want to try two free books from another series?
Call 1-800-873-8635 or visit www.ReaderService.com.

* Terms and prices subject to change without notice. Prices do not include applicable taxes. Sales tax applicable in N.Y. Canadian residents will be charged applicable taxes. Offer not valid in Quebec. This offer is limited to one order per household. All orders subject to credit approval. Credit or debit balances in a customer's account(s) may be offset by any other outstanding balance owed by or to the customer. Please allow 4 to 6 weeks for delivery. Offer available while quantities last.

Your Privacy—The Reader Service is committed to protecting your privacy. Our Privacy Policy is available online at www.ReaderService.com or upon request from the Reader Service.

We make a portion of our mailing list available to reputable third parties that offer products we believe may interest you. If you prefer that we not exchange your name with third parties, or if you wish to clarify or modify your communication preferences, please visit us at www.ReaderService.com/consumerschoice or write to us at Reader Service Preference Service, P.O. Box 9062, Buffalo, NY 14269. Include your complete name and address.

LIH11B